TWO SHOTS QUICK
A N O V E L

Ross A. Phelps

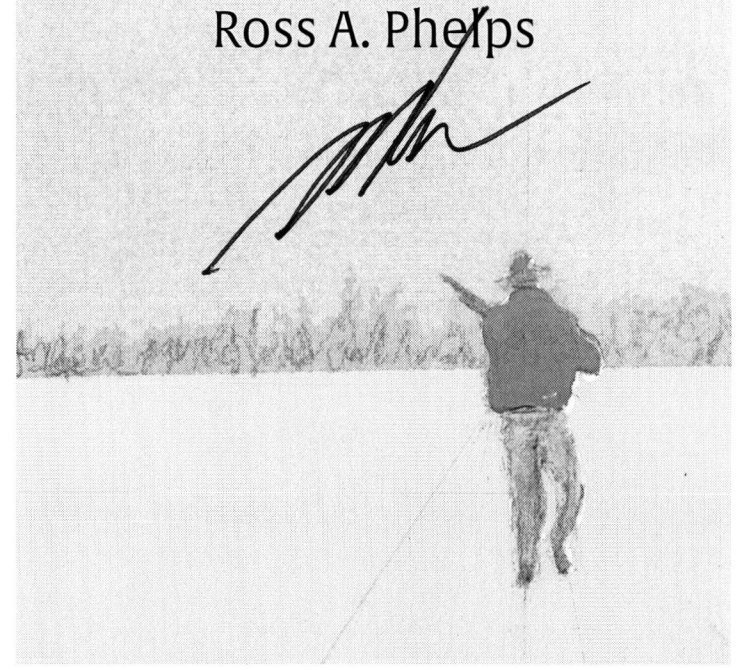

Copyright © 2017 Ross A. Phelps

- FIRST EDITION -

All rights reserved. No part of this book may be reproduced or transmitted in any form or by any means without the prior written permission of the author, including reproductions intended for non-commercial use.

Despite the use of real places and events, this is a work of fiction and no reference to any real person is intended or should be inferred.

ISBN 978-0-9903345-3-8

PUNTILLERO PRESS
La Crescent - Minnesota

For Lara and Mike

Also by the author

Lleyellyn
(First in the Lleyellyn Shay Series)

TUESDAY OCTOBER 20

He sat in the Mustang with the windows down, trying to take advantage of the slight breeze in the bright midday sun.

In the far distance he heard the approaching distinctive cries of migrating Sandhill Cranes. Several large V-shaped flocks, high in the sky, barely visible in the bright blue background, were heading south, sounding for all the world like a grammar school yard full of screaming kids at recess.

He had seen only one vehicle pass by, a little red pick-up, which never slowed down. He was the only one there. He knew no one else would be hunting this stretch of the old rail line this afternoon. It was always first come, first serve.

He heard the faint wail of the noon time siren in Moreloft.

Satisfied that everything was ready, he locked the door, loaded his twelve gauge, and started off down the old railroad grade, now a long strip of prime hunting land.

Lush weeds had grown up along the abandoned right of way. On his left was a flat field of corn stubble. There was the remnant of a harvested soybean crop on the opposite side.

There has to be pheasants here, he thought. *There's no other place for them to hide.*

Almost immediately he saw two hens and a rooster dart across the old rail road bed eighty to a hundred yards ahead.

He moved at a slow steady pace, his Remington Wingmaster held at port arms, one finger on the safety. The wind was at his back.

As he got closer to where he had seen the birds cross, he moved slower, alert for movement.

Times like this, I could use a dog.

Suddenly the quiet was shattered by the racket made by a pheasant taking flight. He had his gun up, and the safety off, before he realized it was a hen. But then, seconds later, another bird arose making even more of an uproar. It gave the unmistakable call of a rooster. He pointed his gun at the bird, led it a few degrees, pulled the trigger, and watched as the bird's wings continued flapping several times, then stopped as the pheasant fell to the ground.

The rooster was laying a few feet to the side of the gravel rail bed in short grass. He retrieved it, shoved it into the game pouch in the back of his jacket, reloaded, and resumed his hunt.

Haven't lost the touch. I'll get my limit soon.

The road bed passed over a small stream, a mere trickle this time of year. A mallard flew up from the far bank, and winged off to the north. The stubble field ended at the waterway. There was a field of standing corn on the far side of the stream that hadn't been harvested. He could see the top half of a John Deere combine parked across the field near the road. Harvesting would be starting soon.

Whatever had been planted on the other side of the railroad bed had already been harvested, and the field plowed.

Ready for spring. Maybe winter wheat, he thought.

He flushed two more cocks that flew up and into the corn field. They were well out of range for a decent shot.

A good birddog would really help here, he thought. *Maybe a Lab, or better yet, a German Shorthair.*

He saw a cock pheasant stick its colorful head out from the weeds in front of him, then turn and move back into cover. He sped up, before veering off the roadbed, and began moving through thigh-high weeds. Suddenly the bird he was after burst into flight off to his left.

He turned, pointed and fired. A feather drifted to the ground, but the bird never wavered as it flew in a bee line over the corn field, gliding out of sight between rows of corn fifty yards away.

If they make it to the corn, they've made it.

He walked slowly, keeping alert, hoping he could flush a bird and get a decent shot at close range before it could get away to the safety of the standing corn.

Out of range ahead of him, another hen flew up and high tailed it to the safety of the cornfield.

Plenty of birds in here.

As he moved along, he could see he was approaching a swampy corner of the field. After that, it looked like more open ground. He knew he'd have better success along the railroad right of way when he got there. The only ground cover would be along the right of way of the old rail road bed itself.

There was a flash of movement off to his left. A rooster was flying from the side of the embankment toward the row of corn paralleling the rail line. Instinctively he fired, the bird dropped, obviously winged, and started running, disappearing between the rows.

"Shit!" he said in frustration. *I'll never find it. But I better look. Probably didn't get very far. Know I hit him.*

He zigged down the embankment and across the ditch that ran along side, then pushed aside some standing corn and stepped between the rows which towered several feet over his head. He could see nothing that looked like a dead pheasant between the first two rows. He moved to the next row, then the next. There it was, lying on its side thirty or forty feet to his left in the space between two rows of corn.

He retrieved the bird, put it in his game pouch with the one he had shot earlier, and started back through the rows the way he had come.

As he turned, he caught movement down between the rows. A man wearing camo was coming towards him, holding a shot gun. It was pointed at him.

"You Terry Walker?" the man said.

He didn't answer, not sure what was going on.

Several weeks earlier...

Two Shots Quick

him of the railroad's cost in producing trial witnesses from their main office in Chicago, or wherever, they'll need to establish the wire's value. Just tell him the offer made by Shay's attorney seems like a good outcome for all concerned."

"You make it sound easy," Watts said, removing his cell phone from his inside jacket pocket.

"I've got his number here."

"Place the call," the judge said, "Use my phone, then hand it to me. What's the security supervisor's name?"

"Beresford. Robert J."

The judge adjusted the volume to speaker phone. They could hear it ringing.

"Burlington Northern Santa Fe Railroad!" the singsong voice of a female receptionist said.

"Mr. Beresford," Watts said.

While they were waiting for the security supervisor to pick up, the judge extended her hand wiggling her fingers, motioning for the county attorney to hand her the phone.

The call was answered in a gruff voice.

"Beresford."

"Please hold for Winona County Attorney Kenneth J. Watts," the judge said, using an authoritative voice, before handing the receiver back.

Watts took a few moments, smiled at the judge, and spoke into the receiver.

"Watts here, Mr. Beresford. I want to bring you up to speed on the Shay case here in Winona County, and the alleged stolen wire."

"About time," Beresford said. "Alleged, hell. Nothing alleged about it. Open and shut. Arrested the son-of-a-bitch yet?"

"No, but I've been contacted by his attorney. Made a settlement proposal. Calls for the railroad to get a thousand dollars in restitution. Just running it by you."

"That's wholly inadequate. He got a little over seventeen hundred bucks for our wire. The railroad wants its money and I want the little thief convicted. And he deserves jail time."

"I understand your position, but you've got to understand mine. The county has limited resources. Bringing him back from out of state will cost the sheriff's office at least five grand," Watts said.

"So what? We're the victim here," Beresford said.

"Shay's attorney presented me with the offer and made some valid points. We have no admission of guilt. No confession from the defendant. We don't have any physical evidence. The wire was melted down before law enforcement was contacted by you. We'd have to subpoena witnesses from your main office. Establish the cost, condition, depreciation and what not of the wire that was allegedly taken. Probably take four or five witnesses from the railroad to lay the foundation. Lots of wasted manpower on your end. Not likely to result in any reimbursement. Your company would be out a whole lot more than a few coils of wire."

"Sounds like you're chickening out on me," Beresford said. "Who's this attorney he's retained? He any good?"

"Watts looked at Simms and winked. He covered the mouthpiece and whispered to her, "Where'd you go to law school?"

"William Mitchell," she whispered back.

"As I understand it, a Harvard grad. Spent several years with a big criminal defense firm in Chicago. Her husband's the new football coach at Winona State. Understand she's tough in the courtroom. Been attracting some pretty big cases in southeastern Minnesota."

Watts covered the phone again, and looked at Simms.

"How many jury cases have you tried?" he said.

"She extended three fingers on her right hand and whispered, "All misdemeanors."

Almost a minute had passed since Beresford had said anything. Finally he came back on the line.

"One thousand dollars to get out from this felony charge is too little, as far as I'm concerned. Get us fifteen hundred and we've got a deal."

"Hang on, I'll call his attorney and see if she can go that high. I'll put you on hold for a sec."

Watts leaned back and smiled at the judge. Well, what do you think, your honor. Fifteen hundred work?"

"Not sure, better ask the defendant's attorney," she said turning toward Simms.

"Tell him twelve fifty. Can't go any higher. I'll withdraw this counteroffer at one o'clock. My client and I are ready for trial, "she said, then looked at the judge. "Think I'm overdoing it a bit?"

"Not at all," the judge said, before turning to the county attorney. "You heard the lady."

Watts looked at the phone and canceled the hold.

"In luck. Got her before she was leaving for federal court. They'll meet you half way. One thousand two hundred fifty. That's a final offer. Said it's open 'til one o'clock this afternoon. Want to think about it?" Watts said.

"Hell no. We'll take it. Can't waste time playing games with no Ivy League lawyer."

Two Shots Quick

CHAPTER 2

FRIDAY JULY 17

Lleyellyn had invited her out to the Boyd Ranch for a picnic. He never mentioned the motion picture that was being filmed there, but there had been an entire section devoted to it in the Sunday Miles City Star. She had read it all. It had been the main topic of conversation at the Big Sky Café all week. The ranch was leased out to a production company for the whole year. They had imported longhorn cattle and were recreating an 1870 cattle drive for the film they were shooting.

She was looking forward to spending time alone with Lleyellyn and joining Irene Boyd and Mr. Montoya, her foreman, at the picnic.

I might even get to meet a movie star, she thought.

o0o

"Hop in," Lleyellyn said to LaDonna Mae. "You drive."

May 19th was a day he knew he'd never forget. It had only been two months ago.

It was the day of the after-rodeo party at the Ritchie place. He and his new friend Tole Winters had been invited by the cute little waitress at the Big Sky, LaDonna Mae.

He'd been introduced to her father and brother and their friends. Tole had gotten to know a retired rodeo champion, Buck Lassen.

It had been an important day for Tole. Buck had pointed out the downside of the rodeo life. Made a big impression on Tole.

Helped him make up his mind. He was now back in Wisconsin planning to attend college.

It had been an even bigger date for Lleyellyn. Since then, about all he had been thinking about was LaDonna Mae. They'd left the party early. She had driven him back to the motel in Miles City, and they ended up in bed together. She was in his thoughts constantly. And now she was at the ranch so they could spend time together.

He was hoping they'd have some time alone, away from Irene and Mr. Montoya.

LaDonna Mae had said wanted to see the ranch. It was a sunny day and there wasn't any work that had to be done around the place.

She was used to driving a stick shift. She smoothly went through the gears and followed Lleyellyn's directions.

"Just follow that track inside the fence," he said. "Goes around the whole place. Thirty six miles, if you can believe that."

She drove a lot better than he did when he first started driving the Jeep. She avoided the dips and low spots effortlessly. And she drove faster than he did.

For a change there was almost no wind. The undulating prairie was spread out before them, the yellowed grass pristine. The motion of the vehicle cooled them a little.

The rolling grassland was unmarked by tire tracks, just the way it was supposed to be when the motion picture crew was ready to film the cattle drive.

They came over a rise and surprised a coyote giving itself a dirt bath in a bare spot in the road.

It indignantly got to its feet and passed under the line fence, ambling off into taller grass, never breaking into anything faster than a walk.

With the bright sun and almost no breeze it was getting hotter quickly.

"Is there a top for this thing?" LaDonna Mae said. "Be nice to get out of the sun."

"Should've brought hats," he said. "There's suntan lotion in the glovebox Want some?"

She stopped. He handed her the bottle of Coppertone.

She applied lotion to her face and the back of her hands and arms.

"Need any help?" he said.

She smiled at him, but didn't reply as she returned the bottle.

He dabbed some on his face and hands.

"Mind if I take my shirt off?" he said, removing his tee shirt without waiting for a reply.

He threw his shirt in the back and tried to put lotion on his shoulders. She helped rub suntan lotion on his back, both of them acutely aware of the physical contact.

"There's nobody out here but us, right?" she said, before slipping off her top, revealing a light blue lacey bra. "What's good for the goose is good for the gander," she said. "Like my new underwear?"

She turned her back to him so he could put lotion on her back. She clamped his hands to her sides with her upper arms when it appeared he might be preparing to apply lotion elsewhere.

"Not much cooler is it?" she said.

"We can cool off at the stock tank when we get to the west side," he said. "It's plenty big for both of us."

They saw the top of the windmill before they crested a high spot, then followed a track towards it and parked in the shade of one of the few trees they had seen.

Lleyellyn pulled off his boots, stuffed his socks inside and walked to the stock tank, looked back at LaDonna Mae with a big smile on his face, removed his pants, and climbed in.

"It's cold in here!" he said. "What are you waiting for?"

He watched her remove her shoes and put them next to his boots. She walked carefully toward him.

"Feet feel hot," she said. "I'm not used to walking barefoot like this. Hurts."

Each time she stepped on a small twig, or a pebble, or something, she gave a string of little 'oohs' and 'ouches' as she moved toward him.

She reached the tank, removed her bra, and then her jeans and matching light blue panties at the same time, and climbed over the edge of the tank, quickly submerging herself up to her neck.

"It's cold! Cold! Cold!" she said. "But, I like it.

The only thing showing above the surface was the top of their heads from their noses up.

"You're sure no one comes out this way," she said.

His only answer was an even wider grin.

"Watched you. Looked like you were getting too big for your britches," she said, giving him a wink. "You know, it feels like we're some place like Southern California, or somewhere. Hot sun. Cold water."

"They have nude beaches there, too. Don't they?"

They relaxed in the water, their eyes glued to each other, wondering who would make the next move.

"Lookie there!" LaDonna Mae said, as she glimpsed movement to the south.

He turned to see what she was looking at. A lone longhorn steer was nonchalantly moving their way.

Had to have gotten loose from the pen, Lleyellyn thought. *Damn things are supposed to stay put so they'll be ready for the cattle drive.*

They watched the mottled brown and white animal as it came ambling steadily closer, clearly intent on getting a drink.

They both remained still. They couldn't sink any lower without holding their breath.

The steer came right up to the tank and started drinking. Its spread of horns was nearly as wide as the length of the tank. It seemed wholly oblivious to the naked skinny dippers.

Must be damned thirsty, Lleyellyn thought.

It seemed to take two or three minutes for the steer to drink its fill. They had enough time to stare at the animal's long purplish-pink tongue as it lapped up water. They could see the hairs protruding from its nostrils, and its long, curled eyelashes.

Finally it stopped drinking, took a step back, then started wandering off, nibbling at some grass growing at the base of one of the windmill supporting legs. When it had eaten a little, it resumed slowly meandering off some fifty yards or so before lying down facing them, holding its head up, seeming to keep an eye on the tank, or on them.

Neither of them moved for several minutes.

"I'm getting out," LaDonna Mae said. "Can't stand that damned old thing staring at me. I feel naked. It's embarrassing."

"Well, we are naked."

She flashed him a grin, climbed out of the tank on the side farthest away from the animal, and hurried tippy toe fashion to the Jeep, again squealing oohs and ouches with every step.

He watched her go, amazed at how graceful and sexy she looked.

When she reached the Jeep he yelled, "You want your clothes or not?"

She didn't say anything, but she started the Jeep and drove up to him.

"Can I give you a ride, Mister? Or would you prefer to stay out here and make eyes at that critter?"

o0o

Irene and Montoya were on the front porch, relaxing in the shade. Irene motioned them over. They parked next to the kitchen door.

"Looks like you got quite a bit of sun," Irene said, looking at LaDonna Mae. "Your face is a little red."

LaDonna Mae smiled.

"I'm fine," she said. "We saw a longhorn out there by the wind mill."

Montoya looked at her for a further explanation.

"All alone. Got out of the pen somehow," she said. "Seemed to be okay."

"Lleyellyn, you better tell the head wrangler," Montoya said. "Probably won't do anything until they're finished filming."

o0o

They waited for Irene and Montoya to go inside to work on preparations for dinner, before getting in the Jeep and moving it next to LaDonna Mae's Gran Am parked near the bunkhouse.

"Check me out, will you?" she said. "Want to make sure I've got all my clothes back on right. And right side out," she added, with a laugh. "Irene thinks we were up to something."

"You look fine," Lleyellyn said. "Like you always do."

As they walked back to the house, Montoya's dog, Mully, went to LaDonna Mae first for some personal attention, then led them to the front of the house.

Montoya was setting up a lawn game.

"Irene loves Jarts," he said. "You're back just in time."

"Jarts?" LaDonna Mae said. "Played it once last Fall. Lot harder than it looks."

Irene came down the steps with the pitcher of lemonade and a stack of plastic cups.

"Figured you'd be getting back about now. Must be thirsty," she said. "Lleyellyn show you the sights?" she added, directing her comments to LaDonna Mae.

"He did. Went way out all the way to the windmill at the west side," she said. "Your ranch is beautiful."

Irene answered with a smile.

"What I think is ladies versus gents. Okay with everybody?" Irene said.

"Great!" LaDonna Mae said. "We playing for money?"

"No, no. Don't want to take advantage of these fellas," Irene said. "Losers get to do the dishes tonight. Okay?"

She looked around at the three of them.

"Seeing no objections, that'll be it, then. Motion's passed. You gentlemen can go first."

Lleyellyn had seen families playing Jarts at the city park in Goodview near home once or twice. He had never played the game. The rules seemed to be similar to horseshoes.

Montoya was good at the game. Lleyellyn's inexperience showed. Irene and LaDonna Mae were near professionals with their uncanny ability to hit the target repeatedly. They played three games. The women won them all.

"Break time!" Montoya said. "You ladies are too good for us. What do you think, Lleyellyn?"

"Must have seen us coming. Regular Jart sharks. We were set up. Didn't stand a chance."

"You'll get us next time," Irene said.

"Next time?" Lleyellyn said, and shrugged. "Not so sure about next time."

o0o

When they were sitting on the porch finishing off the lemonade, LaDonna Mae asked if she could go in and freshen up a little.

Irene invited her to use the upstairs bathroom. LaDonna Mae got her overnight case from her car, then went inside.

Montoya went to check the spare ribs he was grilling.

When they were gone, Irene lifted the lemonade pitcher as an invitation to see if Lleyellyn wanted a refill.

"No thanks, I'm good," he said. "You play a mean game of Jarts."

"Well thank you. Your lady friend and I will be happy to take you men on again anytime. Just say the word."

They were lost in their own thoughts for a few minutes.

"Before I forget," Irene said. "Your grandmother called today. We talked for quite a while."

"How is she?"

"Seems to be doing fine," Irene said. "Misses you. Said for you to call anytime. Sooner the better."

"I will. Haven't talked to her in three weeks, at least."

"Reason she called was about the arrest warrant for you in the State of Minnesota. Said she told you about it before."

"Yes, she did. It's about the copper wire from the railroad," Lleyellyn said. "I get caught in Minnesota, they could throw me in jail. For felony theft."

"Your grandmother is trying to do something about it. Wants you to be able to come back when there's a memorial service for your mother. Won't do it without you."

"Think she'll be able to do anything?"

"Your grandmother thinks so. Said she's trying her best. She's already written the judge a letter."

o0o

LaDonna Mae came bouncing down the front steps. Her hair was neatly combed. She had put on bright lipstick that matched the printing on her *Grand Tetons* tee shirt.

Lleyellyn beamed at her.

"You look marvelous," he said, as he stood up. "I'll be right back."

He sprinted across the yard to the bunk house, Mully racing him to the door. Two minutes later they were back. He had combed his hair and had put on a collared polo shirt.

"Never saw so many dolled up folks for an outdoor bar-b-que before," Irene said. "You two make a handsome couple."

o0o

Montoya had fixed the entire dinner. The slow-cooked falling-off-the-bone ribs were tender, juicy, and delicious. He had fixed potato salad, a relish plate, and a baked bean dish with at least six different kinds of beans.

"Best ribs I ever had,' Lleyellyn said. "I mean it. Everything's great."

"Loved it, too," LaDonna Mae said. "I ate a whole lot more than I usually do. Really, really good."

Irene smiled before adding her two cents.

"Best cook I know," she said. "If Mr. Montoya played Jarts the way he cooks, we'd be doing the dishes."

Montoya didn't say anything, but he was all smiles. Lleyellyn had never seen him in such a good mood.

He put a hefty helping of rib bones in a bowl for Mully. She went after them with enthusiasm.

Irene got their attention while they were still all seated at the table.

"You know," she said, "I was planning to say grace before we ate. No reason we can't do it now."

She lowered her eyes and waited for the others to do the same.

"Okay, then. Let's hold hands."

Before she could start, Molly stopped gnawing on the bones and walked over to the edge of the porch, her ears cocked in the direction of the bunkhouse. They kept their eyes on her. After ten or fifteen seconds, the dog returned to the rib bones.

"Don't know what that was all about," Irene said. "Whatever that was, the bones took precedence, I guess."

When she was sure they had their hands joined, she said a brief prayer.

"God, thank you for the delicious food we just ate. Thank you even more for the people at this table who enjoyed the meal together. We all have many things to be thankful for. Please continue to bless each and every one of us now and in the future. And bless, too, my clients and women in their position everywhere. Give them kindness and peace. And help bring their abusers to justice. We thank you. Amen."

They released their hands slowly. Montoya gave Lleyellyn's hand a little squeeze. So did LaDonna Mae. He squeezed their hands back in return. He felt good being around people he cared about. The only time he remembered saying grace before was at his grandmother's.

"Okay, everybody," Irene said. "Want dessert now, or later?"

o0o

Lleyellyn and Montoya made fast time with the clean-up. They ate Irene's chocolate layer cake sitting on the porch.

"Cake's wonderful," Montoya said.

LaDonna Mae and Lleyellyn added their compliments.

Things were winding down. Montoya said his good nights and excused himself to go to the bunk house. Irene announced she was going inside to watch the nine o'clock news.

"I'll say good night," she said. "You're welcome anytime," she said to LaDonna Mae as she touched her on the shoulder. "Remember, you have to work tomorrow. Don't stay up all night."

LaDonna Mae smiled, then said, "I had a great time. You and Mr. Montoya are the best."

When Irene went inside, Lleyellyn said, "What about me?"

"You?" she said, getting up and sitting on his lap. She gave him a kiss. "You're the best, too. I'll be thinking about you getting in that water tank all the way home," she said. "If that darned old steer wasn't watching, who knows what would have happened."

They kissed some more.

"You sure looked nice today," he said. "And tonight. Like you always do."

"You're sweet," she said. "Didn't get much of a chance to show off my new underwear for you."

"I got a flash of blue, at least."

"Well, there's always next time," she said. "Hey! I've got to get going. Irene's right. I'm working tomorrow."

He walked her to her car, carrying her overnight case. He put it in the backseat and turned to face her, taking her hands in his.

"Thanks for coming out," he said, and gave her a peck on the forehead. "You be sure and drive careful."

She got in and started the car, flashing him a smile as she fastened her seatbelt, and turned on the headlights.

He watched her go, keeping an eye on the tail-lights until they were out of sight.

o0o

It was completely dark when LaDonna Mae reached the highway and turned toward Miles City. She was thinking about her visit to the ranch and her time with Lleyellyn. She became aware her head lights were gradually growing dimmer and dimmer. Then the motor began to sputter. She suspected the alternator. It had been acting up ever since her brother had tuned up the engine.

She was able to creep along until she crossed a culvert and pulled over at a wide spot next to the road.

It was a warm night. The sound of frogs and other creatures filled the air. She recalled the earthen dam that held back a small stream that coursed through the culvert. On the way out to the Boyd Ranch she had seen cars stopped where she was parked. They had been picnicking, and fishing, or swimming in the pond.

Now it was deserted. The moon hadn't risen. The last vestiges of the fading twilight had disappeared. She didn't see headlights in either direction.

She turned the key. Nothing. The battery was dead. She felt around inside the glove compartment and found a penlight she had put there when she first got the car. She switched it on. There was a faint beam. Its battery a near goner. She knew the trunk was empty. Luckily there was a bottle of water in the cup holder.

There was nothing she could do but wait.

o0o

She must have nodded off because now it seemed darker than ever. She heard the crunch of tires on gravel and saw the beams of a pair of headlights as they shone on her car.

A pick-up truck pulled up alongside her. She could barely see through the truck's passenger side window as it was lowered.

LaDonna Mae cranked down her side window.

"You having a problem?" a male voice asked. "Need a lift?"

"Battery's gone dead. You going to Miles City, Mister?"

"I am. Hop in. Plenty of room."

LaDonna Mae stepped out of her car, decided not to lock it because it didn't run anyway. She put her car keys under the driver's seat. Grabbed her bottle of water, closed the car door, and walked to the pick-up.

She opened the passenger door and started to climb in. The interior lights in the pick-up did not come on like she expected. She looked over at the driver, but couldn't see what he looked like in the dark.

"Dark in here," she said, before closing the door.

She heard the door latch lock behind her.

"Something's wrong with the switch," the driver said. "Still under warranty, though."

She realized immediately that she was trapped inside the dark cab.

Suddenly a bright light came on. The driver was wearing some kind of light fastened to a band around his head. In the reflection she could see the vague outline of the man's head, but she couldn't make out any of his features.

She tried to open the door, but it wouldn't budge. She felt panic start to build.

"Please. Let me out!" she said. "I've got a ride on the way. He'll be here soon."

"Not so fast, little honey," the stranger's voice said.

She shrank back against the door and tried the handle again. She tried to lower the window, but it was locked, too.

"Just calm down," the voice said." Let me have a look at you."

The bright light moved up and down from her face to her lap, then back to her face.

"Nice outfit. We'll have some fun."

As she looked toward the driver she saw something move out of the darkness from the driver's side and into her view.

"Know what this is?"

She had seen enough movies to recognize the gun. It was a revolver similar to the one Dirty Harry used in the movies. Biggest pistol she had ever seen.

She didn't answer, but she was terrified, her eyes focused on the gun.

"You do what I say and you'll be okay. Might even like it," the voice said. "Try anything fancy and I'll use this. Understood?"

She squinted because of the bright light trained on her. She weighed her options.

357 Magnum! That was it, she thought. *Is there anything I can do to defend myself?*

"Take off your tee shirt." He said.

She hesitated. She heard movement and saw him move the revolver to his left hand. Then he pulled a knife out of a scabbard on his belt and moved it into the light.

"Your damned shirt," he said. "Now!"

Out of the corner of her eye she saw headlights approaching from a long way off. He saw them, too. As the headlights drew closer he put his hand over the lens of the light on his forehead to dim it as a cattle truck sped by. It never slowed, and was quickly gone.

When he put his hand over the lens she got just a brief glimpse of his hand and wrist. They were light complexioned. She didn't see a watch or any rings. She had a brief glimpse of the steering wheel. She was pretty sure there was a Chevrolet logo in the center.

As the cattle truck disappeared into the darkness, he removed his hand and the light shown as bright as ever. She had not caught a glimpse of his face.

He moved the hunting knife into the light and placed the tip just under her chin.

"Shirt."

She was pressed against the passenger door as far away from him as she could get. He was leaning over the center console with the hunting knife of some sort in his right hand, lightly pressed against her chin. The revolver in his left hand was hidden in the darkness. She would wait for some opening before making a move.

She couldn't see his face, but she could feel his eyes on her as she put her hands on the hem of her shirt and slowly pulled it over her head.

"That's a girl," he said. "You get the idea."

She squinted into the bright light and the darkness beyond. He had moved the hunting knife a few inches away from her chin.

"Nice bra," he said. "Take it off."

LaDonna Mae hesitated. He placed the point of his knife between the cups of her bra.

"Want me to cut it off?"

She was weighing her odds. Stalling. Hoping another vehicle would pass them. Maybe a cop car.

Slowly she reached behind her and unsnapped the hooks, letting the straps fall.

"Take it off. You haven't got much to hide anyway."

She removed the garment, and let her arms cover her nakedness.

"Now we're getting somewhere. Remove your belt."

"She carefully unbuckled her belt and pulled it slowly though the loops of her jeans. He held the knife in front of her with his right hand, and held out his left.

"Hand it to me," he said.

She did as she was ordered.

"Big Cock Country," he said, reading from the inscription on her belt buckle. "Truer words were never spoken. Now take off the rest."

A beam of light reflected off the knife blade and briefly illuminated his face. It was covered by a red bandanna, bandito style. She thought his eyes were probably blue.

LaDonna Mae reached down and removed her left shoe. She was stalling for time, and she didn't want to get her feet tangled up in her pants if she had a chance to make a move.

He reached out with his left hand again, and she handed him her left Nike. She wasn't wearing socks. She wished she was. It would take just that much longer to remove her clothing.

He took the shoe and placed it on the floor in front of the driver's seat, then snapped his fingers impatiently.

She started to remove her other shoe. The light stayed on her upper body and her feet were in the dark. She pulled the lace and managed to tie a knot without him noticing.

She pretended to struggle with the shoe lace, trying to get her shoe off. He looked down and the light illuminated her feet.

"Hurry it up! Pull the damned thing off!"

When she removed the right shoe, he grabbed it and dropped it next to the other one.

"Not done yet, but you're getting there. Pants."

She was backed into the far corner next to the passenger door, and the door handle was digging into her hip. She moved to see if the handle would open the door, but it still wouldn't budge.

Both of them heard a noise at the same time. A single headlight was coming toward them from the direction the cattle truck had gone. At first she thought it was a car with a headlight burned out, but as it came closer she could hear the sound of the engine. Unmistakable. A Harley.

"Put this on!" he said throwing her tee shirt on her lap.

As she slipped the shirt over her head, she saw the motorcycle slow down and pull into the parking area behind the pick-up. The rider turned off the motor. The sound of his radio filled the air with a blaring Merle Haggard tune. She recognized *I'll Never Swim Kern River Again*, one of her dad's favorites."

"Keep quiet! Don't try anything cute!"

She saw the rider get off his cycle and stretch his arms and legs. She watched as he turned to the side and urinated onto the grass.

"He comes over here, he's a dead man, got that?"

She kept silent as she tried to take in as much as she could inside the cab from the light shining through the pick-up's back window from the Harley's single headlight.

Leather seats, she thought. *I'm positive that's a Chevy Silverado emblem in the middle of the steering wheel, just like I thought. And he's got a plastic Jesus there on the dashboard. Arms spread. Facing front.*

The driver was intently watching the motorcyclist through the back window.

Seat color hard to tell in this light. If not white, then a light color.

She made a mental note of as much of the driver as she could see.

Looks pretty tall. Hair over his ears. Some gray. White Stetson. Looks new. No sweat stains. Braided horsehair band with a turquoise doo-dad on the side. Guy looks to be forty at least. Plaid shirt. Jeans. Freshly pressed. Wide, hand-tooled brown belt. Matching Roper boots. Clean shaven, far as I can tell.

LaDonna Mae looked back at the motorcycle. The rider had taken a water bottle out of a saddle bag and was taking a long drink. He but the bottle away, lit up a cigarette, took a long drag, and climbed back on his machine, started the motor and revved it up two or three times before slowly pulling back on the roadway and heading off in the direction of Miles City.

They watched it go, seeing the tail-light recede. They heard it shift through the gears then disappear from both sight and sound.

"Back to the fun. Get that shirt off."

LaDonna Mae removed her shirt. He reached for it and dropped it on the floor over her shoes.

"You know what's next. Get those pants off!"

She pretended to have trouble unbuttoning the button, but she could sense him getting impatient. She undid the button and slid the zipper down. She got her pants off and was sitting there in only her panties.

He grabbed the jeans and placed them on the top of her other clothes as he said, "This is getting interesting. Bra and panties match. Nice touch. Get them just for me? Blue's my favorite color."

Her lingerie was new. Bought just for today. For Lleyellyn.

She was getting use to the dim light reflecting back onto her assailant. His face was hidden behind his bandanna, but she knew, could feel, that he was grinning evilly at her.

"Take them off. Haven't got all day."

She hesitated. He moved the knife blade into the beam of light and held the point an inch from her chin.

"Now!"

Quickly she pulled down her panties, wadded them into a ball and threw them at him. He said nothing, but she knew he was staring at her as he moved the light from her face to her crotch.

"Now the real fun begins," he said.

She heard the sound of a zipper. It looked like he was starting to climb over the console, then thought better of it. He opened the driver side door. Keeping the light trained on her, he started walking around the front of the truck.

When he got directly in front of the passenger side fender, LaDonna Mae sprang from her seat, hopped over the center console, and lunged for the door handle. It wasn't locked! She opened the door, sprinted across the road, and jumped down the embankment to the roadside ditch below.

Her feet hit the roadside weeds. Her momentum carried her forward. With her next step she landed on top of rip rap boulders. Her feet hurt with unbearable pain, but she knew getting as far away as possible was her only hope.

She heard him yell as she landed on her side in the ditch at the bottom of the embankment. Her feet were bleeding. The pain was intense. She scrambled along the ditch. She saw his light shining from the road above, moving along, trying to locate her.

As she moved, she was aware that she had stepped on broken glass and who knew what else. She was losing sensation in her feet. They were becoming numb.

As the light came closer she got a glimpse of the round opening to the culvert that passed under the road.

She ducked into the culvert just as the light caught up to her. A bullet ricocheted off the rip rap at her feet as she ducked inside. She could see the beam of his flashlight moving around in the ditch.

"I know you're in that pipe, you bitch!"

When the beam of light moved away she poked her head out. It was dark and she saw no movement and heard nothing.

He's still up on the road, she thought, wondering what he would do next.

The culvert was a round pipe about three feet high. She could bend over and scramble through it, but if he flashed a light through it she would be a sitting duck.

She listened some more. At first she heard nothing. She waited. Straining to hear him. Finally she heard a sound of movement echoing through the culvert from the other side. She edged away from the mouth of the culvert, waiting to see what would happen next.

There was light coming from the other end, and then the full intensity of the light beamed through the culvert.

He's crossed the road and is on the other side.

It was her chance. She followed the nearly dry streambed from the culvert away from the road oblivious to the damage to her bare feet. She wanted to get as far away from the road as possible. Out of range of the light and out of firing range of his gun.

As she moved forward in the dark, her naked body was brushed by branches and her skin was scratched by stickers and thorns. Finally, the course of the streambed made a turn to the right beyond a clump of bushes. She made the turn and collapsed to catch her breath, straining to see and hear anything in the pitch blackness.

She looked out from behind the bushes and saw the light playing along the side of the road. She had made it at least a hundred yards.

She stayed where she was, gradually catching her breath and keeping a lookout.

I'm out of range, she thought. *He doesn't know where I am.*

The moon had started to rise, giving just a hint of light in the eastern sky. Not enough light to see the road, or his truck, or her car.

From a distance she heard a sound. At first she wasn't sure what it was, but then recognized it as a truck coming her way from the southwest. He must have heard it, too, because she heard a door slam, saw headlights come on, and then the Silverado pulled onto the road and headed off toward Miles City. The approaching sound got louder. She saw two cattle trucks pass, headlights ablaze and diesels roaring.

He's gone, she thought, relieved. *But, now what? I'm out here without a stitch on. Can't hardly walk. Probably bleeding to death.*

She felt the urge to cry, but she pulled herself together. Took several deep breaths, and resolved to get out of her predicament.

I'm not giving up.

Two Shots Quick

CHAPTER 3

SATURDAY JULY 18

She managed to slowly make her way on her hands and knees back along the nearly dry stream bed toward the road. The sky had finally started to lighten and gradually she was able to see her surroundings. She inspected her feet. There were ugly cuts on both of them. She removed a protruding piece of broken beer bottle from her right foot. The blood had started to coagulate on most of the cuts. She applied pressure to the biggest cut on her right foot until the bleeding slowed. There were scratches on her arms and shoulders. It felt like there were scratches on her face, but she couldn't be sure.

When she was finally back at the culvert the sun had risen above the horizon. She was out of sight from the road in the ditch. With the condition her feet were in she couldn't really walk, but she could scramble on all fours.

She stayed hidden as several trucks passed by. How could she be sure they would stop. And if they did, would she be attacked again?

By standing back from the culvert in the bottom of the roadside ditch she could look down the road and see approaching traffic. She ducked down when two pick-ups passed by. One was white.

It couldn't be him, could it?

Finally she saw a square looking brown colored vehicle coming her way. She knew what it was immediately.

I'm taking my chances with this one.

LaDonna Mae scrambled up the rocky rip rap and over the roadside weeds to the shoulder of the road, and waited there, sitting on her left hip and supporting herself with her left hand as she waved to flag down the approaching UPS truck.

The driver saw her immediately, slowed, then pulled over a hundred or more yards up the road.

She saw the backup lights come on and heard the familiar warning ding ding dings of its safety alarm as it backed up. The truck stopped, the driver's door slid open, and the uniformed driver stepped down.

"Holy shit! Girl, what happened to you?"

The driver was a large woman with short blonde streaked brown hair. She was wearing boots, brown mid-thigh cargo shorts, and a UPS jacket.

"My car broke down last night. That's it over there," LaDonna Mae said. "Guy offered me a ride. I got in his truck and he stuck a gun in my face, had me undress, and was getting ready to fuck me. I got loose. I've been out here in the dark ever since."

"Looks like your feet are mangled pretty bad. Can't walk, can you?"

Without waiting for a reply, the driver bent down and picked LaDonna Mae up and carried her over to her truck.

"Open the door, will you?"

LaDonna Mae turned the handle and slid the door open wider. The driver maneuvered her onto the seat.

"I've got a first aid kit in here. Plus, some emergency winter survival stuff. Give me a sec."

The driver took the first aid kit out of a compartment in front of the passenger door.

"First, I'm Doreen. What's your name?"

LaDonna Mae introduced herself, and the two women shook hands.

"Here's what I'm going to do," the driver said. "First, I'm going to bandage your feet. Looks like the bleeding's about stopped. Pressure bandages will stop the rest. Then I'm going to get something to cover you up. Then I'll call 911. Tell dispatch what happened. Then I'll take you to the emergency room in Miles City. Get you checked out. Sound okay?"

"It does," LaDonna Mae said. "You've done this before?"

Doreen smiled as she finished bandaging the right foot.

"I've come across an emergency or two in my time. Can't say I've had a Lady Godiva before, though. You're the first."

After the bandaging of the left foot was finished, the driver opened the back door of the truck and pulled out a flat box from a compartment near the spare tire. She removed a package from the box and returned to the front of the truck where LaDonna Mae was seated.

"Survival blanket, it says here," she said. "We'll see if we can't turn it into suitable attire."

She tore open the package and removed a tightly folded thin looking blue blanket. As she unfolded the blanket she said with a smile at LaDonna Mae, "Good color for you. Matches your eyes."

LaDonna Mae watched as the driver removed a pocket knife from a pouch on the side of her cargo pants, and proceeded to cut a circle in the middle of the blanket.

"Slip this over your head," she said.

LaDonna Mae did as instructed, pulling her head through the newly cut opening poncho style.

"Okay. That works. Let me tie some of this twine around your waist to make a belt," she said, pulling a length of jute from a spool she took from under the seat. "Keep this stuff around in case I have to repair a package. Got tape, too. Can improvise almost anything."

"Thanks. I feel a whole lot better with something on," LaDonna Mae said. "I'll be happy to pay you back for the blanket and the first aid stuff."

"Like hell. They're for emergencies. Today that's you," Doreen said, then reached around LaDonna Mae and dug into a cooler next to the driver's seat and handed a bottle of water to her. "You better drink some of this."

LaDonna Mae took the bottle and drank until it was empty. "Thanks. Tasted great."

"When's the last time you had something to drink?"

"Thought I had a bottle with me when I got in the truck. Maybe not. Not exactly sure," she said. "Last drink I remember was before I left the ranch. Maybe about ten, ten thirty. Somewhere in there"

"Here, have one of these," Doreen said, handing her an energy bar she removed from her jacket. "You must be starving."

As LaDonna Mae unwrapped the energy bar, Doreen said, "As you can see, there's no passenger seat in this rig. You'll have to sit on the floor. Can you manage that?"

She didn't reply, but scooted off the driver's seat and over to the right side of the cab.

"Okay. Let's go. I'll contact dispatch. Should have you at the E. R. in less than an hour."

LaDonna Mae let the half eaten bar slip out of her hand, and curled up on the warm floor of the UPS truck. She was asleep before they had traveled half a mile.

o0o

She slept soundly, lulled to sleep by the steady hum of the truck's engine. She started to wake up when the passenger door was flung open and two hospital orderlies peered in.

"We can take it from here," one of the orderlies told Doreen. "There's an investigator in the lobby wants to talk to you," the orderly said, then turned to LaDonna Mae and added, "And you, too. But after you get checked out by the doctor."

She was lifted out, and placed on a gurney. As they started to wheel her into the emergency room, she turned to Doreen, "Thanks. Thanks for everything."

"No problem, kiddo. I'll stop by when I'm finished with John Law. See how're you're doing."

o0o

She was wheeled up to the ER receiving desk, answered a few general background questions, then almost immediately was placed in an exam room.

"Someone will be with you in a minute," the attendant who wheeled her in said, before she left, closing the door behind her.

It was the first time she's had a chance to look at herself in good light. There was a mirror over the sink. Her hair was matted down and had burrs and small twigs stuck in it. There were scratches on both arms. She moved the chair forward so she could get a better look. Both cheeks had several scratches and scrapes and there were insect bites on her forehead and neck. She noticed a fresh dark red scab on the bottom of her chin.

That's where the asshole held the knife, she thought.

There was a quiet knock on the door. A woman wearing light yellow scrubs entered. LaDonna Mae glanced at her name tag which indicated she was from Special Patient Services.

"Good morning, Miss Ritchie. I'm Roseanna Cummings. A doctor will be in to see you momentarily."

LaDonna Mae watched as Cummings sat down at the desk and swiveled to look at her.

"My job is to interview women who have been assaulted. Particularly assaulted sexually. After the doctor sees you, you will be interviewed by a law enforcement officer concerning details of the attack. Then, after you have been attended to, I believe a counselor will visit you. Think you can answer some questions for me?"

"I think so. Depends, I guess," she said. After a pause, she continued. "What do you want to know?"

"I understand from the friend brought you in, you were forced at gun point, and also at knife point, to completely disrobe against your will. Is that right?"

LaDonna Mae, didn't say anything, but she nodded her head.

"If you need time, let me know, okay?"

Again LaDonna Mae nodded her assent.

"Did the assailant attack you sexually. Put another way, did he do anything to you of a sexual nature?"

"Well, he made me take my clothes off so I was sitting there without a stitch on with him staring at me. But no, he didn't actually touch me with his hands or anything. He held a knife at my chin, that count?" she said, pointing at the cut on her chin.

"Did he.... Excuse, me." Cummings said, trying to get her words right. "You are a mature young lady. Have you ever as a consenting adult engaged in sexual relations with anyone?"

LaDonna Mae looked up, realizing that this was probably a necessary question.

"Yes. I have a boyfriend, if that's what you mean."

"Okay, Cummings said, "Did your assailant last night penetrate you in any way at all sexually?"

"No!" LaDonna Mae said. "I got away before the bastard could. I know he was going to try."

"Good for you. You did the right thing. I have no further questions. An investigator will be asking for details about the crime," Cummings said. "If you had answered yes to my last question then I would have followed up with more questions and taken a swab to obtain DNA to try and identify the perpetrator. Won't need to use the rape kit."

Cummings stood up, and extended her hand. LaDonna Mae shook her hand as Cummings said, "You were very brave, young lady. I've talked to quite a few women who weren't so fortunate. I'll tell the nurse you are ready for them."

oOo

A nurse came in, had LaDonna Mae remove her poncho and slip into a hospital gown. The doctor followed a few minutes later, examined her cuts, scrapes and bruises, then unwrapped her feet and made a careful examination of each one.

"Sounds like you are lucky to have made it in one piece, Miss Ritchie," the doctor said. "You've got some relatively routine abrasions, lacerations, and contusions about your body. You know what an abrasion is, it's a scrape. Laceration is just a fancy word for cut. A contusion is a bruise. We'll clean those up, but on an antibiotic ointment, and they should give you no trouble."

LaDonna Mae watched the doctor, who was gauging her reaction.

"Your more pressing problem, as I'm sure you know, are your feet. They have experienced severe trauma. There are deep cuts in both of them. Bruising, Most certainly infection. We'll clean those and stitch up the cuts. Should turn out okay. But, and here's the thing, you'll have to keep your weight off your feet until the swelling goes down and the stitches are removed. And until any infection has been negated."

"How long will that take?"

"We'll take the stitches out in about ten days or so. Hard to predict when the swelling will subside. You follow my instructions, maybe not much longer than that. Okay?"

"You're the doctor," LaDonna Mae said, flashing a slight smile.

"There's one other thing. You have a small penetrating wound right under your chin. That could be infected. It'll take a stitch or two to close it up without leaving a permanent scar. May leave a minute one. Won't be very visible on the bottom part of your chin in any event."

"I remember him sticking his knife under my chin. Didn't know he actually cut me, the bastard."

"Don't know where that knife's been. You'll have your tetanus shots brought up to date and of course an antibiotic prescription for the infections to your feet and chin. Okay?"

LaDonna Mae gave a slight nod.

"Any questions?'

"No. And thank you, doctor."

"All righty," he said as he stood to leave. "I'll see you in the operating room and again after we're done."

o0o

As soon as the doctor left, a nurse wheeled her to a shower stall where she sat on a stool while the nurse helped her shampoo her hair before she bathed off the dirt and grime she had picked up during her ordeal.

After her shower, LaDonna Mae was prepped for surgery and wheeled into the operating room. The last thing she remembered before she woke up were three faces behind white masks staring at her.

One of them must be the doctor, she thought, but she didn't know which one.

o0o

"Surgery's over," the nurse she had seen before told her. "You're probably still a little disoriented. Try and rest a little."

Immediately she fell into a dream free sleep. The faint sounds of the various monitors she was hooked up to gradually became louder. She was aware that she was in a hospital room and remembered why she was there.

When she opened her eyes, Lleyellyn was standing right there, looking at her. She smiled at him.

"You're here. How'd you find out about me?"

"Irene got a call. She brought me along. You know she's the county's domestic abuse counselor, don't you?"

"I do," she said. "She out there waiting to talk to me?"

"I think what happened to you is what she's here for," Lleyellyn said. "She didn't tell me why she's here. Just told me about what happened."

LaDonna Mae reached a hand toward Lleyellyn. He took it and gently held it as he asked her how she was feeling.

"I feel okay. Maybe a little groggy from the surgery. My feet are cut up pretty bad. They had to sew up several cuts," then she removed her hand from his and pointed to her chin. "I've got a couple little sutures here. Didn't even know he cut me."

They stared at each other for a moment before Lleyellyn bent down to give her a gentle kiss on the cheek. She quickly told him what she remembered about the incident as they held hands.

"But, I escaped," she said, smiling at him.

"I'm sure glad you did. Proud, too," Lleyellyn said, before continuing. "Say, I'm supposed to let Irene talk to you. Then I think the sheriff's office needs a word. I'll be outside."

"Thanks," she said. "Come back when they're gone."

As soon as he left, Irene entered and sat down next to the bed.

"Honey, the nurse says you should be good as new before long. How you feeling?"

"Better. Little groggy. Not too bad. Oh, and thanks for bringing Lleyellyn into town with you."

Irene smiled and took her hand.

"I'll get right to the point. You know I'm the domestic abuse counselor for the county. Right?"

LaDonna Mae gave a nearly imperceptible nod.

"Women who are beaten up or otherwise assaulted often have things they want to talk about. My job is to listen and to help with anything you need help with. I'll be happy to talk with you now or anytime you want to talk. Is there anything I can help you with now?"

"No. I'm fine now. Just so damn happy I got away from that goddamn asshole. Excuse me. But you know what I mean. Wish I had more information to give the sheriff. It was dark. Just know what he tried to do. That he cut my chin. Even took a shot at me when I was getting away. Just glad I'm here where it's safe."

"You may have bad dreams about your experience. Remember to call me when you want to talk. This entire thing was not your fault. What you did to get away was very brave. I'm sure you'll do fine."

"Thanks, Irene. Thanks for stopping by," she said. "And thanks for inviting me out to the ranch. I had a great time."

"Okay. Now don't forget. Just call. I'll leave you now. There's a deputy that needs a word with you."

After Irene left, the nurse came in, checked the monitors and the drip, fluffed up the pillow and said, "Ready for your next visitor?"

"I guess."

The young woman who came in after the nurse departed was wearing a sheriff's uniform with a brass star above her left breast and a name tag that said Deputy Stevens on the opposite side.

"Miss Ritchie, I'm deputy Marie Stevens. Need to ask you a few questions, if that's all right with you."

"I'll do my best."

"I've listened to the 911 tape and interviewed the UPS driver so I have a general idea what happened. What can you tell me that might help us identify the perp, or his vehicle?"

"All I can tell you about the vehicle is that it was a pick-up. It had to be a four-wheel drive because I had to step up on a running board to get inside. It was dark, so I didn't see much. Saw a Chevy, or Chevrolet logo in the middle of the steering wheel. Think it was a white truck, or at least a light color. Pretty sure it was one of those fancy Silverado models. Real big rig. Other thing I saw was a plastic Jesus stuck in the middle of the dashboard. It was looking ahead. Seems like it maybe glowed in the dark. That's about it."

"Upholstery?"

"Oh, yeah. Leather. I think light colored," she said. "Beige or tan. Maybe even white. Hard to tell at night."

"What about the perpetrator? The driver."

Had a scarf pulled up over his face. Had on a white Stetson-type hat with a horsehair band and a turquoise thingy on the side, the right side, side nearest me. Brown roper boots, broad brown belt, creased jeans and a long sleeved shirt. Dark. Didn't see a watch. No rings. And no glasses."

"Good memory for details," the deputy said. "Anything physical? What did he look like?"

"Pretty well hidden by the bandanna. I think he had blue eyes. I'd guess he was maybe forty, forty-five," she said. "And the gun he had. You know about that?"

"Right, big pistol like Dirty Harry had in the movies," the investigator said. "What were you wearing?"

"Jeans. Nikes. Tee shirt. Matching blue underwear," LaDonna Mae said. "Had a billfold with my driver's license and stuff. They been found?"

"Not that I know of," the deputy said, meeting her eyes. "We're looking."

"Wish I could be of more help."

"Any details about your stuff? Might be helpful."

"Well the underwear was brand new. Just bought at Eileen's Style Shoppe. Vanity Fair brand. Her best," LaDonna Mae said. "Matching light blue top and bottom."

Anything else?"

"Well, my buckle was kinda unique," she said. "Gift from my brother. Had a pheasant on it," she added, then after a pause continued, "*Big Cock Country* was written across it."

"How about your tee?"

"White," LaDonna Mae said. "*Grand Tetons* printed on the front. In red."

"You described what happened to Miss Cummings from the hospital staff, didn't you?"

LaDonna Mae nodded yes.

"May I talk to her about what she found out from you?"

"Sure."

"Okay. Would you sign this authorization? She can't talk to me about you without your consent. Patient confidentiality."

"Hey, no problem," LaDonna Mae said, before signing the consent form.

As soon as deputy Stevens stepped out, the nurse returned. "Anything you need?"

"Maybe some sleep. Is Lleyellyn still out there?"

"Yes he is. Shall I send him in?"

"Yes, please."

Lleyellyn came in a few seconds after the nurse left the room.

"One thing I want you to do. Would you call my Dad? I haven't told him about ... ," she said, gesturing to her feet. "Well, I haven't told him anything."

Before Lleyellyn could reply, LaDonna Mae was asleep.

oOo

The phone was answered on the second ring.

"Ritchie's," a voice Lleyellyn recognized as Jimmy's said.

"Hey! It's Lleyellyn. Your Dad there?"

"Sure. Just drove in. I'll get him. Hang on."

It seemed to take several minutes before LaDonna Mae's father picked up the telephone.

"Jim Ritchie," he said.

"Mr. Ritchie, this is Lleyellyn. LaDonna Mae asked me to call you."

There was silence on the other end of the line.

"Well, sir, she hurt her feet last night. She had to have some stitches. She's here at the hospital in town."

"How'd she do that, for God's sake?"

Lleyellyn told Mr. Ritchie the whole story.

"She's sleeping right now. Doctor says she has to spend the night. Probably will discharge her tomorrow."

"Thanks, son, for calling. If she wakes up before we get there, tell her Jimmy and I will be there as soon as we can."

oOo

Irene drove into the yard and dropped him off a few feet from the bunkhouse steps. Mully came running up, and Lleyellyn gave the dog a good ear rub and went inside as Irene make a sweeping turn and stopped near the house.

Just as Lleyellyn started up the steps, Montoya opened the door and stepped aside to let him in.

"LaDonna Mae was attacked last night," Lleyellyn said. "On her way home from here. She got away, but screwed up her feet. Had a bunch of stitches. She's in the hospital."

Montoya put a hand on Lleyellyn's shoulder.

"Irene told me about it," he said. "Let's go in my room. You can fill me in on the details."

o0o

Shay sat on the bed while Montoya sat at his desk with his chair swiveled around so they were facing each other.

"Start at the beginning. Take your time."

"LaDonna Mae and I were on the porch talking after we finished dinner. You and Irene were watching the news or something. We stayed out there a while, just talking, you know. She left about nine thirty, ten, or so. Not exactly sure of the time. She wanted to get at least a little sleep before she had to go to work. Her shift starts at ten. Said she noticed that her headlights started going dim a little ways before she reached the highway. Even on high beams. Pulled over at that wide spot near the pond we pass a mile or two down the road toward town."

"Know the place," Montoya said. "She been having any car trouble before that?"

"Don't think so. Didn't mention it to me."

"Sorry to interrupt. What happened next?"

"She was hoping someone would stop. Give her a lift to town. Said a truck or two whizzed by, but nobody paid her any attention. It was pitch black and she didn't have any light at all. At any rate, a pick-up finally stopped. Guy rolled down the window and asked if she wanted a ride to Miles City.

"It was dark out. Pitch black. She couldn't get a good look at him. When she opened the door to get in the lights didn't come on in the cab like usual. Driver told her they weren't working. She got in. High step. Why she figured four-wheel drive."

"Know what make?"

"Later she thought it was a Chevy. Four by Four. Silverado model, probably. Big. Had leather seats. Light colored. Tan maybe. Thinks the truck was white, or at least light in color. Hard for her to tell for sure in the dark."

"Sorry, again. Go on."

"Well, as soon as she got in the door seemed to lock itself automatically. The guy turned on one of those lights you can wear strapped around your head. Sorta like a miner's lamp. Real bright. She couldn't hardly see anything. At some point she could make out he was wearing a bandanna over his face. Train robber style."

Lleyellyn was talking faster and faster. Montoya handed him a Mountain Dew from his mini fridge. Lleyellyn took a couple swallows.

"Okay, thanks," he said, wiping his mouth with the back of his hand. "Bastard pulled a gun. Told LaDonna Mae to remove her clothes. When she didn't do it fast enough, he held a knife under her chin. Cut her, too. Needed a couple stitches."

He took another gulp of the soft drink.

"When she was sitting there naked he unzipped his pants. She heard it. Then he opened his door and started around the truck to where she was sitting. She saw her chance, jumped over the console, and ran across the road. She jumped down the embankment. Fucked up her feet on the rocks and broken beer bottles. He took a shot at her, but didn't go after her. Got scared away when a truck went by, she thought."

Lleyellyn paused to take another sip of his soda and collect his thoughts.

"She hid in the brush until it started getting light out. Finally hitched a ride with a UPS driver. Lucky. It was a woman driver. Knew first aid, too."

Montoya stood up, grabbed himself a Diet Coke and closed his eyes while he thought about what he had just learned.

"She know what type of gun?"

"She could see it in the light when he pointed it at her. Said it looked just like the big pistol Dirty Harry had in those Clint Eastwood movies. Told the deputy she thought it was a Three Fifty Seven Magnum."

"Doubt that," Montoya said. "But any gun pointed at you looks big, I suppose. Think she knows anything about firearms?"

Lleyellyn shrugged. He didn't know.

"I'm sure that was a 44 Magnum Eastwood used in the movie," Montoya said. "Smith and Wesson. With at least an eight-inch barrel."

After they both took another sip, Montoya said, "She notice anything about the guy?"

"Said she got a glimpse when a motorcycle pulled in behind them while the driver stretched and took a leak. Guy with the gun turned out his light and kept a close eye on the motorcycle. That's when she got a good look at the bandanna and stuff. He kept the pistol in his hand. Tried to remember all the details she could. She thought he looked tall. Probably mid forties. White Stetson. Saw a horsehair hat band with a turquoise doo dad on the side. Was wearing a long sleeve shirt. Pressed jeans. Roper boots. Brown. Wide, tan or brown belt. That's it. Oh. She thought maybe he had blue eyes."

"Good for her. Pretty observant. Anything else?"

"She remembered he had a plastic Jesus on the middle of his dashboard. Said it was facing toward the front," he said. "Said when the lights were out, it seemed to glow in the dark."

"That's interesting. Haven't seen too many of those around lately. Have you?"

"Not that I remember," Lleyellyn said.

After they finished their soft drinks, Montoya said, "Let's grab a bite to eat. Think over what happened. We can talk again in the morning."

Two Shots Quick

CHAPTER 4

SUNDAY JULY 19

Breakfast was waiting for them when they got to the house.

"Felt like hot cakes today," Irene said. "There's bacon."

"Smells good," Lleyellyn said.

"She's an expert at hot cakes," Montoya said, sitting down and pouring coffee for Irene and then himself. "You're not a coffee drinker," he said looking at Lleyellyn.

Lleyellyn didn't say anything, but filled a glass with water from the tap before joining them at the table.

Irene watched them as they started eating.

"I've been awake half the night thinking about what happened to LaDonna Mae," she said. "What are the odds that the first person to stop to help her out would be someone prepared to attack her? Someone able to lock the door. And no interior light. And a gun. A knife, too. That weird light around his head. And the bandanna. Almost like he was expecting her."

"I agree, seems funny to me, too," Lleyellyn said.

"What I think happened," Montoya said, "Is that someone did something to her car so it would have to stop somewhere out in the middle of nowhere. Give him the opportunity to go after her."

They ate in silence for a few moments, each lost in their own thoughts.

"He must have got to her car before she left the ranch," Lleyellyn said.

"Exactly," Montoya said. "We'll have to take a look at her car. See if we can figure out what the hell happened."

"The car's still parked where she left it, I bet," Irene said. "Lleyellyn, give her a call. See if it's okay with her if we bring it back here."

"You do that. Tell her I'll try and get it running. Shouldn't be too hard to find out what happened," Montoya said.

o0o

Lleyellyn was worried about LaDonna Mae, wondering how she was recovering.

Lleyellyn called the hospital. He was connected to LaDonna Mae's room by the receptionist. She answered on the second ring, and was happy to hear from him. She put his worries to rest immediately.

"I got a good night's sleep," she said, sounding like her old self. "Breakfast tastes really good. Supposed to see the doctor. He's on his rounds. Hoping I get discharged soon. Probably in a day or two. Maybe even today."

She described her progress and treatment, and what the medical staff had told her so far.

"I'm missing some work, but I should be as good as new," she said. "I'm really hoping they catch the asshole as soon as possible."

"Call me after the doctor stops in," Lleyellyn said. "Let me know if you need anything."

"Thanks for calling," she said. "Love you."

"Me, too," Lleyellyn said. "Love you, too." Before hanging up he added, "Another reason I called, Mr. Montoya thinks he can get your car fixed up. Doesn't think there's anything too much wrong with it. You okay if we tow it back here to the ranch so he can work on it in his shop?"

"You bet. I was worried about leaving the car out in the middle of nowhere," she said. "Keys are on the floor under the seat."

o0o

They took Irene's Ram truck to retrieve LaDonna Mae's car.

"Ever have to tow anybody?" Montoya said.

"No, not really," Lleyellyn said. "I've had to push a few times when we ran out of gas."

On the way to LaDonna Mae's car, Montoya explained the finer points of towing a disabled vehicle.

o0o

The key was right where it was supposed to be. Just to make sure, Montoya tried to start the car using the key, but the battery was still dead.

Montoya backed Irene's Dodge so it was ten feet in front of LaDonna Mae's Gran Am. There were two hooks bolted to the frame of the car behind the bumper.

"We'll fasten this rope to the hook on the driver's side. Should tend to keep the car to the left of the center line," Montoya said, before fastening the other end to the Dodge's bracket supporting the trailer hitch. "Don't want this damn ball to go flying."

"You get in her car. Put it in neutral like we talked about. Remember, keep the slack out of the tow rope. I'll try and go at an even speed. You steer like normal. Apply the brakes if the rope has any play in it, or you start to gain on me. I'll signal you with hand signals if I want you to slow down or stop. Make sense?"

"Sounds easy enough," Lleyellyn said. "Let's go."

"With the electrical system down you won't have power bakes or power steering. Keep that in mind," Montoya said. "Just use a little more umph."

They had no trouble towing the car back to the ranch. The hardest part was making a u-turn when they first started out. After that it was smooth sailing. They only saw two trucks and a single car all heading in the opposite direction the whole way.

When they pulled into the yard, Montoya got out and walked back to Lleyellyn.

"Mechanic tools are in the shed out back. Not sure you've been in there. We'll just take her real easy. We can push it in by hand when we get close."

They eased up to the shed. Montoya quickly undid the tow rope and coiled it over his arm, then unlocked the shed door, and rolled it open.

The shed was spacious with a cement floor and fluorescent lights hanging from the ceiling. A big red tool chest stood against a side wall, and an older pick-up was parked in the back. There was plenty of room for LaDonna Mae's car.

Montoya rolled down the driver's side window and steered as he pushed from the outside with Lleyellyn helping from the rear.

"Hold her right there!" Montoya said.

He opened the door, set the emergency brake, and pulled the release to open the hood.

Montoya hung the tow rope on a nail, before taking a drop light from a hook near the workbench. He undid the cord and hung the light over the engine compartment. He leaned forward to get a better look, maneuvering the light so he could inspect the belts and pulleys in the front of the engine.

"What I thought," he said. "Damned belt's been loosened. Battery wasn't charging When it petered out there was no power getting to the spark plugs. Could easily have been done on purpose."

Montoya played the light beam over the belt assembly and motioned Lleyellyn closer to take a look.

"This gizmo automatically keeps the slack out of the belt so it doesn't slip," he said, pointing to a place near the front of the engine with the tip of a screwdriver. Thing's spring loaded. It's been monkeyed with. Recently. See how loose the belt is?" he said, moving the belt from side to side. "Not sure what he did to it, but see those fresh scratches? Sure as hell did something. Knew what he was doing. No doubt about it."

"You think whoever did it followed her until the car stopped? Had the whole thing planned out?"

Lleyellyn said.

"Damn right. Now we just have to figure out who that was."

Before taking Irene's pick-up back to the house, Montoya tried adjusting the tension on the belt.

"Might have to replace a part," he said. "But this might do for now. We could have Irene follow us back to town once we get some juice in the battery."

Montoya got a battery charger from a shelf.

He showed Lleyellyn how to hook it up to the battery in LaDonna Mae's car.

"Nothing to this," he said. "Hook the red clamp on the positive terminal like this. See the plus sign? Then clamp the black one to the frame. Now all you have to do is plug the charger into the wall. See that the knob is set for a twelve-volt battery. Then we flip this switch to the fast charge setting. Should be fully charged in a couple hours."

o0o

They parked Irene's pickup near the kitchen door.

"Let's go back to my room and talk some more," Montoya said, before turning and heading for the bunkhouse. "Give me a minute, will you? I have to get this grease off my hands."

Once they were seated in Montoya's room, they got right to the point.

"Whoever fiddled with the car had to have done it before LaDonna Mae started back to town."

"My conclusion, exactly," Montoya said. "Had to have been done right here at the ranch. Right where her car was parked."

"When? is the question," Lleyellyn said.

"Let's face it. None of us was around the car the whole time she was here. Weren't paying attention. Someone could have got to it when we were fooling around on the lawn, having dinner, or whenever. I doubt if she locked the car. Would only take half a minute to pop the hood, and disable the tension device, if you know what you're doing."

Lleyellyn looked at Montoya and shook his head.

Remember when Mully stopped gnawing on those rib bones we gave her and was looking toward the bunkhouse?" he said.

"I do," Montoya said. "Could've happened then."

"There's a damned rapist here somewhere," Lleyellyn said. "Someone with the movie outfit, I'll bet. Has to be. A crew member, maybe an actor, or at least an extra. Wrangler. Somebody like that. No one else has been around. Right?"

Montoya didn't reply, but he reached over and picked up a yellow legal pad from his desk and turned it to a clean page.

"Let's write down what we know. What she told you. First, she said he was driving a four wheel drive full size Chevrolet truck. That's a C/K. She also mentioned Silverado, right? That's the fancy model."

He wrote down the words 4x4 Chevrolet pickup C/K (Silverado model). Then continued writing as the two of them discussed what LaDonna Mae had recounted.

> Tan (or light ?) leather upholstery
> Glow in the dark plastic Jesus on the dashboard
> White Stetson with horsehair band and turquoise clasp
> Pressed jeans
> Brown roper-style boots
> Wide leather belt, brown
> Long sleeve shirt
> Miner's type light
> Blue eyes
> Mid-forties
> Tall
> 44 Magnum S&W pistol
> Sharp pointed knife
> Missing blue panties
> Missing blue jeans
> Missing blue bra
> Missing tennis shoes (Nike)
> Missing billfold, license, credit card

"It's a pretty long list," Montoya said. "We better add, alternator belt loosened."

He held up the tablet. Lleyellyn scanned the list.

"Know her tee shirt said Grand Tetons across the front. You probably saw her belt buckle. Said Big Cock Country," he said.

Montoya added the information to the list.

"We know quite a bit," Montoya he said. "What do you think we should do?"

"Maybe contact the sheriff?" Lleyellyn said.

Montoya looked at Lleyellyn, a serious look on his face.

"Here's the problem with that. They'll say we compromised the evidence by moving her car and readjusting the tension on the belt. Probably think everything is just speculation. And since LaDonna Mae escaped, they won't give it top priority. Out here in the middle of nowhere law enforcement is spread pretty thin."

"I can see that. Like what happened when my mom was murdered. Law enforcement didn't work too hard at finding the murderer. And they knew who he was," Lleyellyn said. "We'll have to track down the guy ourselves."

Montoya nodded his agreement, and then said, "Like we did before."

"Where do we start?"

"We better check all the Chevy pickups used by the movie crew. Especially four by fours, and any Silverado models. I've seen several go in and out of the parking area. Check out any other white pick-ups, too. Need to find out if there's any with a plastic Jesus on the dash."

"Lot of them are gone for the weekend," Lleyellyn said. "Think we should wait to Monday when they get back?"

"Makes sense."

CHAPTER 5

MONDAY JULY 20

Montoya sat down next to Shay on the bunkhouse steps. Mully was nosing around under the porch. The lights were on in the movie compound. But it was quiet. The moon hadn't risen.

"Let's run down what we know again."

He took a folded sheet of yellow lined paper from his shirt pocket, and they reviewed the list they had compiled the day before.

"She remembered a center console," Lleyellyn said. "The guy couldn't climb over it."

Montoya added 'center console" to the list.

"She say anything else?" Montoya said.

"Not really. Said the Jesus looked like that statue on that hilltop in Buenos Aires or Rio, or wherever. Said it was facing toward the front. Thought it was magnetized," Shay said. "It glowed in the dark."

"Well, probably held on with Velcro. Maybe glue or something. Dashboards are mostly plastic these days. Maybe fake leather or Naugahide. Magnet wouldn't work."

They remained silent for a while thinking. Finally Montoya broke the silence.

"We know there's a couple dozen pick-ups in that lot over there. At least half of them are white. When we're sure everybody's asleep, we'll go take a look. See if there's a plastic Jesus or maybe a Velcro patch or a glue spot on one of the dashboards."

Two Shots Quick

CHAPTER 6

TUESDAY JULY 21

At a few minutes after midnight they met in Montoya's room. Shay was handed a flashlight.

"You start with the truck closest to us. I'll start at the other side of the lot. We're just checking the white ones. Don't try and open any doors. Don't want to set off any alarms," Montoya said.

o0o

Lleyellyn walked quietly to the parked line up of pick-up trucks. Mully walked along beside him. He didn't see Montoya but knew he was making his way to the far side of the parking area.

Shay kept an eye open for anyone in the area. No one was moving around near the motor homes or tents. The area seemed deserted.

The first truck he came to was a light colored Ford 150. It looked white in the moonlight but could have been any light color. Beige, perhaps.

He looked inside the cab. There was a pair of leather gloves on the dash in front of the steering wheel. He used the flashlight to check the middle of the dash. No statue. No Velcro. No residue of glue or putty.

As he walked around the front of the Ford, Mully gave a slight yip and took off after something. He watched the dog go and saw a rabbit dash across the lighted area in front of the supply shed beyond the bunkhouse.

Shay stood still and looked around again for signs of life. There was no one he could see. He moved on.

The next vehicle was another Ford. A 250. A little older. Duallies on the back. Several Copenhagen cans were clustered on the driver's side of the dashboard. In the center was a radar detector securely fastened to the dash. No sign of a statuette or any evidence that one had been there.

As Shay moved onto the next vehicle, he caught a glimpse of Montoya at the other end of the row checking out other trucks.

The majority of parked vehicles were pickups. Shay checked out two Jimmys, an older Chevy, and a Dodge Ram, before Mully was back. No indication of a statuette in any of them.

As he was passing several dark colored pick-ups, Montoya stepped out in the open and waved him over. Shay followed Mully, and they joined Montoya by a white pickup.

"Take a look at this. Says *Silverado* right here," Montoya whispered, pointing to an emblem on the side.

He motioned for Shay to move closer. Shay looked over Montoya's shoulder as he flashed his light on the center of the dash board.

"See that?"

Shay tilted his head to get a better look. In the middle of the dashboard about three inches from the windshield was a dime sized circular spot. Something green was visible on one side of the area.

"Looks like something was glued on right there," Montoya said. "I think that green stuff is felt. Off the bottom of the statue."

"Sure seems like it," Shay said as he used his flashlight to check out the interior of the cab. "Light colored leather. Tannish. Just like what LaDonna Mae described, don't you think?"

Montoya removed a notebook and pencil from his shirt.

"Read me off the vin number, will you? It's right there on the corner of the dash," he said, pointing to the number with the beam of his flashlight.

Shay read off the vehicle identification number and double checked it as Montoya read it back from his notes. Montoya moved to the front of the truck and jotted down the license number. It was a California plate.

They stood there looking at the truck for a moment. They both saw the flashing red light in the middle of the dash above the console.

"With that alarm system, nothing we can do now," Montoya said.

o0o

"We've gotta find out whose truck it is," Shay said.

"If we were law enforcement we could call the DMV and find out in seconds. But we aren't. We'll just have to keep an eye out and see who's driving it. Maybe ask around. Someone might know who it belongs to."

"Well, we know where to start," Shay said. "I'll ask around in the morning."

"You'll need a reason to do that. Think on it. See if you can come up with a reason you need to know," Montoya said. "I'd like to figure out a way to check out the vehicle. Search it. Maybe the plastic Jesus is in the glove compartment. Who knows?"

o0o

Lleyellyn Shay was gassing up the Jeep when Montoya walked over and put several steel fence posts in the back end.

"Got any idea how we can find out who owns that truck?" Shay said. "I'm thinking maybe a sign-up sheet. Have all the owners write in their license plate numbers and names."

"Better idea. We'll punch a hole in a tire. Let the air out of the spare. Owner will need help fixing the flat," Montoya said. "Maybe he'll ask us for assistance, or have us call the tire service at the Co-op in town. Find out his name then."

"Could work. Probably figure we'd know who to call."

CHAPTER 7

WEDNESDAY JULY 22

About two in the morning, Montoya grabbed Shay's shoulder and gave it a little shake. He awoke immediately.
"Let's go. I've got what I need."
They walked to the parking area like they did the night before. As usual, Mully was keeping them company.
They approached the white pickup from the front.
"You stand back there. Keep a look-out. See anything, just call the dog. I'll take care of the tires," Montoya said.
The spare tire was on a bracket under the rear of the truck bed. Montoya crawled under the truck. Shay caught a glimpse of a flashlight beam and heard the pssst of escaping air. Montoya crawled out from the rear of the Chevy and moved to the side of the left front wheel. He slid under the truck and punched a hole in the interior side of the tire using an awl.
Lleyellyn saw the truck slowly tilt to the front left. Montoya removed his knife from the scabbard on his belt and used it to cut an L-shaped flap in the sidewall to obliterate evidence of the puncture.
When he was back on his feet, he motioned to Shay, and they returned to the bunkhouse, keeping out of sight. They were sure no one had seen them. Mully stayed outside.
"Tire's unfixable. Might look like road hazard damage. Guy must have run over a sharp piece of angle iron or something," Montoya said. "Wonder how he made it here without noticing it, though," he added with a smile. "See you in the morning."

o0o

Before breakfast Montoya told Lleyellyn to park the Jeep in front of the bunkhouse.

Shay backed the Jeep out of the machine shed. He saw Montoya standing near the bunk house steps holding the handle of a heavy duty jack. As soon as he parked the Jeep and set the emergency brake, Montoya shoved the jack under the axel of the left side front wheel. He pumped the jack handle to raise the vehicle.

"Lug wrench is in the back," Montoya said. "Take off the wheel. I'll get some tools."

Lleyellyn hadn't quite got the wheel off when Montoya was back, pulling a cart with an air compressor and a tool box.

"Lay that wheel down. Let the air out," Montoya said. "Know how to do it?"

By way of answer, Shay stuck the end of a Phillips screwdriver in the valve stem and let the tire deflate. To hurry the process along, Montoya stood on the tire until the bead was loose from the rim and the tire was completely flat and separated from the rim.

"Looks like a flat that needs fixin' to me," Montoya said. "Let's grab breakfast. See if this will be bait enough to catch Mr. Silverado."

o0o

When they came out of the kitchen after finishing breakfast and helping with the clean-up chores, Shay was surprised to see someone sitting on the bunkhouse steps on the far side of the Jeep.

Mully took off and cautiously approached the stranger, tail lowered, ears up.

"Mully, get back here!" Montoya said, approaching the stranger. "Can I help you?"

"Hope so. See you're fixing a flat. Think you can help me out? I've got two of 'em."

As the stranger stood up, Lleyellyn made the introductions.

"I'm Lleyellyn," he said. "This is Mr. Montoya, our ranch foreman. You with the movie outfit?"

"You bet," the stranger said. "I'm Cass," he said, shaking hands first with Montoya then with Shay. "Cass Montgomery."

Montgomery was six feet tall or better, about forty Shay thought. Wearing jeans and a red polo shirt. They both noticed the sharp creases in his denims.

"Where's your vehicle?" Montoya said.

"I'm over in the parking area. Chevy 4 X 4. Silverado. White. California plates."

Montoya removed his hat and scratched the side of his head.

"Tell you what. We'll get this Jeep fixed up. Shouldn't take long. Then we'll drive over and take a look. Where 'bouts in the lot are you?"

Montgomery told them where his truck was parked, then started walking back to the lot.

"I'll be waiting behind the wheel," he said, looking over his shoulder.

o0o

Montoya slid the Jeep tire in place while Shay tightened the lug nuts. He filled the tire to the proper p.s.i. before Shay lowered the jack.

"Throw the jack and stuff in the back," Montoya said. "There's something I need. Take just a sec."

He started the Jeep. Mully jumped in the passenger seat, but quickly leaped in the back when she saw Montoya approaching.

"Good Mully!" he told the dog before climbing in. "Here's just what we need," he said, showing a half foot length of one-inch angle iron to Shay. "The road hazard."

As Shay drove slowly toward the parking area Montoya filled him in on his plan.

"I'll take a look see under the truck. You get the jack in place and start raising it up. I'll do the talking."

Shay stopped the Jeep nose-to-nose with the Silverado. Before the driver got out of his truck, Shay had the jack on the ground and was positioning it in place on the hard packed dirt.

"I'll take a gander," Montoya said, as he got under the truck. He slid back out in a few seconds holding the piece of angle iron. "Here's the culprit. This piece of scrap iron seems to have punctured your tire."

Montoya handed the piece of metal to Montgomery who glanced at it before dropping it on the ground.

"I don't remember hitting anything. No blow out."

"Hard to explain." Montoya said. "Damn thing punctured the sidewall. Might have been sticking out of the ground right around here somewhere. Be my guess, anyway."

Before taking all of the weight off the tire, Montoya loosened all of the lug nuts. He then signaled for Shay to finish jacking up the truck. When the tire was clear of the ground, he removed the nuts, pulled off the wheel, and laid the tire on its side.

"Here's where that angle iron was protruding," Montoya said. He picked up the scrap of angle iron and pushed in into the L shaped incision he had made earlier. "Seems to fit."

"Fuck that," Montgomery said. "Can you fix it?"

"Sidewall's shot. This tire's unrepairable. What about your spare?"

"Check it out. Flatter than a door nail."

The spare was lying behind the truck where it had been left when Montgomery removed it from the rack under the bed. Montoya made a show of checking it over, before turning to look at Montgomery.

"There's a problem with the valve stem," he said. "Easily fixed."

Montoya removed the inside of the valve stem from the damaged tire and inserted it in the spare. He glanced at Shay who turned on the portable air compressor and filled the tire.

Montoya checked the air pressure with a gauge, then moved the tire into position so Shay could bolt it in place. That finished, Lleyellyn lowered the jack, and torqued the lug nuts snug.

"Good as new," Montoya said to Montgomery as he straightened up. "Better get a new tire when you get to town. Or you can call the dealer in Miles City. Have one dropped off."

"Okay. Will do. Sure glad you guys were handy. What's the damage?"

Montoya held up a hand, palm forward.

"No damage. Glad we could help. Lucky this happened here. Who knows what would have happened if you suffered a puncture like that at highway speed."

o0o

Lleyellyn was clearing the noon dishes, and putting them in the sink when the phone rang. Irene picked up the phone.

"Boyd Ranch. Irene speaking."

She listened to the caller, then said, "Mr. Montoya's the ranch foreman, he's right here."

Montoya took the receiver and said, "Montoya. Can I help you?"

"Cass Montgomery here," the caller said. "You fixed my tire this morning."

"Right. How can I help you?"

"You mentioned calling a dealer in town to get the tire replaced. Any suggestions?"

Montoya looked at Shay and gave a wink, before answering.

"Got a guy from High Plains Co-op coming out tomorrow afternoon. Bringing out some tires for our John Deere. They bring 'em out, balance, and mount, and haul away the old ones. Pretty proficient at the job. Could get them to bring a tire out for you."

"Should I call them?" Montgomery said.

"Give me the tire size, make. I'll call for you. I was about to call to verify the time for tomorrow anyway."

Montoya listened for a few seconds, then said, "Call back. I'll be at the phone."

Montoya answered when the call back came a minute or so later.

"Okay. Here's what's on the tire. Goodrich. P265/75R16. All purpose tire."

Montoya read the information back.

"Should I call you when it's here tomorrow?"

"Tomorrow's a busy day for me. Could be tied up all day. Can I just drop my truck off?"

"That'll work. Be sure and leave the key on the floor. Tire guy might have to move to a level spot or something."

Montgomery said he would leave the truck before the start of work in the morning.

Before hanging up Montoya asked Montgomery a question and waited for his answer. After the call ended, he looked at Irene and then at Shay.

"Montgomery's a veterinarian. Has to keep an eye on the livestock. Has to certify that no animals are abused or injured in the filming of the picture. Federal law, I guess."

Two Shots Quick

CHAPTER 8

THURSDAY JULY 23

When they finished breakfast in the morning, Montgomery's white 4X4 pickup was parked in front of the bunkhouse. Shay opened the door and saw the key in the ignition.

"Key's in it," he said, as he straightened up and looked at Montoya.

"See if the glove compartment is locked," Montoya said. "Or if the ignition key will unlock it."

The compartment was locked, and the key didn't fit the latch. He walked over to Montoya and said, "Locked."

"Figures. Ever drive one of these?"

"Only stick shift I've driven is the Jeep," Shay said.

"Give it a try. Works the same. Drive it back to the machine shed. I'll be out in a jiffy."

Shay got behind the wheel, shifted into low and eased the truck forward. He managed to make it without stalling.

o0o

"Keep a look out for Montgomery. I'm gonna open the glove compartment."

Shay watched as Montoya opened the passenger door and placed a cigar box sized leather case on the seat.

"You've seen the graduation certificates I got at Granite City," he said. "I also took some, shall we say, elective courses. Lock picking 101 was one. Taught by one of the best. Safe cracker from Fargo. Was a locksmith before he got caught."

Montoya selected several small implements and worked away on the glove compartment lock. In less than a minute they heard a click and the door of the compartment fell open.

Montoya starting removing the contents item by item. What caught their eye immediately was an antiqued brass belt buckle engraved with a picture of a Ring-necked Pheasant in relief and the words *SO DAK – BIG COCK COUNTRY.*

Montoya held the buckle up for Shay to get a good look.

"LaDonna Mae's, don't you think?"

"Must be," Lleyellyn said. "Looks just like it. Can't be too many like that around. I'm sure it's hers."

Some of the other items were in small boxes and envelopes. Montoya removed them carefully and placed them on the floor. There was a copy of the vehicle registration and an insurance card. Under the papers in the far corner was a white plastic figure of a mature Jesus with out-stretched arms. He held it up for Lleyellyn to see. Then handed it to him.

"It's it!" Shay said. "Has to be. Just exactly like she described."

He turned the plastic Jesus upside down. There was green felt on the bottom. Shay got behind the steering wheel and compared the bottom of the statuette with the half circle trace of green felt on the dashboard. They matched perfectly.

Montoya handed the insurance card and registration to Shay.

"Here's a pen," Montoya said. "Copy down Montgomery's full name and address, will you?"

As Shay wrote down the information on the back of his left hand, Montoya went through the other envelopes and the boxes.

In one of them he found a small tin of aspirin and several books of matches. One of the envelopes was addressed to the Clerk of Court in Denver and had a parking ticket attached. The last item was a box that said Deluxe Checks on the outside.

Montoya carefully opened it and saw shear light blue fabric. He removed the item, straightened it out and held up a pair of women's panties for Shay to see.

"LaDonna Mae's?" Montoya said.

Lleyellyn recognized the blue panties immediately. They were the ones he remembered from their little dip in the stock tank.

"Hell, I don't know," he said, embarrassed to admit he had seen LaDonna Mae in her underwear. "Look like they're small enough. Right color, seems like. Probably fit her."

Montoya checked the label.

"Says Size 3."

"Not too sure about sizes," Shay said. "Sure could be hers. Bet they are."

o0o

The first thing Lleyellyn did when he got back to the bunkhouse was copy down Montgomery's full name and address from the back of his hand.

o0o

The tire truck from Great Plains Co-op showed up about noon. While the tire experts from the co-op started working on the J-D tractor, Montoya and Shay took the things they had found to the bunkhouse.

"Arrange this stuff on the bed," Montoya said. "I'll get my camera."

Shay placed the buckle in the middle of the bed and placed the panties below it. He placed the parking ticket and the other items next to the buckle. Montoya returned with a digital camera and took several pictures including close-ups of the buckle.

"Turn the buckle over, will you?" he said. "And fix those panties so the label shows."

Montoya finished taking pictures, and checked the camera to see if the images were clear.

"I'll put the camera away, you can put this stuff back in the truck the way we found it. Anything missing, Montgomery'll know it was us."

Shay put the panties back in the box, and returned everything to the glove compartment.

Montoya came back, looked over what Shay had done.

"Looks pretty good. Maybe push the plastic Jesus back a little more. Far right rear corner."

Shay did so, before closing the glove compartment.

Montoya pressed the latch to see if it locked itself.

"I'll have to use my locksmith training some more," Montoya said. "Not much call for using these tools to lock something."

Montoya selected the same tools he had used to open the lock. Shay watched him as he manipulated several of the slender picks at once. It took nearly twice as long, but they finally heard a click. Montoya checked the latch. The glove compartment was locked.

A few minutes later, the co-op crew drove up in front of the bunkhouse with their service truck.

"John Deere's set," the driver said, looking at Montgomery's truck.

"I put the spare on the left front," Montoya said. "The cut up one's in the bed. Figure you should put the new tire on the left front, too. Put the spare back where it belongs. Damn thing hasn't been used, but it looks kind of dried out. Probably do in a pinch. Not the best spare in the world. Aged out."

After the guys from the co-op left, Shay drove the Chevy pickup back to the parking area and left the key under the floor mat on the driver's side.

Two Shots Quick

CHAPTER 9

TUESDAY JULY 28

Lleyellyn knew the recipe by heart.

He sliced the linguisa into half inch segments, sprayed a little Pam in the frying pan, and started sautéing them. Quickly, he halved, and chopped an onion and added it to the pan.

While the meat and onions were slowly frying, he opened two cans of Butter Beans and poured them into a kettle and placed it on the stove at medium heat. He opened a can of tomato sauce, mixed it into the beans, then reached over and gave the onions and sausage a stir.

When the onions were translucent he added the linguisa and onions to the beans and stirred the mixture. He turned the heat down on the kettle to let it simmer while he sliced the French bread, placed the butter out, and set the table.

Lleyellyn was about to call everyone to dinner when he heard the crunch of gravel as a vehicle approached the house, stopping near the kitchen steps. He thought it might be Montgomery again.

Irene answered the knock at the door.

"Evening, Ma'am," a tall middle-aged gentleman dressed in a western cut suit with matching pale blue boots said, removing his white Stetson. "Mrs. Boyd, I'm Will DeLong, director of the picture."

"Of course, Mr. DeLong. Remember you from college. You're looking great," she said. "Please, call me Irene." She smiled at him. "Won't you come in for a minute. You can meet my foreman and his assistant."

Irene held the door open as he stepped through the vestibule and into the kitchen.

"We've got a visitor," Irene said. "Mr. DeLong here is the director of the picture they're shooting."

"You better call me Will. We go back a long way," he whispered to Irene as he passed her.

Montoya stepped forward, hand out stretched.

"Manuel Montoya," He said by way of greeting. "I'm Irene's foreman." As they shook hands, he continued. "And this is Lleyellyn. Lleyellyn Shay. My assistant. And, as you can see, tonight's chef."

Shay felt conspicuous wearing an apron and standing at the stove. He put the stirring spoon down, and shook hands with the director.

"Nice to meet you."

"Don't be fooled by the kitchen attire," Irene said. "Around here, we take turns fixing supper. We're having Minnesota Bean Surprise. Lleyellyn's secret recipe"

DeLong glanced at the stove, then said, "Smells good," before directing his attention to Irene.

"Reason I stopped by. We're having a wrap party next week. Friday. August seventh. Wanted to invite you, all three of you, to the party. Libations start at six. Barbeque to follow. Hope you can all be there."

Irene glanced at Montoya, then at Shay.

"Appreciate the offer. We accept," she said. "Whose turn is it to cook Friday?" She smiled. "Oh dear, my turn. Great! A day off from my cooking duties."

"Okay, great. See you next Friday evening," DeLong said, flashing a smile at them. "We'll have a chance to talk then," he added, as he looked at Irene.

Montoya took a step forward.

"Question for you, Mr. DeLong. Are you about done with filming?"

"We've got everything we need for the film except what needs to be done in studio. But, of course, still need to get shots of cattle on the move, and so forth. We'll keep the wranglers on until the cattle are gone. Unit director will stay, of course. Camera men, grips, sound engineers. Animal safety guy. Everybody else will be finished up by the end of the week-end. With the weather reports we've been getting, I'm not too hopeful we can shoot what we need next week. Not supposed to be any rain headed this way until the middle of the month. Just have to wait for Mother Nature to do her thing."

"Okay, then. Just one more question," Montoya said. "When you finish up with the cattle, how long before everyone will be gone?"

"Contract with the livestock company lets them stay on pasture until the snow flies. They'll be here a while. Then they'll round up the cattle, load 'em and ship 'em back where they came from." DeLong said.

"That pasturing part was part of our deal," Irene said, looking at Montoya.

She turned her attention back to the director.

"Well, thanks again, Mr. DeLong," Irene said. "Always glad to see you again," she added with a smile. "See you next week," then looking a little sheepish, she continued, "Will any of the actors be at the party?"

"You bet," DeLong said. "Can't have a wrap party without the stars." He paused. "Oh, and please, all of you, just call me Will."

He opened the back door, then looked back at them.

"As you might imagine, this is a western themed party. Western, that is cowboy attire, is expected."

"Won't be a problem for us," Irene said, as she shut the door behind the director. Then looking at Shay she added, "But you can leave the apron at home."

o0o

Sandra Simms grabbed a bite for dinner at the Blue Heron, and walked the two blocks to her office. She was a sole practitioner doing public defender assignments on a contract with the Office of the State Public Defender. She liked working late when there was no one around to interrupt.

She turned on her desk top computer and checked her emails. The Court Administrator's office had efficiently sent her a copy of the court file on the State v. Lleyellyn Fellows Shay felony case together with the other pertinent information in the court's file.

She scanned the court records, found Shay's contact number, and called the number listed for the Boyd Ranch, the defendant's employer. She knew it was a few minutes past seven in the Mountain time zone and hoped she would be able to catch her new client without difficulty.

Someone picked up after the third ring.

"Boyd Ranch. Irene speaking."

"Good afternoon," Simms said. "May I speak to Lleyellyn Shay, please?"

There was a brief pause, but she heard Irene say, "Lleyellyn, it's for you."

A chair scraped, then she heard, "Lleyellyn here."

"Mr. Shay. My name is Sandra Simms. Judge Jensen here in Winona appointed me to be your public defender regarding the charges about the railroad's copper wire. I need to talk to you a minute. I've got good news for you. Can you talk now?"

Lleyellyn looked at Irene and shrugged.

"Sure. Go ahead."

Simms explained what had happened in the judge's chambers, the settlement discussions the judge instigated after Lleyellyn's grandmother had written to her, the fact both the county attorney and the railroad were on board.

"The bottom line is this. You send me a check made payable to the Burlington Northern Railroad. Just say BNSF. And the office of the Winona County Attorney, in the amount of One Thousand Two Hundred Fifty Dollars. The judge will then quash the arrest warrant and dismiss the criminal complaint with prejudice. No criminal record. No jail. No fine. You'd be free to come back to Minnesota. With prejudice means the charges cannot be refiled."

Simms paused. Shay was silent.

"Interested?" Simms gently prodded.

"Well sure, but why? Seems too good to be true."

"It is a good deal. The judge thinks you've suffered enough. Realizes you had to get away from home. Mr. Watts seems to agree. The sheriff's office, too."

"What do you think, Miss Sears, er ... ?"

"Simms. I'll be honest with you. I'm a new public defender. Just passed the bar last fall. But I really think this is a great deal. Only issue, do you have the money?"

"Money's okay," Lleyellyn said. "Say, would you mind explaining this to Irene? Irene Boyd. She's my boss. I trust her."

Simms repeated the details of the offer to Boyd.

"And to be honest with you, this was the judge's idea. She knew Lleyellyn when he was little, knew the tough time he had with his step-father. Thought he needed to get away, and the copper wire deal was done out of necessity. I also think both the judge and the county attorney didn't care much for the railroad security supervisor. His grandmother's letter to her is what started the ball rolling. It's a good deal, but it's up to Mr. Shay. I can't finalize it without him."

"I'll have a word with him. Can you hang on a minute?"

"No problem."

She heard muffled voices as though someone had a hand over the receiver. After a short time Lleyellyn came back on the line.

"I agree. Thanks. How soon do you need the money?"

"How long will it take you to send me a check?"

A hand was held over the mouthpiece at his end for a few seconds.

"Where should I send the check?" he said.

He noted down the address.

"I'll mail the check tomorrow. Mail man comes by right after lunch."

o0o

Lleyellyn felt relieved to have the Winona County case resolved. All three of them were in good spirits as Shay assembled a salad, put the bread in a basket, and set the table. He served his bean dish in soup bowls and the tomato and basil salad on small plates.

"Smells good," Montoya said.

"Nice presentation," Boyd said. "Like the way you fixed these tomatoes. Another recipe from your Home Ec class?"

"Family recipe, really. My grandmother grows tomatoes. Knows a million ways to fix them This is one of the easiest," Shaw said. "If you've got fresh tomatoes."

Irene took a bite of Lleyellyn's bean dish, then glanced at them before wiping her mouth with a napkin.

"Tasty," she said, before continuing. "I don't know about you, but I'm sorta looking forward to the wrap party. You?

"Might be interesting," Montoya said. "See how those Hollywood types act around the rest of us."

"Me, I want to see how Mr. DeLong dresses in so-called authentic western attire," Irene said.

"Think he'll wear that light blue outfit with the Robin's egg blue Ostrich-skin boots and that baby blue Stetson?"

"Authentic, alright," Montoya said. "At Hollywood and Vine or at the Sun Dance Film Festival."

"You know," Irene said, "The Will DeLong I knew back in college was different than he seems today. Back then he was pretty clean cut. Not a loud dresser or a hippy. But, I remember, he had a great singing voice. We were in choral groups together."

"What do you think I should wear?" Shay said, looking at each of them in turn.

"What you've been wearing is about as authentic as you can get. The boots and your big hat seem perfect," Montoya said,

"And that big rodeo prize belt buckle you picked up from that guy in town. Wear that. Makes you look like a real cowboy," Boyd said.

o0o

He called LaDonna Mae. She was doing better after being discharged from the hospital.

"Doctor wants me to stay at home for a while," she told Lleyellyn. "Not supposed to do much until my feet are fully healed."

He didn't mention the wrap party, knowing she'd be disappointed in not being able to attend.

Two Shots Quick

CHAPTER 10

THURSDAY JULY 30

After breakfast, Lleyellyn helped with the dishes then went out to the bunkhouse to get his check book and the notes he made when his public defender called. Montoya was setting on the steps when Lleyellyn came back outside. He was brushing Mully, and picking off burrs.

"Darned dog chased something," Montoya said, pointing to a small pile of stickers he had removed. "Hasn't learned to stay out of the thistles. Eager as a pup."

"She knows to ignore prairie dogs. Coyotes, too. Probably just likes the attention," Lleyellyn said, holding his hand out for the dog to lick. "What about this wrap party?"

"Entire movie crew's invited. Cast. Us, too. Irene wants to meet the stars. Might be interesting."

"I think so, too. Think Irene is really looking forward to it."

He went in the house, made out a check the way his lawyer had told him to, borrowed an envelope and stamp from Irene, then addressed the envelope to Miss Simms in Winona.

He picked up two letters that had been left out on the table to be mailed, and walked out to the mail box and left them there for the mail carrier. He made sure the red flag was up so the outgoing mail wouldn't be missed.

Two Shots Quick

CHAPTER 11

MONDAY AUGUST 3

It was another busy District Court Monday morning in courtroom three at the Winona County courthouse. As usual, there were nearly two dozen people making initial appearances.

Sandra Simms was standing at the back of the courtroom conferring with someone from her office. As soon as one of the County Attorney's hearings wound up with a defendant being released on her own recognizance, Simms walked to the counsel table and whispered something to Watts.

"May we approach?" Watts said, looking at the judge.

The judge motioned the two attorneys forward. She held her hand over the microphone so their conversation would remain confidential.

"Your Honor," Watts said, "Counsel just handed me the restitution check from Lleyellyn Shay. Made payable to the Burlington Northern Santa Fe Railroad, actually it says BNSF, and the Winona County Attorney in the full agreed amount. One thousand, two hundred fifty dollars. I'm satisfied, assuming the check clears."

"My assistant just called the bank," Simms said. "Confirms adequate funds are on deposit. The check's good."

"Sounds good to me," the judge said. "Good job Miss. Simms."

The judge glanced at the court reporter and went back on the record by nodding to the reporter to resume transcribing the proceedings.

"I've just been advised that the County Attorney has received a valid, verified check in full satisfaction of the previously agreed upon restitution in the matter of State v. Lleyellyn Fellows Shay. Accordingly, upon the motion of Mr. Shay's counsel, Sandra Simms, and the agreement of the prosecutor, Kenneth Watts, I hereby formally dismiss the charges against Mr. Shay, with prejudice. And, of course, without further court costs to either party. Please prepare an order to this effect for my signature."

The Judge again covered the microphone and motioned the two lawyers closer.

"Good job Mr. Watts. You too Miss Simms, congratulations on resolving your first felony matter. Time to put the first notch on your briefcase."

o0o

"Phone's for you," Irene yelled from the kitchen door.

Lleyellyn crossed the yard and entered the kitchen. Irene handed him the phone.

"Hello," he said. "This is Lleyellyn."

"This is Sandra Simms in Winona. Your public defender. I've got some good news for you."

He waited, hoping for the best.

"Got your check. Was in court today. The Judge dismissed all criminal charges and quashed the arrest warrant. No reason you can't return to Minnesota any time you want."

"Wow!" he said. "That's great. Thanks. Thanks for everything."

"One you should thank is your grandmother. She got the ball rolling," Simms said. "Congratulations."

"Surprised it happened so soon."

"Me, too. A little," Simms said. "Another thing, dismissal was with prejudice. That's good. Means the charges can't be refiled. Officially, there's no record."

Lleyellyn was at a loss for words.

"You still there?" Simms said.

"Yes. Sorry," Lleyellyn said. "Can't hardly believe it."

"It's true. I'll send you a copy of the judge's Order."

"I can't thank you enough."

"You already have," she said. "Good luck, Mr. Shay," she added, before saying, "Good-bye."

Irene was looking at him when he hung up the phone.

"Criminal charges have been dropped in Minnesota," he said. "Whatever my grandmother did, it worked."

Irene gave him a hug.

"That's great. Your grandmother will be happy. Better let her know."

Irene left the room.

Lleyellyn knew his grandmother's phone number by heart. She answered after two or three rings.

"Grandma, it's me, Lleyellyn."

She was glad to hear from him and happy with the news of the dismissal.

"You're the one that did it," Lleyellyn said. "My lawyer said you contacted the judge. That's what started everything."

She deflected his praise, preferring to talk about him and what he was doing in Montana. He could tell she had learned a lot during her phone conversation with Irene.

She knew about the movie being made and about his friend LaDonna Mae. She hadn't heard about the assault. He told her about it, but didn't mention Cass Montgomery, her attacker.

"She's doing good. Planning to be back at work as soon as she can."

"You take good care of that girl. Irene speaks very highly of her," his grandmother said.

Later, after they had talked about other things, his grandmother said, "When your gal friend is fully recovered, maybe the two of you can come back here. I'd like to meet her. We could even hold the remembrance for your mother then."

CHAPTER 12

THURSDAY AUGUST 6

Shay was returning from his fence inspection duties, Mully dutifully ensconced in the Jeep's passenger seat. As they approached the buildings, they saw the mail man pulling away from the mail box at the end of the driveway. The red flag was up. Without slowing down, Lleyellyn continued along the road and stopped at the mail box. There were several envelopes and a small box inside.

Lleyellyn drove back to the garage, parked the Jeep, then walked to the house. He placed the stack of mail on the counter and grabbed a 'Dew and a bag of nacho chips. He went out on the porch and sat in one of the wicker rocking chairs. Mully was waiting, looking at him expectantly.

He slipped the dog a few chips and sipped his soda.

As he relaxed his mind wandered back to his trip home to Minnesota and their encounter with Mal across the river in Wisconsin. He had thought about Mal's death. His part in it. And Montoya's. It bothered him, but not as much as he thought it would

We did the right thing. What else could we have done? Mal murdered my mom.

Mully had nearly finished off the nacho chips when the door opened and Irene joined them.

"Thanks for getting the mail, Hon. These two are for you."

Both envelopes looked official. The first was from the Wells Fargo Bank in Miles City. Inside was his checking account statement. He checked his balance. $2,953.47. There had been no withdrawals, and no checks had been paid out.

Two Shots Quick

Tole hasn't cashed his check for the saddle. Wonder what's keeping him, Lleyellyn thought, remembering the saddle bronc rider he'd befriended on his trip west on the train.

When Tole left for Wisconsin to start college, Lleyellyn had agreed to sell his Association Saddle and send him the proceeds. The check had been mailed weeks ago.

The check he sent to his lawyer made out to BNSF and the Winona County Attorney didn't show up on his statement, either. He knew Simms had received it. It would show up on the next bank statement.

The other letter was from Liberty Mutual Insurance Company. There was a letter inside and another paper. The letter was addressed to him.

Dear Mr. Shay;

Enclosed please find a draft made payable to you in the amount of Ten Thousand Forty-seven Dollars and Eighteen Cents ($10,047.18).

This sum represents the proceeds of the life insurance policy on the life of your late mother together with accrued interest. You were the sole named beneficiary of this policy.

Please accept the Company's sincerest condolences for your loss.

Sincerely yours,

Conway L. Webster
Assistant to the Vice President

He handed the letter to Irene and showed her the check.

"We'll go into town so you can put this in the bank," she said. "Very foresighted of your mother wasn't it?"

o0o

Lleyellyn came out of the bunkhouse buttoning a clean shirt as Irene pulled up in her blue pickup. She got out and walked around to the passenger side.

"Lleyellyn, I want you to drive. At least until we get to the state highway. This'll be way easier than the Jeep."

He climbed in behind the wheel.

"Take your time. Adjust the seat. And the mirrors," she said.

The seats operated electrically. He moved the seat up and back. Adjusted the inside rearview mirror by hand and checked the side mirrors. They seemed good. Then after glancing briefly at Irene, he looked over at Montoya seated on the bunkhouse steps with Mully, flashed a wave, put the truck in first gear, and slowly moved forward.

Irene stopped him with a hand signal.

"Seat belt," she said.

He fastened the seat belt before putting the truck in motion again, gaining speed gradually, the gears meshing nicely as he accelerated and motored down the drive. He stopped at the road, carefully looked both ways, turned onto the black top, and headed east, picking up speed smoothly.

"Good start," Boyd said. "Drive like you've done this before. Remember, you've got a fifth gear on this rig."

Lleyellyn shifted into fifth and maintained a steady pace along the county highway.

They were silent for several minutes.

"I want you to learn to drive on public roads so you can get your driver's license," Boyd said. "Lot more things you can do for us if you have a license."

Shay had no trouble handling the pick-up all the way to the state highway. Several cars and a cattle truck passed them going the opposite direction, and he maneuvered around a county work crew repairing a bridge without difficulty. When they saw the *Stop Ahead* sign as they approached the state highway, Irene had him pull over and they exchanged places.

Irene got behind the wheel, quickly readjusted the seat, fastened the belt and the mirrors, and headed toward town.

"We'll try this a few more times, then you can take your driver's test. Better get you the DMV booklet in town so you can read up on Montana traffic rules and regulations."

Lleyellyn was thinking about taking the driver's test, when Irene interrupted his thoughts.

"I'll have Mr. Montoya set up some poles in the yard so you can practice parallel parking. That's always the hardest part. But I'm sure you'll have no trouble."

"Hope so. This is a damned … excuse me, this is a darned big truck."

"We'll see how it goes. Maybe we can even borrow a little car. An automatic. Those things practically park themselves," Irene said, then after a pause added, "I got my driver's license so long ago they didn't even have a behind-the-wheel part. At least out in this part of the state. Never had to parallel park. In fact, I don't think I've ever had to really parallel park my truck. Ever."

"When we get to town I'll drop you off at Wells Fargo. You do your banking. See if you can talk to one of the personal bankers. See what she suggests you do with your life insurance money."

"Not sure what you mean," he said.

"They'll suggest an account that might earn you additional interest. Worth asking about."

o0o

When they returned to the ranch, Montoya told them that LaDonna Mae's father, Jim Ritchie, and his son, had dropped by to pick up his daughter's Grand Am.

"Gave me a call when they got home," Montoya said. "Said the car ran fine. No issues with the battery."

Two Shots Quick

CHAPTER 13

FRIDAY AUGUST 7

Montoya came out of his room at the end of the bunkhouse as Lleyellyn was standing by his bunk tucking in his shirt. Montoya was wearing tan western cut jeans, dark cordovan boots, and a light brown checkered western-style long sleeved shirt. Everything was freshly pressed or shined.

"I'm going to talk to some of the wranglers at the party. Try to find out what they've been told about filming the cattle drive. Like to know when they plan to start, stuff like that," Montoya said. "I'd like you see if that Montgomery guy's there. Maybe you can talk to him a little. Try and find out what he's supposed to be doing when the herd's being moved."

"Think he'll talk to me?"

"Just be friendly. Ask him about his tire and his truck. Flatter him a little. He's a blowhard. Won't be able to shut him up."

"Anything else I should do?" Shay said.

"Have a good time. Check out the women folk. Play your role. Retired bull rider. Buckle to prove it. They'll be asking you for autographs." Montoya said with a grin.

Montoya returned to his room to get his hat.

Lleyellyn threaded his belt through the loops in his jeans and centered the buckle Buck had given him, the one Buck had won riding bulls in Cheyenne. He pulled on his Tony Lama seconds and squared the broad brimmed straw hat he had bought at Highplains Haberdashery. He checked his appearance in the bathroom mirror and turned just as Montoya was locking the door to his room.

Montoya was wearing a wide brimmed flat crowned light brown hat he had never seen before. Looked like a Stetson. He had knotted an orange kerchief around his neck.

Lleyellyn wasn't sure what to say.

Montoya held up his hand.

"Don't say anything. Look like that DeLong guy, don't I?"

"You look good. Successful like. And at least you're not wearing a baby blue get up like he was," he added with a grin.

"Got that going for me. Want them to think being foreman is a big deal. A lot of those people are actors. I'm just playing my role," Montoya said. "And you look your part. Ex rodeo performer, assistant ranch foreman, Montana cowboy. You'll do fine. Everybody'll want to talk to you."

"I'm not too sure they won't know I know damned little about cattle ranching."

"Just smile a lot. Silent cowboy type. Man of few words. Ask them questions. Everyone loves to talk about themselves."

o0o

They left the bunk house and walked across the yard to the house together.

"Mully! Stay!" Montoya said.

The dog trotted back to the bunkhouse and sat on the porch in front of the door. It looked like she was pouting.

"Good girl. Keep an eye out."

Mully looked at them, her head resting on her front paws.

They walked to the house. Shay held the door open for Montoya, then followed him into the kitchen.

"Be there in a second," Irene yelled from upstairs. "Want anything, help yourself."

Lleyellyn took a double take when Irene came downstairs. She was dressed in a long fringed skirt and a scoop necked white blouse accentuated with a large silver and turquoise necklace. Her hair was in an upswept hairdo held in place with silver clips. In contrast to her normal cosmetic free look, she was carefully made up. Lipstick, rouge, eye shadow – the whole ball of wax.

He glanced briefly at Montoya, then smiled at Irene.

"You look very nice," he said.

She was smiling as she twirled around so they could see her entire outfit.

"Not every day a lady gets a chance to hob knob with movie stars," she said. "You gentlemen look great. Glad to see you're wearing your new hat, Mr. Montoya. Suits you."

Montoya gave a rare but brief smile.

"Well that's nice of you to say. You do look mighty stylish. You'll be the belle of the ball."

"And you, Mr. Shay," she said with a smile. "Every bit the cowboy. And your buckle's fantastic."

"Okay, then. Enough compliments. Let's blow this pop stand." Montoya said.

o0o

The party was in full swing when they reached the largest of the tents. A band was playing in the far corner and people seemed to be taking their places at various white tablecloth covered tables around the room. There was a long table on a platform at the far end of the room with a podium in the middle.

They were greeted at the entrance by Will DeLong who was standing with an attractive impeccably dressed woman a few years younger than he was.

"Irene, so glad you're here. Your spread has been just what we were looking for. I'd like to introduce you to my wife. Celeste, this is Irene Boyd, the woman I've told you so much about. We knew each other at MU. She's the proprietor of this ranch."

Celeste flashed a practiced smile as she turned to face Irene.

"I've heard a lot about you. Will says you were the first cattle rancher he thought of when this film project came up. You have a wonderful place."

"Why thank you. I've known your husband for more years than I care to count. Glad to have you all here."

Irene turned toward Montoya and Shay and introduced them as her foreman and his assistant.

"Find your name tags on that table," DeLong said. "Seating is assigned. There's place cards on the tables. The number of your table is on the lower left corner of your name tag. Tried to mix people up so everyone can meet someone new. Call it a cross culture experience. Have fun."

Shay found his name tag at the far end of the table among the names starting with *S*.

LLEYELLYN SHAY
Boyd Ranch
Assistant Foreman

He glanced at the name tag before peeling off the back and positioning it on the left pocket of his shirt. His assigned table was clearly marked as *Table 16*.

Irene came up to him. Her name tag was in place.

IRENE BOYD
Boyd Ranch
Owner/Manager

"Will you look at this? I'm at the head table," she said, as Montoya moved to join them.

"Let me help with that," Boyd said, taking the name tag from Montoya and peeling off the back. She centered it below his left shirt pocket and stuck it in place.

MANUEL MONTOYA
Boyd Ranch
Ranch Foreman

"Now we're all official. Looks like you are over at table six. Lleyellyn's at sixteen," she said. "I'm up there somewhere, at the head table."

Other guests were looking for their assigned seats. The wait staff, all attired in black pants and tops and wearing similar white cowboy hats, were making the rounds from table to table, taking drink orders and handing out appetizers.

"Better find our seats," Montoya said. "Don't want to miss out on the libations."

"Good idea," Boyd said, before turning to Lleyellyn. "Now, you have a good time."

o0o

Table 16 was in a corner, as far from the head table as possible. Shay found his place at about the same time as a young man about own his age walked up to it, looking for his place card.

"Hi! I'm Lleyellyn," he said glancing at his table mate's name tag which read *Karrey Cadon – Grip*. "Grip. I'm not sure what a grip is," he added, seating himself at the next chair.

"I'm just one of twenty or so. A stagehand really. We move cameras around. Stuff like that," Cadon said.

Their assigned seats were on the side of the table facing the podium, one empty seat between them. They had an unobstructed view of the head table.

"How long you been in the movie business?" Lleyellyn said.

"Finished film school at USC a few weeks ago. This is my first real film job. Interned for a semester. Strictly sound stage stuff in LA. Lucked out with this project."

Shay picked up a program that was under his plate. Before he could open it, he noticed Cadon leaning forward to read his name tag.

"Assistant Ranch Foreman. Must have been raised around here, right?"

Shay felt a little sheepish. He didn't want to admit he had been working on the ranch for only a few months and that he really knew very little about ranching, or Montana, or much of anything that his stated occupation would seem to indicate.

"New at the job. Got finished with school in May. Just happened to be in the right place at the right time. Mostly I take orders from the foreman. Or help out the owner."

"Raised around here?"

Before Shay could come up with an answer, they were joined by a thirty-something woman wearing a fringed denim skirt, western cut boots, and a satin yoked cowboy shirt.

"Karrey, you were right. Back of the room, away from the action again," she said sitting down across from them with her back to the head table.

"Melissa, this is Ll ... ," Cadon stammered, having trouble pronouncing Lleyellyn's name. "Mr. Shay. He's the Assistant Ranch Foreman."

"Name's Lleyellyn," he said. "I see you're a Script Assistant."

She smiled and they shook hands.

"Script Assistant. Does that mean you help write the script?"

"Hell no. Don't I wish. Last movie they called us all Script Girls. Now that's politically incorrect. I'm a Script Assistant. Really, what I do is deliver script changes, write overs, whatever, to the director and his assistants and the cast. Should just say Gofer on this damned tag."

The room was filling up and several more people joined their table. Checking name tags, he spotted a Wrangler, a Gaffer, a Best Boy, a Wardrobe Assistant and several other unfamiliar job titles. Everyone at his table looked to be in their twenties or thirties.

Montoya found table six near the front of the room with a good view of the head table. He saw Irene standing behind the head table talking to Will DeLong, the director. They were laughing about something. DeLong gave her a peck on the cheek and helped her take her seat by pulling out a chair for her. As the director left, Irene picked up the program, glanced at it before looking up and catching Montoya's eye. She gave him a wink, then turned and selected a cocktail from the waiter that appeared next to her.

Several people showed up at table six and greeted Montoya. There was an Assistant Director, a Unit Supervisor and several other men and women who he took to be middle management for the film. He recognized that there was a definite hierarchy: the big-wigs were at the head table, then management of one sort or another at the first row of tables, then various functionaries in the tables farthest away from the podium.

"Buenos dias," an Asian gentleman in pristine western wear said to him from beneath a large ten-gallon hat. "Mi llama is Norman Zxiong."

"Well how do you do, Norman. Wanshang hao," Montoya said. "'Fraid I don't speak Spanish," Montoya added, noticing that Zxiong's name tag identified him as an Underwriting Representative.

"Sorry about that, I think you have a Latin look."

"I have some south of the border blood, you are correct on that, but I'm Montana born and bred. Third generation, in fact."

"I see you're the ranch foreman. Must run this place," Zxiong said. "Where'd you learn Mandarin?"

"Well, I learned a few basic phrases in several different languages when I had some spare time on my hands. That was the extent of my Chinese you just heard," Montoya said. "And you know, there's not much to do as foreman when your movie crew's taken over. Most times we run our own string of livestock. Then I get to earn my pay."

The three-piece band playing softly in the corner was barely audible over the crowd noise.

The tables were filling fast.

Two still photographers and a video cameraman were circulating, taking pictures of the guests.

Montoya spied Montgomery at a table directly in front of the head table. He was taking a drink from a cocktail glass as he eyed the crowd.

He made eye contact with Montoya, gave a slight nod, then stood and walked over to him.

Taking something from his shirt pocket, he said, "Here's a check for what I owe you for the tire. Sure appreciate the help."

Montoya took the check, glancing at Montgomery's name tag which identified him as *Livestock Protection Agent*. Before he could say anything, Montgomery turned and moved back to his seat.

The check was made out to *The Boyd Ranch* and drawn on the account of *Animal Protection Professionals, LLC*. It was for the exact amount the Co-op had charged for their services and new tire.

He hoped Lleyellyn would find out more from Montgomery. He himself hadn't learned a thing about what the Livestock Protection Agent would be doing during filming of the big cattle drive.

o0o

The house lights dimmed and a spot light shown on the center of the head table. The director stood behind the lectern.

"Good evening friends," DeLong said. "First thing I want to do is recognize one special person. I want to give special thanks to her," he said turning toward Irene Boyd who was seated on his left.

She smiled broadly, and gave a self-conscious wave.

"Irene Boyd is the owner of this ranch."

He looked again at her and motioned her to the podium.

"Irene would you step over here. I want to tell everybody how this film came to be made here in the middle of Montana on the Boyd Ranch."

She hesitated, then stood up and moved over a few steps until she was standing next to the director.

"The two of us go back a long ways, don't we, Irene?" he said rhetorically.

Irene didn't say anything, but looked at him and smiled.

"We both attended the University of Montana at the same time. I was majoring in Geology, Irene in Social Science or some damn thing. We both joined the glee club as freshmen. She was the first real, honest to goodness, cattle rancher I'd ever met. But she could really sing, too. When this project came up, Irene was the first one I called. I knew I needed a place to film the cattle drives. Asked her for some suggestions. The Boyd Ranch fit the bill perfectly. Most important thing in this industry is who you know. Irene's spread is about six miles square. Thirty-six sections. Some 23,000 acres. Almost all of it pristine. Perfect for our needs. Can't thank you enough, Irene."

Irene stepped to the microphone. She looked around the room, seeming to make eye contact with everyone like a seasoned public speaking veteran.

"Thank you, Will," she said. "I want to welcome everyone. I'm proud of this part of the State of Montana."

After surveying the crowd, she turned her attention back to DeLong.

"I have to tell you, it was a surprise hearing from you after so many years. I never dreamed I'd shut down my entire cattle operation for a couple years so the ranch could be used to film a movie."

After a pause for a sip of water, she continued.

"I was intrigued by the idea of a motion picture showing an authentic old time cattle drive. I'm proud of the fact that my great grandfather established this outfit, what is still called the Boyd Ranch to this day. He started out with a small herd of longhorns that he helped trail north from Oklahoma. I had to agree with you then, Will, and I agree with you now. This does seem to be the perfect place to shoot your picture."

o0o

DeLong continued with the introductions of others at the head table including the people bank rolling the project, members of the cast, and the production team.

Next to Zxiong at Montoya's table was a man about his own age with a weather beaten face and prominent grin lines. Montoya leaned around Norman Zxiong to get a good look at his name tag. *Leland Fordham*, it read, *Supervisor (Stunts/Wra*nglers).

Montoya slid his chair back and leaned over in Fordham's direction behind Zxiong. He tapped him on the shoulder.

"Excuse me," Montoya said. "I'd like to introduce myself. Manuel Montoya, I'm the foreman here at Boyd Ranch. Couldn't help read your name tag. Looks like we might be in the same business."

Fordham backed his chair up, took a good look at Montoya, and shook hands with him.

"You bet. Mostly I keep an eye on the cowboys we have here. Main job is to supervise the actual cattle drive we've got planned. Otherwise, I try and keep the wranglers on their toes and out of trouble," he said. "Make sure the livestock's cared for."

"Sounds like what I do when we're operating like a real cattle operation. During this movie making thing I've got no cowboys and no cattle. Expect we'll be back in the ranching business in the Spring," Montoya said.

The director was making other introductions. Zxiong turned to look at them, annoyed with them for talking during the speech.

"Let's step outside," Fordham said. "I could use a smoke."

Once outside, they exchanged histories on each other's ranch back grounds. Montoya told him about growing up on a cattle ranch north of Miles City, and that both his daddy and his granddaddy had been ranch foremen.

"Runs in the family," he concluded.

"Well, Fordham said, "I got in the business mostly by accident. My folks wanted to expose us, by that I mean me, my brother and two sisters, to life outside of Chicago where we lived. Took us to a dude ranch in Arizona. I was thirteen, maybe fourteen. Called the Tanque Verde Ranch, a little east of Tucson. We were there ten days. Rode a horse, even helped herd their tame string of cattle. I was hooked. Spent the next school year reading everything I could about horses, cattle, cowboys. Somehow my dad got me a job at Tanque Verde. Started out as a porter, showing guests their rooms, hauling luggage, delivering room service. Managed to spend time helping out in the stables, too. Rode horses a lot, and actually learned how to ride. Some of the wranglers were real pros. I must have been a quick learner. Went back the next summer. Became a wrangler, and then a trail boss. I met DeLong there. He had taken the family to the ranch for a week. Not long after that he called me about a movie project he was planning. Been working in the business off and on ever since."

They compared notes some more. Fordham was having an issue with saddle sores on his horse, and Montoya had a few suggestions.

"If I'm out on the trail," he said, "I've had pretty good luck just cutting a hole in the saddle blanket right over the raw area. When I get back to the stable, I usually use that diaper rash ointment, Desitin, ever heard of it?"

"Know it well. Changed a diaper or two in my day."

"Nuskin works, too."

They returned to their seats. Nothing was happening at the head table. Montoya slid his chair back, then moved closer to Fordham. Zxiong was busy making notes on the back of the program.

"Met a fella yesterday. Last name's Montgomery. Seated over there. White Stetson. Know him?"

Fordham nodded, and leaned closer, keeping his voice low.

"Damned nuisance. Calls himself an Animal Safety Representative. Makes sure no animals are harmed. Necessary evil, I guess. Studio wants to make sure they can list as a credit that no animals were injured in the making of the picture."

"That's a good thing, right?" Montoya said.

"Absolutely. But when you've got three or four hundred cattle and a string of riding horses things happen. Everyday things. Nothing to do with movie making. Had to put a steer down couple days ago. Busted up hind quarter. Double compound fracture. Had to be put out of its misery. Nothing we could do. More an act of God. Nothing caused by filming a movie scene. Montgomery had a meeting. Wrote up a big report. Warned us we were risking loss of certification."

Montoya was going to reply, but Fordham continued.

"Can't blame the guy for doing his job. But I'll be honest with you. No one likes the guy. Try and avoid him. Female staff keep their distance. I haven't seen anybody talking to him over there. Ladies will most likely have moved on. Rumor has it, he comes on too strong. Thinks he's a real Romeo or something. He's pretty much a loner. To be honest, he's about the only thing about this job I hate. I'm not alone. Can't stand the son-of-a-bitch."

"Tell me how you really feel," Montoya said, stifling a laugh. "He's the only one I've known that my dog doesn't like. When he was up at our shop, Mully backed away from him tail down and sat next to me. Never saw her do that before."

o0o

They escorted Irene back to the house when the party started winding down.

"I had a wonderful time," she said. "Maybe a few too many cocktails. You enjoy yourselves?"

They both agreed with her that it had been a great party.

"Nice bunch of folks," Montoya said. "People I talked to seemed pretty normal."

oOo

When they got back to the bunkhouse, Lleyellyn told Montoya what he had found out.

"You were right. Montgomery liked talking about himself. Told me he would be keeping an eye out on the livestock during filming. Likes to use binoculars and a night vision spotting scope. See if animals aren't being treated right. Loves his job. He's his own boss. Told me it's mostly detective work."

CHAPTER 14

MONDAY AUGUST 10

After talking to LaDonna Mae briefly on the phone, Lleyellyn offered to help Irene clean up the kitchen.

"LaDonna Mae's getting restless sitting around the house," he said. "Doc told her she's doing great, but said she had to be patient."

"Wonderful. We'll go into town so you can see her as soon as we can."

o0o

. Leland Fordham was sitting on the steps of the bunkhouse talking to Montoya, idly scratching Mully between the eyes. Montoya was using a whetstone, carefully sharpening his knife. He had just told Fordham that he would find a spot for him at the next roundup at the Boyd Ranch, when they saw one of the wranglers running toward them.

He was one of the cowboys Montoya had seen at the banquet. The cowboy paused a moment to catch his breath.

"Problem in the cattle pen! Steer has a broken fore-leg. That goddamned Montgomery's making a scene. Need to do something. Not sure what."

"Hold on a sec," Montoya said. "We'll take the Jeep."

Montoya backed the Jeep out of the shed. Fordham got in beside him. The wrangler and Mully climbed in the back.

They arrived at the corrals and pulled up next to Montgomery and several cowboys who were standing around, relieved when the foreman arrived.

"You're in deep shit, Fordham," Montgomery yelled. "You've got an injured animal that you're not taking care of."

They could see a longhorn steer with an obvious leg injury standing alone fifty yards from the fence. Its left front leg was bent at an oblique angle twelve inches or so above the hoof. An obviously irreparable leg fracture.

"I'll put the poor beast out of its misery," Fordham said. Then turning toward one of the cowboys said, "Jerry, take my keys and get my pistol out of the glove box for me, will you?"

"You're not killing an animal on my watch," Montgomery said. "Get the goddamned veterinarian here. See what he can do."

The steer let out a painfully woeful sound and hobbled a few steps ahead on its three good legs, the broken leg dangling off at angle to the side.

"Look Mr. Montgomery," Fordham said. "I've been around livestock for all of my adult life. I know and you know there's absolutely nothing that can be done for an animal with a leg like that. I want to put the animal out of its agony now. Only humane thing to do. Like they do to a race horse with a fractured leg."

The cowboy came back and handed Fordham a holster with a long barreled revolver inside.

"I'm the animal protection officer here," Montgomery said. 'We're waiting for the vet, got that?"

The steer gave another mournful wail and stepped unsteadily forward a few more agonizing steps.

Fordham and Montgomery glared at each other. The cowboys looked away from the injured animal. Mully sat next to Montoya looking at him.

Without a word, Montoya squeezed through the fence. Mully started to follow.

"Sit, Mully!" he said, then started walking slowly toward the injured steer. He undid the flap on the scabbard he had fastened to his belt with his right hand and carefully removed his knife. With his left hand he took a white handkerchief out of his left rear pocket and held it above his head, like a flag of surrender.

The steer watched Montoya approach, caught sight of the handkerchief, and focused both eyes on it.

Montoya continued moving even more slowly until he was about six feet in front of the steer. Then he moved the handkerchief to the right, the animal's eyes tracking the movement of the white cloth.

Montoya slowly moved the white cloth back and to his left, then slowly started lowering it. The steer's eyes remained glued on it as Montoya took two short steps closer and dropped the handkerchief so it fluttered to the ground directly in front of the animal.

The steer lowered its head as though it was going to sniff the white cloth.

Montoya quickly leaned between the animal's wide horns. The glint of his knife flashed in the bright sun. He made a quick motion and the animal collapsed in a heap, dead before it hit the ground. He had severed the spinal cord at the base of the skull.

Fordham and the others at the fence were speechless. Montgomery stalked away without saying a word.

Montoya cleaned the blood off his knife by wiping it across the dead animal's neck, then put it back in his scabbard, turned and walked back to the fence.

"Never saw anyone do that before," Fordham said to Montoya. "Nice work." Then he turned to the wranglers standing nearby. "I'd like you boys to field dress that critter. Save the head for the taxidermist. Boss'll want it mounted. Jim you know what to do. Be sure and save the liver for me."

o0o

Fordham rode back to the bunkhouse with Montoya. Mully raced ahead of them. Lleyellyn was coming out of the bunkhouse as they drove up.

"Guess what your boss man here did," Fordham said. "Put a severely injured steer out of its misery like a galled darned matador. Better even."

Shay looked at Montoya, waiting for an explanation.

"Sorry cuss had a dangling broken front leg. No way to fix it. It was in agony. That damned Montgomery was raising a fuss about the proper protocol. All I did was walk out there and do what had to be done. Only thing to do, really," Montoya said.

"Kinda understating the situation," Fordham said. "Your pal here walked up to that critter, distracted it with his handkerchief, then reached over the horns with his right arm and severed the spinal cord with a damned pocket knife. Animal fell like a sack of bricks. Dead before it knew what hit him. Craziest thing I ever saw. Bravest, too."

Shay looked at Montoya for a further comment.

"He's exaggerating. Wasn't no pocket knife. I used this miniature Bowie knife I usually carry. Thing's razor sharp. Remember, I was raised around livestock. I've known cattle since I was first able to walk," Montoya said. "Got the animal's attention with the handkerchief. Could see it following the motion. When it tracked it and lowered its head, I saw my chance. Reached in. The space between the base of the skull and the first vertebra was plain to see. Longhorns don't run to fat."

"How'd you know that would kill it instantly?" Shay said.

"Some reading I did at Granite City. Read about it in the *Encyclopedia of Bullfighting*. Guy that dispatches a mortally wounded toro at a bullfight is a *puntillero*. Job's to do exactly what I did."

"What if the bull had suddenly raised its head?" Fordham said.

"I didn't think it would," Montoya said.

"What if you'd missed. Hit bone or something?" Shay said. Montoya looked at him.

"I didn't think that would happen, either."

o0o

Lleyellyn and Montoya were sitting at the kitchen table drinking iced tea when Irene came downstairs.

"Will DeLong called a little while ago. They were filming as you put down an injured animal. Said it was the damnedest thing he's ever seen. Just what did you do?"

Montoya was looking intently at a drop sliding down the side of his glass. He shrugged.

"I had to do something. Animal was in agony. Nothing anybody could do for it. Had to be put out of its misery. I just did what you have to do. Not a big deal, really."

"Well, Will said you handled yourself better than any bullfighter he's ever seen. Going to show me the film," she said. "Though I'm not sure I want to see it."

Irene poured herself a glass of lemonade, and then sat down at her usual place nearest the stove.

"Reason he called, wants to maybe use the film of you and that bull in the movie. Needs to get you to sign a contract. Wants you to have your agent call him," she said, smiling.

"Agent?" You know I don't have an agent," Montoya said. "Except my parole agent. That count?"

'Well, we've got Lleyellyn right here. Remember that newspaper story about his friend Tole, the bronc rider. You were his agent, weren't you?" she said, looking at Shay.

"Well yeah, sort of. Didn't really know what to do. Got some pictures, talked to a reporter, helped him out a little when he broke his arm. Stuff like that."

"Well, you can help me out a little," Montoya said. "Ask around. Maybe talk to some of the people you met at the party. Quite a few of them went to college for film making. Find out just what an agent does. What kind of a paper they might want me to sign. Talk to the director. See if you can get him to tell you what he's thinking."

"Think he'll tell me anything?"

"Only one way to find out."

CHAPTER 15

TUESDAY AUGUST 11

After the breakfast dishes were cleaned up, Shay went to the movie outfit's office tent looking for one of the people he had talked to at the wrap party. The place was nearly deserted. There was a woman at a desk staring at a computer screen.

"Looking for Kerry Cadon," Lleyellyn said. "He around?"

The woman didn't look up, but said, "Just saw him loading a trailer. Just out the back, through there."

Cadon was standing behind a trailer holding an aluminum box. He glanced up as Lleyellyn approached.

"You! The assistant foreman, right?" Cadon said, by way of greeting. "Looking for me?"

"I am," Lleyellyn said. "Got a minute?"

Cadon shoved the box he was holding in the back of the trailer, and sat down on another aluminum box sitting nearby.

"Grab a seat," he said, nodding toward an empty space at the tail end of the trailer.

"What can I do ya?"

"You went to film school, right?" Lleyellyn said.

Cadon nodded, and said, "I did. You're right."

"They teach you anything about agents? And contracts?"

"Sure. Some. That stuff's mostly handled by lawyers. Intellectual property guys. Talent agencies. People like that. Why you asking?"

"You heard about our foreman, Mr. Montoya, putting down that injured steer, didn't you?"

"Wasn't there when it happened. Heard about it. Saw the film. One of the cameramen just happened to be in the right place at the right time. Everybody's been talking about it."

"The director called. Wants to include the film footage of the incident in the movie, Wants Montoya's agent to call him."

"He got an agent?"

Shay looked at his boots, then met Cadon's eyes.

"Asked me to be his agent. That's why I'm talking to you. Tell me what an agent does. What I should do. Stuff you learned at UCLA."

"USC," Cadon said.

"Sorry."

"University of Southern California. The mighty Trojans. Hate the Bruins. At least that's the usual line on campus. You go to college?"

"Just graduated high school."

"Tell you what. Help me load the rest of these boxes, then we can go back to my trailer. I can give you some information. Got a book there could help."

o0o

Cadon had a shelf filled with books about the motion picture industry. They talked for over an hour. He told Lleyellyn about the contractual side of the film industry and the role of agents.

"I'll loan you this book for a couple days. Written by one of my professors. Should tell you the basics. What you'll need to know so you won't sound like an idiot."

CHAPTER 16

WEDNESDAY AUGUST 12

Shay was up half the night thumbing through Cadon's book. Reading the parts that he thought would help. Making notes. He fell asleep about three in the morning, but was up by six. He jotted down the things he learned that should be in a contract for Montoya. He hadn't asked Cadon how much money he should ask for.

o0o

Cadon was just getting up to bus his breakfast dishes when Shay entered the mess tent.

"Morning, Kelly. Got a minute?"

"Sure, what's up?" Cadon said, while sitting back down at the table. "Have a seat."

"First of all, here's your book. Thanks. Helpful. Learned a lot," Shay said. "I've got a question for you."

"Shoot."

"I know what stuff's supposed to be covered in an Actor Agreement. But what I don't know is, what should I ask for? How much is the film of Mr. Montoya putting that animal down worth?"

Kelley Cadon looked around the room, scratched his head, then faced Lleyellyn.

"This is a pretty big budget picture. Final cut will run close to two and a half hours, I'd bet. Your friend's scene might be what? Twenty-five, maybe thirty seconds?"

"Seems about right."

"Look at it this way. If they had planned the scene they would have needed a stunt man. They couldn't intentionally harm any livestock. Maybe they'd have to recreate the scene digitally, or something. Cost a hell of a lot to film it and get it right. Montoya doing what he did, didn't cost them a dime. He put a doomed animal out of its misery. Saved the producers a lot. Can't be too bashful making a demand."

"Think what, five thousand dollars?" Lleyellyn said.

"Not enough. Remember, you can always come down if you ask for too much."

"Any suggestions?"

Cadon looked him in the eye, smiled, and said, "It's a hell of a scene. Adds a lot to the picture. Just keep that in mind. Don't be bashful. Remember, you're the agent."

o0o

The phone rang several times before a feminine voice said, "Mr. DeLong's office. May I help you?"

"My name's Lleyellyn Shay. Manuel Montoya has asked me to speak on his behalf. Mr. DeLong wants to discuss Mr. Montoya's scene yesterday."

"Well yes. Glad you called," the receptionist said. "You know, I've seen the footage. Everyone has. Your friend was very courageous." She paused. "Hang on a sec, I'll talk to Mr. DeLong."

A half minute later she was back. "Can you come by now?"

o0o

DeLong's trailer was off by itself in back of the office tent. DeLong was standing in the open door when Shay walked around the side of the tent.

"Lleyellyn Shay, right?" he said, extending his hand.

As they shook hands, Lleyellyn said, "That's right. I'm representing Manuel Montoya. He asked me to come over and talk to you."

DeLong motioned him to follow. They entered the mobile home. DeLong sat behind a big desk. Lleyellyn sat down in a leather side chair across from him.

"You're the assistant foreman, if I remember."

"Right."

"Ever represent a performer?"

"I've been an agent for a saddle bronc rider. Tole Winters. Nothing involving motion pictures."

DeLong stared at Shay for a half minute.

"You sure you have Montoya's okay to speak for him."

"Well, yes. He asked me to. Of course, anything I come up with will need his final okay. He's good with this."

DeLong handed Shay a one-page document headed *Actor Contract – License Agreement*.

"Get your buddy Montoya to sign this and I'll give him two thousand dollars cash today, and of course less your agent's commission. A standard two hundred. Ten percent."

Lleyellyn took the paper and scanned it. He had seen several sample actor contracts in the book he had borrowed.

"Mr. DeLong, we appreciate the offer. I see your proposal is for all rights in all markets. I'm looking for something a little more specific."

"What do you have in mind?" DeLong said, a condescending smile playing on his face.

"Let's put aside the money issue, for a moment," Shay said. "We need to work out domestic, foreign, re-release, television, and digital rights. My client will need five film and five DVD copies of his scene with license or permission to use them for personal and promotional purposes. He requests that he be identified in the cast credits and as a stunt performer. His likeness on promotional material for the film will be subject to his prior approval."

DeLong held up his hand, stopping Shay before he could go on.

"You another goddamned USC film graduate?"

Shay smiled, but didn't answer the question.

"I'm familiar with motion picture cast contracts," Lleyellyn said, thinking of the manual he had studied the night before. "I am also aware that this particular scene is an unusual opportunity. For the picture, and for my client. It would be virtually impossible to purposely film such a scene. But we both know it will, shall we say, enhance your picture."

DeLong leaned back in his chair and put his hands behind his head as he looked up at the ceiling.

"Okay, Mr. Assistant Foreman. I can tell you the language is doable. Now let's talk money. What's your demand?"

Shay reached in his shirt pocket and removed a sheet of paper, unfolded it, and placed it on the table.

"I'll cover each point separately, but first I want to talk about the head of that bull. The one that was taken to town to be mounted by a taxidermist."

"What about it?"

"I'd like my client, Mr. Montoya to get it. It would look great here at the ranch."

"I'm sure it would. However, thing's already spoken for. Going to be auctioned off for charity at the world premiere," DeLong said. "Deal's already signed."

Lleyellyn looked down at the floor, scratched his head, and didn't look up until Delong continued.

"Tell you what I can do. Half the auction proceeds for the damned mounted head go to a charity chosen by the owner of the herd. Other half, I get to choose. Probably the old actors' home in Pasadena. But tell you what. I'll give part of my share to Montoya to donate as he wishes. Say twenty percent of the whole thing, which'll leave me with thirty percent," DeLong said rising from his chair. "Okay?"

"Sounds fair, sir," Shay said. "Depending if we get the dollars right."

"Right you are. We're at the brass tacks point. How much money you thinking of?"

Lleyellyn picked up the sheet of papers with his scribbled notes.

"Okay. Here goes. U.S. rights for theater screenings, one hundred ten thousand."

He glanced at DeLong who was sitting back in his chair.

"Overseas rights. Asia, fifty-five thousand. Europe, same. Middle-east, Africa. Australia and New Zealand, sixty thousand combined. South America the same. These are for all for theater release," he said, glancing at the director who was busy making notes.

When DeLong looked up, Shay continued.

"Digital rights, North American, all foreign markets licensed for ten years. Ninety thousand."

Shay raised his eyes. DeLong was sitting back, arms on the armrests, a slight smile on his face.

"You done?"

"Pretty much."

"You sure you're new at this game, kid? Must've done your homework. You in law school or something?" DeLong said, giving Lleyellyn a brief smile.

Lleyellyn smiled back, but kept his mouth shut.

Two Shots Quick

DeLong swiveled around and faced the credenza behind his desk. He punched numbers into a calculator and drummed his fingers next to it. Finally he turned and faced Montoya's agent.

"I have to check with my people," he said. "I want your client's scene in the picture. He'll have to agree to some additional filming to set the scene. Need to make him one of the cowboys herding the cattle. Film him sitting around the campfire, maybe. Riding a horse. Hell, I'll need him sharpening his knife. He'd have to agree to up to twenty hours before the cameras. He'd have to join the union and all that crap. There's a lot more than just a yes or no to your proposals."

DeLong stood up.

"I'll have a full answer for you tomorrow. Stop in about one. Right after lunch. See if we can't put something together."

o0o

Montoya and Irene were both in the kitchen when he walked in.

"I think we're getting close to a deal."

"Sit down. Tell us about it," Irene said. "We've been talking it over. Mr. Montoya's thinking maybe three thousand dollars. I'm betting ten."

Lleyellyn walked over to the refrigerator and extracted a Mountain Dew.

"Anybody want anything?" he said, before popping the can and sitting at the table.

"I think a little more than that," he said, smiling at each of them in turn. "I think he'll go a hundred grand."

"You've got to be kidding," Irene said. "My lands!"

He looked at Montoya.

"You're kidding right?"

"No. I'm serious. And there's more," Lleyellyn said.

They watched as he took several sips from the soda.

"That's just for the U. S. theater rights. There's overseas rights. And then digital rights. All together should be over two hundred thousand."

"What's the catch?" Montoya said.

"Well, I'm waiting for the completed contract. But I think we're close. He'll have the written document tomorrow. We can go over it and make sure the numbers are right."

"There are some other things. The bull's head taken to the taxidermist. That's going to be auctioned off at the world premiere in Los Vegas. Same week as the National Finals Rodeo. Auction proceeds all go to charity. You," he said, looking at Montoya, "Get to designate the charity that gets twenty percent of the proceeds."

Montoya didn't say anything. Irene sat there with her lips parted.

Lleyellyn kept his eyes on Montoya.

"You'll have to be filmed sitting round the campfire with the other cowboy actors, maybe some shots of you riding a horse. No more than twenty hours, total. Just to set up the scene you're in. So you don't just appear out of nowhere in the picture."

"Anything else?" Irene said.

"Couple of minor things. I want the name Manuel Montoya to appear in the film credits. As an actor. And as a stunt man. You'll have to register with the union. That's a rule for this picture. If they ask you to make personal appearances they'll have to provide first class airfare for you and another person of your choice, provide top notch lodging and meals. Oh, and pay you fifty bucks an hour, portal to portal."

"My goodness, Hon, how'd you end up getting all these things?" Irene said.

Lleyellyn pushed his hat back and smiled.

"Guy I met at the party studied at USC. Knows a lot about the film business. Has a job as a grip now, but hopes to move up. Loaned me a book about the movie business, film contracts, and stuff. I studied it last night. Guy made a few suggestions."

He took another sip of his drink, looked at them and smiled, then continued, "Delong offered two thousand five hundred dollars for everything. I may be new at this, but I knew that was bulls..., excuse me..., too damned low. I was ready. I made a counter-offer. I expect he's going to accept it almost exactly as I just said. Know for sure when the written contract is ready."

CHAPTER 17

THURSDAY AUGUST 13

They were eating breakfast when one of the director's gofers knocked on the door.

Shay answered the knock by opening the door.

"You're Mr. Shay, aren't you?" one of the young women who had been seated at his table at the wrap party said. "This is for you. From Mr. DeLong."

Lleyellyn thanked her and took the large manila envelope she handed him.

He undid the clasp on the envelope and removed three thick typed documents. There was a memo clipped to the top page. He read it aloud.

"I've incorporated your requests in this formal contract. It should be signed by you and Montoya in the presence of a notary. There are two duplicate originals for your records." It was signed "DL."

Irene and Montoya watched him as he thumbed through the contract, before he looked up at them.

"Twenty-three pages. Looks like gobbledygook to me."

"Irene started clearing dishes while Shay continued reading the first page.

"We need some legal advice here," Irene said. "I'll call my attorney. We can go into town. Show it to him. See what he says."

o0o

Irene and Shay drove into town to meet with the lawyer. Montoya stayed at the ranch to keep an eye on things.

"You've done a great job representing Mr. Montoya. This contract is a piece of work. Too bad there's no Philadelphia lawyers around here," Irene said. "Mr. Glencoe will have to do."

The law office was up a flight of stairs above the drug store. They stood outside the office door for a moment while Irene caught her breath. The frosted glass door said *Wallace D. Glencoe, Law Office* in gold letters shadowed in black.

The receptionist behind the counter looked up as they entered, letting her half spectacles slide half way down her nose.

"Irene. It's good to see you. Mr. Glencoe will be with you in a sec," she said. "Would either of you like some coffee? Water?"

"Couple waters will do fine. Justine, this is Mr. Montoya's new assistant. Lleyellyn Shay. Justine Cooper."

"Pleased to meet you, Ma'am," Lleyellyn said, smiling at her.

"I've heard all about you. LaDonna Mae at the café told me about you and your other cowboy friend. Good to put a face to the name. Have a seat. I'll get those waters."

Justine was just returning with two bottles of water when attorney Glencoe came out of his office.

"Irene!" he said, giving her an embrace. "What brings you to town this fine day?"

"Wally, I've got a legal document we need you to go over. This is my new man. Lleyellyn Shay."

After Shay and Glencoe shook hands, Irene continued.

"Need you to look over these papers for me, or for us. For Mr. Montoya, really, I guess."

He took the contract from Irene and motioned them into his office. They took chairs facing his high backed office chair, while Glencoe started scanning the contract. After a few moments, he looked up.

"This is a pretty high powered legal document. You know I'm not an intellectual property type lawyer. I'll need to peruse this document carefully. Maybe consult with a colleague. Tell you what. Give me a chance to do my homework. Can you come back after lunch? Say two, two fifteen. I'll have something for you by then."

"That's fine. We have things to do in town anyway," Irene said.

Glencoe held up a hand to stop them from leaving.

"Just one question. Why do you have this proposed contract anyway?"

"It's kind of a long story. Lleyellyn here negotiated an agreement for Mr. Montoya to appear in the movie they're making out at the ranch. This is the formal response."

"Must have done a hell of a job negotiating. They're talking some pretty big numbers here."

Glencoe waived them off, and started reading the contract in earnest.

When they got to the street Irene said, "I've got a few errands to run. We've got about two hours. With LaDonna Mae home from the hospital, I'll be happy to run you out to her place, if you want."

"You bet. That would be great. Can I use your cell to call her first?"

Irene removed her cell from her purse and handed it to him. He knew the number by heart. He dialed. It was answered after the first ring.

"Hi! It's me, Lleyellyn."

Irene couldn't hear what was being said at the other end, but Shay was nodding and smiling.

"Irene will drop me off in a few minutes."

He hung up the phone and looked at Irene.

"She's going to have some lunch ready. You know how to get there, right?"

"I do," Irene said. Just a little north of town. One mile, maybe a little less."

o0o

Lleyellyn spotted the Ritchie place as they approached.

"I'll give you, I mean LaDonna Mae, a call when I leave town to come back to pick you up. Should be a little before two. Say hello to her for me. Have fun," Irene said as she pulled up to the ranch house, let him out, and left.

He walked up the steps to the screen door. The inner door was ajar.

"Come in, it's open," he heard LaDonna Mae say.

She was sitting on the sofa. Both feet covered in white bandages encased in black Velcro-strapped hospital-type walking boots.

"I'd get up, but it's still a little bit tough right now," she said. "They took the stitches out at least ten days ago. That didn't hurt at all, but they're still a little tender." She smiled. "Come over and sit next to me. I'm not contagious."

He stepped around the coffee table and slid next to her on the coach. She leaned her face toward him and they kissed each other, long and hard.

"Sure wasn't expecting to see you today," she said, brushing a strand of hair from her forehead. What are you doing in town?"

He told her about the lame longhorn steer, and how Montoya put it out of its misery with the knife he always carried. She interrupted before he could go on, and told him where the lunch fixings were. He made them sandwiches from the roast that was in the refrigerator, then resumed his narration while they ate lunch.

No one knew it then, he had told her, but some cameramen were filming and captured everything Montoya did. Everyone who saw the footage thought it was an amazing and brave thing. The director saw it and wanted to use the scene in the picture.

"Mr. Montoya knew about me being the so-called agent for Tole Winters at the rodeo. He asked me to meet the director and see what they were willing to pay. First I talked to a guy I met who just graduated from film school at the University of Southern California. I looked over some sample agreements he had in the book he loaned me. Bottom line is, I asked for a lot of money, and basically they agreed. Irene is having her lawyer look over the legal papers now."

"That sounds great," LaDonna Mae said. "Can't believe we might see Mr. Montoya up on the silver screen."

They finished their sandwiches and Lleyellyn said he wouldn't mind having seconds. When he sat back down with sandwich number two, he set the plate down on the coffee table and took LaDonna Mae's hands.

"Tell me about you. I've been doing all the talking," he said. "How're your feet really doing?"

"I got some pretty deep cuts from the broken glass. A little infection's left in my left foot. Antibiotics are working. Guess how many stitches I got?"

Lleyellyn made several guesses, but they were all wrong.

"Twenty-seven in my left foot and sixteen in the right. I've started putting weight on my feet. Standing up. Taking some steps. Doctor expects I'll heal up real good, but it'll take a while. Still some swelling," she said. "I'll just be glad when I can take these damn hospital boots off, and move around a little more. Hope to go back to work in three or four weeks, if not sooner. Doc says that's within the realm."

"Have you heard from the sheriff?"

"This morning. Found some of my clothes along the road. Guy mowing the roadside discovered them. My jeans, belt and top were found together. No underwear. And my belt buckle was gone. Supposed to being showing me what they have," LaDonna Mae said.

"Say where they were found?"

"A mile or two from where I escaped from the truck. West side of the road. They're going to search for my Nikes and my underwear along that same stretch of road today."

"That buckle. The one your brother gave you, right?"

"Yeah. The one that says *Big Cock Country*. Remember?"

"How could I forget?"

oOo

Lleyellyn stood up to take the dirty dishes back to the kitchen when they heard a vehicle crunching up the driveway.

"Irene's back already," LaDonna Mae said. "Give me another smooch before you go."

"She was supposed to call first," Lleyellyn said. "Must've forgot."

After they kissed, Lleyellyn said, "Irene told me she wants to talk to you before we go. Private, she told me. I'll get her if it's okay with you."

"Sure, I'd like to see her. I'm not going anywhere."

oOo

Lleyellyn waited in the truck while Irene went inside. He knew Irene was talking to LaDonna Mae about the attack in her official capacity as a sexual abuse counselor.

Irene came out ten minutes later.

"If we drive fast enough, we'll be back at Wally's right on time."

She pulled onto the highway heading toward Miles City, hitting sixty-five before slowing down to fifty as they entered the forty-five mile zone on the edge of town.

As they pulled into an open diagonal space across the street from Glencoe's law office, Irene said, "Despite her stitches, LaDonna Mae is doing really well. You don't have to worry about that gal, she's going to be just fine."

o0o

When they entered the waiting room Justine stood up immediately, and ushered them into the lawyer's office.

"You're right on time. I've had ample time to review the proposed agreement. Even talked to a colleague of mine out in Burbank. That's near Hollywood, as you probably know," Glencoe said.

"Well, Wallace," Irene said. "What's the verdict?"

The attorney looked at Lleyellyn and smiled.

"Mr. Shay you have negotiated a very good agreement. Contract looks to be in order. They didn't try and pull any disqualifying language. I'll go over the figures they're proposing in a minute. There is only one main concern at this juncture."

Glencoe removed his glasses, and started polishing them with a white handkerchief as he looked first at Irene, then at Lleyellyn."

"The agreement is signed on behalf of the production company handling the picture. Called Longhorn Film Ventures, LLC out of Fountain City, Arizona. I could find out nothing about this Limited Liability Company except that it is in good standing in the State of Arizona as of October 10th last year.

What I don't know is who the members of the company are and what their financial wherewithal is."

He raised his hand to halt questions from Boyd or Shay. He took a drink of water, and smiled at them both in turn.

"These production companies are the way business is done in the film industry. No problem there. What we have to do is make sure the money is there to pay in accord with the written terms. I've prepared a letter for you to deliver to Mr. DeLong in response to his written document. Here's a copy for each of you to follow along as I read it aloud. Stop me if you have any queries."

The letter was less than a page long.

Wallace D. Glencoe
Attorney at law
P. O. Box 12
Miles City, Montana 59301

[Date]

Mr. Will DeLong
Principal – Director
Longhorn Film Ventures, LLC
c/o Boyd Ranch
Miles City, Montana 59301

Re: Unnamed Film in Progress at the Boyd Ranch (proposed) Contract with Actor Manuel Montoya and Longhorn Film Ventures, LLC (an Arizona Limited Liability Company)

Dear Mr. DeLong:

I am writing on behalf of Manuel Montoya and his defacto agent, Lleyellyn Shay, my clients.

Mr. Shay has shown me the proposed Contract with Actor which you provided to him recently.

The contract language is acceptable.

What is required before this document is executed by my clients are the following:

First: At the time the contract is executed by or on behalf of the limited liability company, the sum of One Hundred Twenty-five Thousand Dollars and no/100 Cents will be paid by cashier's check issued by Wells Fargo National Association (or other bank to be pre-approved by my clients) made payable to Manuel Montoya and Lleyellyn Shay.

Second: An amount equal to all additional sums due pursuant to the contract (which I calculate to be $305,000.00 US) shall be placed in escrow in an interest bearing trust account administered by my office to be paid when due as delineated in the Contract with Actor. (Accrued interest shall be used to administer the escrow account.)

Assuming you will be agreeable to these requirements, I will be most happy to arrange a closing either at my office or at the Boyd Ranch.

He concluded the letter: Yours very truly, Wallace D. Glencoe.

Both Irene and Lleyellyn had carefully followed along while the letter was being read.

"Any questions?" Glencoe asked.

"No. Makes sense. You think the figures are okay?" Lleyellyn said.

"This is one of those once in million lucky breaks. Be glad the cameras were rolling when Mr. Montoya did his thing. I think it's a good deal for him. And for Longhorn Film Ventures, LLC, Glencoe said. "I'm betting they'll agree to everything, and have a check for you tomorrow."

"What do I do now?" Lleyellyn said.

"I'll insert today's date and fax this letter to the director immediately. You head back to the ranch. Wait for DeLong's reply. Let me know if you hear anything. I'll do the same at this end," he said standing up behind his desk. "Have a nice trip back. Tell Mr. Montoya congratulations for me."

He walked them to the lobby.

"Nice meeting you young man," he said. "And always happy to see you," he added, reaching for Irene's hand and giving her a European-style peck on both cheeks.

o0o

Montoya was working on dinner when they got back to the ranch and entered the kitchen.

"What did you find out?" he said looking at them each in turn.

"He thought the contract looked good. Needs assurance that the production company can come up with the dough. Faxed DeLong a letter. Demands part of the money up front. Hundred twenty-five thou to be exact, with the balance held in an escrow account maintained in Glencoe's private clients' trust account," Irene said. "Wally thinks we'll get a prompt reply."

o0o

It was Lleyellyn's turn to do the dishes. He was just finishing up when the phone rang. Irene picked up the receiver.

"Boyd Ranch, Irene speaking."

She was quiet as she listened to the caller.

"Tomorrow's fine. How about eleven? Will that be okay with Justine? What about DeLong?"

The caller spoke for a few moments before Irene said, "We'll be ready at eleven unless you call back and change the time. Any time tomorrow should work for us."

The caller said something else. Irene listened intently.

"Sure, I'll put him on," Irene finally said, before handing the phone to Montoya. "Mr. Glencoe wants to talk to you."

"This is Montoya."

Montoya listened to Glencoe carefully.

"Thanks. I'd like you to do that. Want to keep the IRS happy," Montoya said, before looking at Lleyellyn and smiling as he continued. "Want to keep my agent happy, too."

The call ended.

"We're going to sign the papers here tomorrow at eleven," Montoya said. "Mr. Glencoe can't be here but Justine, his secretary, will be. She's a State of Montana notary public and can take care to see that everything is properly signed, sealed, stamped, and delivered."

Irene looked at them both.

"Wally told me the one additional issue was an Escrow Agreement governing the funds to be held in his trust account. He worked it out with DeLong's LLC and their legal department. You gentlemen can sign that paper tomorrow, too."

"Big thing. They're paying a hundred twenty-five thousand bucks tomorrow. Certified Check. Great job Lleyellyn," Montoya said. "Oh, and one more thing. Glencoe suggests we endorse the check over to him. He'll run it through his trust account, hold back enough for income taxes and deposit my share and your agent's commission in our personal checking accounts in town."

"Makes sense to me. Wally knows what he's doing. He drew up the papers when I agreed to lease this place so the film could be made here," Irene said. Then looking at Montoya she added, "You ever tell Lleyellyn what his commission is?"

"Glencoe suggested twelve and a half percent. I agreed. And well worth it," he added, turning to Shay and giving his shoulder a squeeze. "Great job you did. I mean it."

CHAPTER 18

FRIDAY AUGUST 14

The next morning, Justine showed up at the ranch a few minutes before eleven, DeLong a couple minutes later.

Glencoe's secretary checked to make sure there had been no alterations to the documents, and carefully inspected the checks. She showed the parties where to sign, and applied her notary seal and signature to make everything official.

After the three complete sets of the original papers were all properly signed and distributed, and the checks handed over, they shook hands all around.

"Next thing for you, Manuel," DeLong said, "Is to get you on film doing some fill-in scenes. You free after dinner?"

"Can be. Sure."

"Meet at the office tent at seven. Wear the same clothes you wore when you dispatched the animal. Be sure and bring your knife."

After DeLong left, Justine sat down with Montoya and Shay and told them she would be taking all the papers back to the office. She got their account numbers and the other information she needed, then had them endorse the check which was in the amount One Hundred Twenty-five Thousand and no/100 Dollars ($125,000.00 US) made payable to Manuel Montoya and Lleyellyn Shay.

"Mr. Glencoe suggests you let him keep necessary funds for you in his trust account to cover the state and federal income taxes you'll owe. He'll figure out the quarterly estimates, and send instructions so you can make timely payments."

"Works for me," Montoya said.

Lleyellyn just nodded.

Mr. Glencoe's secretary gathered her things together and was getting ready to leave.

"Oh, before I forget. Mr. Montoya, you should fill out one of these forms. It tells what charities you designate to receive your share of the proceeds when the mounted bull's head is auctioned off. Just fill it out and mail it back to us in this envelope. Mr. Glencoe suggests you get the full legal name and official address of your designated charity."

o0o

"This calls for a toast," Irene said when Justine had gone. "I've got a bottle of champagne left over from New Year's."

Montoya popped the cork and filled three wine glasses. They drank a toast.

"To Hollywood!" Irene said.

Montoya and Lleyellyn each smiled at her, then took sips of the bubbly liquid following Irene's lead.

"I've been thinking it over. With my share of what they get from the charity auction of that longhorn, I want each of you to designate a charity. Each of us will pick one. Plan to divide my share three ways. Any ideas?" Montoya said. "You go first Irene."

"I'm thinking of the women's shelter in Miles City. Help out a lot of my clients. They always need funds."

"I know there's a charity that helps parolees from the South Dakota State Prison find jobs when they're paroled. Helped me get a ticket back to Montana, anyway. I'm leaning that way," Montoya said.

They both turned toward Shay.

"Never had to think about giving to charity," he said. "I think the kids at the alternative school I went to in Winona could use a little help. And there's a place helps abused women in Winona County. Not sure of the name. Helped my mom a little. That's what I'm thinking, anyway."

"Well, we can find out the full names of these organizations," Montoya said." Then I'll let Justine know so she can have the lawyer make it official."

o0o

Montoya showed up at DeLong's office trailer a few minutes before seven. He was introduced to an assistant director and taken out behind the headquarters area where several cast members he had seen at the wrap party were waiting around a campfire.

Several cameras were set up and ready to go.

He sat next to Leland Fordham, the head wrangler he had met earlier. They talked quietly while the cameras rolled.

He was asked to remove his knife and sharpen it as he talked, one camera moving in for a close-up.

Satisfied with filming around the fire, Fordham brought him a horse. Montoya climbed aboard and followed directions as more film was taken.

Finally, he was asked to put on a rain slicker and sit on the horse under a sprinkler while more filming took place. He was directed to look at one of the cameras and smile broadly as a spotlight simulating lightning flashed on and off several times.

After a half hour they thanked him and told him they had what they needed.

o0o

Back at the bunkhouse, Montoya asked Lleyellyn how LaDonna Mae was getting along.

"LaDonna Mae still has some trouble walking. Until a couple days ago, hadn't been able to take more than a few steps at a time. The stitches been out quite a while, but there's a trace of infection left in one foot. Sometimes she had to use a wheelchair to get around. Tells me her feet hurt when she walks too far," Shay said. "But she says she's making good progress, though. Planning to go back to the Big Sky soon."

"Bothers me to see that Montgomery fella around. Creepy son-of-a-bitch. She hear anything from the sheriff?" Montoya said.

"They found some of her other clothes in a ditch," that's about all.

o0o

They were sitting in Montoya's room in the bunkhouse. Lleyellyn had just finished talking to LaDonna Mae on the phone. He wanted to do something. The way Montoya handled things in the past, he knew the foreman was probably feeling the same way.

When Montoya started talking, he knew he was right.

"You know what I did to the guy who raped Irene when we were in high school. I know I paid a high price, but I still feel justice was done. Same with your stepfather. Bastard got what he deserved. Both cases, the authorities didn't get the job done. Didn't try too hard. Same thing seems to be happening here with LaDonna Mae's situation," Montoya said.

"There's no doubt Montgomery's the guy. The plastic Jesus and her belt buckle are proof enough for me, don't you agree?" Lleyellyn said.

"There's that. And there's more. The pickup's the right color. Some of the females in the movie crew avoid him. Even Mully's afraid of him. All adds up to solid proof far as I'm concerned," Montoya said.

"What can we do? What's appropriate? He didn't actually rape her, but he sure as hell tried. Luckily she escaped. How do you handle an attempted rapist who practically ruined someone's feet?"

"Let's think about it overnight. Talk about it before breakfast."

Two Shots Quick

CHAPTER 19

SATURDAY AUGUST 15

Lleyellyn was shaving when Montoya entered the bathroom.

"I've got an idea," Montoya said. "About Montgomery, I mean."

It was more like a plan than an idea. Lleyellyn listened as Montoya went over his thinking in detail.

"Hell of an idea," Shay said. "My only question is, 'When?'"

"They're waiting to film the big cattle drive scene as soon as we get a rain storm. Should be in the next couple days. If you can believe the weather forecast. Montgomery will be busy making sure no animals are harmed in making the picture. He told you he'll be out and about when the drive starts, didn't he? With binocs and night vision goggles, right? We can make our move then."

"What do we need to get ready?" Shay asked. "Need anything special?"

"Nice to have a handgun. Another of those Savage automatics maybe. Something easy to hide," Montoya said. "Being on parole, I don't have access to firearms out here. You don't either. Might be out of luck there," Montoya said.

"This is Montana. Must be a lot of guys packing. Maybe we can borrow one."

"Well, we don't want anyone to know we have a gun. Wouldn't want it traced back to either one of us."

Two Shots Quick

CHAPTER 20

MONDAY AUGUST 17

Irene had breakfast ready when they walked in the house.

"We're going into town today," she said, passing the platter of ham and eggs to Montoya. "Know you have to see your friend at corrections. And honey," she said, sitting down and looking at Shay, "We're going to get you your driver's license. Eleven o'clock appointment."

Lleyellyn raised his eyebrows in surprise, but didn't say anything.

"I'll call corrections before we leave, let them know I'm coming." Montoya said, before turning his attention to Lleyellyn. "You ready for a road test? Ever parallel park a big truck like her Dodge Ram?"

"Tell you the truth, I've never parallel parked anything. Not sure I'm ready for a driver's test."

"Now look, you've read over that booklet I gave you about Montana driving laws, right?" Irene said. "And you've had no trouble with the Jeep you've been using around here."

"Sure. But your truck's a whole lot bigger than that little Jeep. Think I need to practice some."

"It won't be a problem. I have to stop in at the county office building to check on some case assignments. That's where the driving examiner's office is. Corrections is there, too. I'll call ahead. Borrow a smaller vehicle for you. Something easy to park. An automatic. You'll have time to practice with it before your appointment with the examiner. Don't worry. You'll do fine."

Has more confidence in me than I do, Lleyellyn thought.

oOo

They were ready to leave at seven thirty.

"Lleyellyn, you drive," Irene said handing him the keys. "You okay in the back seat?" she asked Montoya, who simply nodded and got in. "Shall we bring Mully?"

The dog didn't wait for an answer, but climbed in on the passenger side when Irene opened the door, and immediately got into the backseat next to Montoya.

After adjusting the seat and buckling the seat belt, Lleyellyn said, "We're off,"

He started the truck, shifted into low and headed toward the road. He looked both ways before turning onto the pavement, shifted through the gears and headed toward Miles City.

Everyone seemed lost in their own thoughts. Irene turned on the radio and tuned into a local station. They heard the weather report, the local news, and the ag report. Markets were steady They were forecasting rain.

"When you get to that substation or cell tower place or whatever the heck it is, would you pull over," Irene said. "I've have to call and get you a suitable car. Cell phone always works there."

oOo

Irene got out of the truck to get clearer reception when she dialed her call to the county government building.

"Misty," Irene said cheerily. "This is Irene. Say, you know everybody in the building. I need to borrow a car for a couple hours. Who's got a smaller car? Automatic transmission. Friend needs it for a driver's test today."

Irene held her hand over the phone, "Misty's went to look out the window. See whose cars are in the parking lot."

A minute or so later, the telephone conversation resumed.

"Sounds perfect. Why don't you check with her. See if we can borrow it. We'll put some gas in for her. I'll call you back in five minutes."

They let the dog out to sniff around and do its duty.

"Misty said a new intern in the building has a little Dodge Neon. Should be perfect. If she's willing. She's checking."

Mully did her thing and got back in the cab. Irene called Misty again and spoke briefly.

As she put her cell phone back in her purse, all she said was, "It's all set. Let's go."

o0o

It was nine twenty-seven when the pulled into the parking lot adjacent to the county building.

"Lleyellyn, you come with me. Get you squared away with that little Neon. Mr. Montoya can take care of his business. Meet back here about one? Grab your own lunch?" Irene said.

"That works," Montoya said. "I'm going to meet the guy at the bank when I'm done at the DOC. Couple of other things I've been meaning to do. See you at one."

He hooked a leash onto Mully's collar and let her out of the truck. Together they walked toward the street.

o0o

The county building was a big three-story rectangle. The lobby inside the main entrance was cool. A counter in the corner was manned by a young woman behind a sign which read *INFORMATION*.

"Irene!" the young woman said, coming out from behind the information desk and giving Irene a big hug.

"Misty, great to see you. Thanks for the help with the car," she said, holding Misty at arm's length. "This is our new man. Lleyellyn. Meet Misty."

"Hi!" Misty said, shaking Shay's hand. "You've got a great place to work. I love Irene. Mr. Montoya, too."

Irene held up her hand.

"Lleyellyn's the reason I need to borrow the car. He's taking his driver's test this morning. That big old truck of mine is just too big."

"Here's the key," Misty said, handing it to Lleyellyn. "Car belongs to a new intern in the assessor's office. Don't know her. Name's Allison. Just know her dad works somewhere in the building. Different office. She told me it's a yellow Neon. Parked in space thirty seven. Said she was sorry the car's a bit of a mess. Not much gas in the tank, either, she said."

"It'll be fine. Thanks a million," he said.

"Let's go give it a try," Irene said. "You need a licensed driver in the car with you when you're driving. Right?"

o0o

The Neon was dust covered and mud spattered. Lleyellyn opened the door. The floor on the passenger side was filled with empty soda pop cans and fast food wrappers. He tossed enough of the trash behind the front seat so Irene could get in. The back seat area was no better. It was littered with similar items. Irene got in the passenger seat as soon as there was sufficient leg room.

"Beggars can't be choosers," she said. "Let's see if it starts."

Lleyellyn turned the key and the car started instantly. It seemed to run quietly. He adjusted the seat and the mirrors. He checked the gauges. They all worked, but the fuel gauge was a needle-width above the E.

"Seat belt," Irene said.

He buckled up, and looked at Irene.

"Thanks. I better not forget that."

Then he started the car, shifted into drive and headed out onto the street.

"First stop, gas," he said.

He had no trouble handling the car.

"Runs a lot better than it looks," Irene said. "After we gas up we can drive around. Park a few times. Do whatever."

o0o

Lleyellyn remembered the Petrol truck stop. It was where he had started his trip back to Minnesota.

This time he pulled up next to one of the pumps in the section marked *AUTOS ONLY*. Irene went to visit the Ladies room. He walked inside to prepay for unleaded regular.

"I'll fill it up," he told the woman behind the counter. "Be back for the change when I'm done. Not sure how much it'll take."

"You want a car wash? Two bucks when you fill up."

"Sure."

The tank took fourteen point two gallons. He got his change from the clerk and received a car wash token.

He drove around to the rear of the station where the automatic car wash lane was. He was the second car in line. While he waited he picked up all the trash inside the car, and threw it into a garbage can, and used the free vacuum to clean up the carpets. When it was his turn, he pulled ahead into the car wash and waited while the automatic hoses, brushes and automated sponges did their thing. After hot air blew off most of the wet spots on the car he drove around to the front of the station where Irene was waiting.

"Looks like a new car," Irene said. "This was Allison's lucky day."

o0o

Irene had him stop and park at the first seven empty parking spaces they came to. After the first one, he had no trouble with the other six.

"This car's easy to drive. Thanks for arranging it," he said.

"I think you'll do fine. Let's go back and park in the lot at the county building. You can go inside, and let them know you're ready for your driver's test. You won't need me. I'll go up and take care of my business," Irene said. "Good luck. Remember, seat belt."

o0o

The motor vehicle office was crowded with people renewing their auto registrations and driver's licenses. He checked in and was told to take a seat adjacent to the desk that said *ROAD TESTING BY APPOINTMENT ONLY*.

No one else was waiting. Fifteen minutes later a woman in her mid-thirties came in followed by a uniformed officer wearing a patch that said *MOTOR VEDHICLE DIVISION – EXAMINER*.

The woman was in tears. The examiner stopped her before she headed for the exit.

"I'm sure you'll do fine next time. Don't forget to keep those seat belts fastened."

The examiner went into his office and emerged a few minutes later holding a clip board.

"Shay."

"That's me," Lleyellyn said, extending his hand which the examiner ignored.

"I'll follow you to your car. Just get in and do what you would usually do. I'll get in the front seat, passenger side. Follow my instructions. Obey all traffic laws and rules of the road. Any questions?"

"No, Sir."

Shay walked to the car, unlocked it with the key, got in, made sure the passenger door was unlocked and waited for the examiner to get inside. He fastened his seat belt, pretended to adjust the already adjusted mirrors, then stared the car, and waited for instructions.

"Back up, go to the exit, and turn right."

Lleyellyn checked the rearview mirrors, shifted into reverse, looked over each shoulder, then slowly backed out. As he approached the exit he flipped the turn signal for a right turn, got to the exit without difficulty, and waited for traffic to clear before easing forward and entering the right hand lane. He smoothly accelerated to thirty miles an hour, the posted speed limit, despite the fact that traffic ahead of him was doing at least forty.

The examiner didn't say anything for several blocks. He was writing something on the papers on his clipboard.

"Turn left at the next signal light, then park in the first available parking space you come to."

A block from the approaching signal light, Shay turned on his left turn blinker, moved into the left lane and then into the left turn lane. The traffic light was red. He stopped before the white line, then proceeded to complete his left turn when the left turn arrow turned green. He signaled to move into the right hand lane, before spotting an empty parking space half way up the block.

He rolled down the window and gave a manual stop signal as he pulled adjacent to the empty parking space, then forward so that he was even with the car in the space ahead. He checked his side view mirrors for approaching traffic, looked over his left shoulder to double check for cars or bikes, then smoothly backed into the parking space twelve inches from the curb. He turned off the ignition and awaited further instructions.

"Mr. Shay, you've done an excellent job. I intend to pass you. I've got just one question."

Lleyellyn looked at him, not sure if he had done something he wasn't supposed to or not.

"Was this car cleaned up and washed when you got it?"

"Pretty much. We borrowed the car so I'd have a vehicle for this test. Why?"

"Hell. It's my daughter's car. Gave it to her when she graduated community college. She's an intern in the County Assessor's Office. This is the best this car's looked since the day we gave it to her. Look like this when you got it?"

Lleyellyn didn't want to get Allison in trouble with her father. After all, she had loaned him the car.

"Pretty much. Couple of pop cans in the back. Sure is a nice car. Appreciate her letting me borrow it."

"You know Allison?"

"No. Friend of mine does. My boss made the arrangements."

"Who's that."

"Irene Boyd, owns The Boyd Ranch."

"I know Irene. Who doesn't. Say hello for me. Name's Isaac Slossman," he said shaking Shay's hand. "Sorry I didn't shake your hand back there. Have to keep up appearances. At any rate, congratulations. You're now about to become a fully licensed driver certified by the State of Montana."

o0o

Lleyellyn met up with Irene in the lobby. As they were heading to her truck they heard someone shouting behind them.

"Miss Boyd! Miss Boyd!"

They turned and watched a young woman about Lleyellyn's age approaching them with a broad smile on her face.

"I want to thank you for cleaning up my car. And the gas. Thanks."

"Allison, right?" Irene said.

She shook hands all around.

"We appreciate you letting us borrow it," Irene said. "Lleyellyn here needed it for his driver's test. My Dodge truck is pretty hard to cram into a city parking space. He's the one drove it through the automatic wash and picked up some beverage cups and things."

"Well, I know he did more than that. Sure impressed my dad. He's the DMV evaluator. Didn't know you were going to use my car for the driver's exam," she said. "Dad called me and congratulated me for finally cleaning up my car."

They smiled back at her.

"He said his client told him the car was cleaned up when he borrowed it," she said looking at Lleyellyn. "I don't know what you said, but my dad was really happy. Taking me out to lunch today. His treat."

"No big deal. Had no trouble with the test," Lleyellyn said. "Your dad seems like a pretty nice guy."

"Tell you the truth," she said. "The car looks better now than when my dad gave it to me. You can borrow it any time."

o0o

Before getting in the truck, Irene said, "You drive."

They got in the pick-up and fastened their seat belts.

"Gal in front of me failed the test. Forgot to buckle her seat belt. Automatic disqualification, I think. Has to wait a month to repeat it. She left in tears."

"She won't ever forget to buckle up again," Irene said. "Head down to the Petrol station. Mr. Montoya said he'd be waiting for us in the coffee shop."

o0o

Montoya was waiting for them at a corner booth. Mully was at his feet under the table.

"Saw you were driving," Montoya said, looking at Shay as he slid in next to him. "Must've passed."

"He did. Borrowed an intern's little Neon. Ran it through the carwash and picked up some trash from the floor and back seat. You won't believe this. Her dad was the driver's examiner."

"Probably gave me a passing grade because his daughter's car looked better than it usually does," Lleyellyn said. "He was happy. His daughter was happy. And so am I. Glad to have that out of the way."

While they were waiting for their orders, Irene said, "Now you'll need a vehicle. Want to look around in town, see if you can find something you like?"

"Sure. But I'm not sure what to look for. Might pick out a lemon, or something."

"Mr. Montoya knows a lot about vehicles. Helped me choose my truck. And the one before that, too. We'll go with you. Find something you like, we'll throw in our opinions if you want."

o0o

At Irene's suggestion, they drove to the Dodge – Chrysler dealer on the edge of town.

"Bought my truck here. And two or three before that. Think they're straight shooters," Irene said. "You know one of the shop guys, right?" she said, looking at Montoya.

"I do. One of my class mates at Granite City," he said, before turning towards Shay. "Kinda vehicle you looking for?"

"A good used one. Reliable. Cheap as possible," Lleyellyn said. "Pickup, maybe."

Irene parked in a space in front of the used car department.

Shay was surprised when a woman about Irene's age came out to greet them.

"Got a potential customer for you," she said by way of greeting. "Lleyellyn's our new man. You know Mr. Montoya, I think."

"I do. Lleyellyn?" she said shaking his hand, and then Montoya's. "Any friend of Irene's a friend of mine. Which one of you is the customer? Not this dog is it?" she added, patting Mully's forehead. "Good looking pooch."

"I am, Ma'am. Just looking. Need something reliable, not too expensive."

"Don't we all. Come into the office. Took in a couple of units yesterday. Let's see what I've got."

They let Lleyellyn take the lead as they followed the woman into an office marked Gwen Garrisson – Owner.

"Take a seat. I'll call back to the used car department," she said, picking up the telephone and dialing an intercom number. "Wally, Gwen. Bring me the sheets on those vehicles you brought in yesterday. Not any crap. Just the better ones. Thanks, hon."

They waited a few minutes until Wally came to the door and waited until Gwen beckoned him in.

"Maybe you know Irene Boyd here," she said. "This is Mr. Montoya, her foreman, and Lleyellyn, her new man. Looking for something reliable. Not too expensive. Got anything that'll fit the bill?"

Wally looked at Montoya.

"Manny. Good to see you. You're looking good. Job must agree with you."

"You, too. Glad to see you're putting your automotive skills to good use."

Wally simply nodded at Montoya as he handed two sheets of paper to his boss.

Garrison looked over the sheets.

"Take these in trade?" she asked Wally.

"Yes, Ma'am. That first unit was from a guy bought it here new. Other one's a New Mexico car. Trade in on a new Chrysler."

She showed one of the documents to Wally.

"Take these gentlemen out and show them this one. I need to catch up on chit chat with Irene."

"Unit's still in the back lot. Haven't had a chance to check it out. Have it detailed. Ready it for sale," Wally said, leading them to the rear of the service department building and behind a fence at the rear of the dealership. "But I'll tell you, owner brought it in regular for maintenance. Took good care of it."

A dozen or so vehicles were lined up in the lot. Two of them had been in serious collisions.

"This is it," Wally said, unlocking the door to a red Ford Ranger. "Take it for a spin, I'll go over it when you get back," he said handing the keys to Lleyellyn.

Lleyellyn scratched his head, then looked at Montoya for instructions.

"Go ahead. You're the customer. I'll catch up with Wally."

Lleyellyn was as careful as he was when he took his driver's test. He adjusted the seat, fastened the seat belt, checked the mirrors, and looked over the instruments, noting that the truck had a manual transmission. Four on the floor.

As Wally and Montoya headed toward the service department, he depressed the clutch and shifted into low. It wasn't much different than Irene's Dodge or the Jeep. He eased ahead, moved out of the lot, and turned onto the roadway.

The pick-up ran smoothly. He turned on the radio. Worked fine. The air conditioner was in good working order. He didn't see any issues in the several blocks he drove.

Back at the dealership, he got out and walked to the service department. Montoya and Wally were in the office, each with a soft drink in their hands.

"Back already?" Montoya said. "Run okay?"

"Yeah. I like it. Seemed good to me. Far as I can tell."

"Wally's going to check it out," Montoya said. "As a favor to me. Not for the dealership."

"Bring the truck around to the side bay," Wally said. "I'll put it on the lift. Give you my two cents."

Lleyellyn retrieved the truck, drove around to the bay and followed Wally's signals as he positioned it over the lift. Wally raised the vehicle, looked over the tires, tugged on the wheels, checked for leaks and so forth. Then he lowered the truck, popped the hood and inspected the hoses and belts before checking the wiper blades and the paint and seals.

"Start 'er up, will you?"

Lleyellyn got in, started the truck and got out to watch.

Wally took a stethoscope from a multi-drawer tool box next to a work bench. He positioned it at various places on the engine block. Then he removed the dip stick and smelled it.

"Okay, turn it off," he said.

After Lleyellyn got out of the truck, Wally checked the brake and gas pedals and looked over the upholstery.

"Let me take it for a test drive," Wally said. "Only take a few minutes."

Wally drove out of the lot, and onto the roadway. They heard the tires squeal as he accelerated rapidly, then squeal some more as he come to a skidding stop.

"Wally knows his stuff," Montoya said. "Dad owned a garage. Grew up around cars. Learned more stuff at Granite City. He'll tell it to you straight."

They could hear the sound of the pickup as it disappeared from view.

"Wally and I have always had each other's backs," Montoya said. "Getting me a little handgun. It'll be under the passenger seat when your truck's ready to go."

Montoya's friend was back in twenty minutes. He parked the Ranger next to the service department and got out.

"Runs like a Swiss watch," Wally said, getting out of the truck and handing the keys to Lleyellyn.

He glanced at Montoya and gave him a nod, which Lleyellyn didn't see.

"Based on the wear and tire on the pedals, I think the odometer is right. Checked our records. Prior owner had us replace the timing belt and hoses and stuff at sixty thousand. Engine sounds good. I used the stethoscope to listen to the valves, pistons, cam shaft. Like listing to a patient's heartbeat. Can listen to the individual cylinders. Can tell if anything sounds not right. Just another tool," Wally said. "Everything sounds good. Couldn't smell any burnt oil. You have any questions?"

"No, sir," Lleyellyn said.

"I'll tell you one thing. Tires and battery are just okay. But serviceable. Should be good for about a year."

"Thanks," Lleyellyn said. "I feel pretty good about the truck."

"Tell the boss about the tires," Wally said. "Might do something."

oOo

Garrison and Irene were enjoying coffee in the owner's office when Lleyellyn and Montoya walked in. Mully was sitting on the floor next to Irene. There was a water dish next to her.

"What do you think?" Garrison said.

"Seems like a nice truck," Lleyellyn said. "Wally didn't know the price."

"Let me look at the sheet again," Garrison said, picking up the paper she had checked earlier.

"Took this in trade. Pretty favorable deal. You being a friend of my friend Irene here, and all, I'm thinking twenty-six hundred. Plus tax and license fees, of course."

Lleyellyn looked at Montoya for guidance.

"Go ahead, talk it over. Irene and I haven't finished our coffee," Garrison said, looking up and giving him a smile.

He was aware of Irene and Montoya watching him.

"It is a nice little truck. But it needs a set of tires and a battery. Wiper blades are about shot. Think it's due for a lube and oil. And hasn't been detailed. I'll take it for your asking price if you throw in those items. I've got cash," Lleyelllyn said. "I mean a local check."

Garrison stood up, and extended her hand to Lleyellyn. As they shook hands, she said, "Irene, young man here seems to have a good head on his shoulders. See why you hired him. I'll draw up the papers and we'll get the new tires and things done while you wait.

Garrison left the room.

"You've got your checkbook, right?" Irene said.

"I do."

"Seems like you got yourself a new truck. I'm sure Mr. Montoya and his friend gave you some good advice. I think Mr. Montoya and I'll head back to the ranch. You stick around 'til your truck's ready. Take it for a ride. No need to hurry home," Irene said. "Maybe you'll have a chance to drop by and see LaDonna Mae. See how she's doing. She'll be glad to see you."

o0o

After Irene and Montoya left with the dog, Lleyellyn completed the paperwork with Garrison, then sat in the waiting room and helped himself to a can of Dew and a donut.

Thirty minutes later Wally pulled up next to the waiting room and beeped the horn. The Ford Ranger had been run through the car wash and the red paint was dazzling in the sunlight. Wally got out and handed him two sets of keys.

"Ready to go. Lubed, oiled, washed, new tires, battery and wipers. Armoralled damn near everything," Wally said. "Oh, filled the gas tank, too. Enjoy the truck."

"Thanks," Lleyellyn said. "Looks almost new."

"One more thing, Wally said. "I put a package under the seat for Manny. See he gets it, will you?"

"Sure, Lleyellyn said. "And again, thanks for everything."

He got in, inserted the key, started the engine, gave Wally a thumbs up, and drove slowly out of the dealership.

I can't believe it, he thought. *Driver's license, new vehicle, all today. Things are working out for a change.*

o0o

Before heading out to the Ritchie place he stopped in at Joanne's Floral and Gift and bought a bouquet of mixed flowers for LaDonna Mae. The clerk put the bouquet in a clear glass vase and attached a yellow ribbon.

"Want a gift card. Help yourself. No extra charge."

He picked out a card that had yellow roses on the front, and wrote "LaDonna Mae, Been missing you. Love, Lleyellyn" on the inside. The clerk taped it to the vase.

o0o

He saw LaDonna Mae's car parked near the barn as he pulled up. He parked near the porch on the side of the drive. As he was reaching to pick up the flowers, he heard another vehicle approaching.

A UPS truck pulled up next to the front steps. The driver stepped out of the passenger door, and hurried up the steps. She saw Lleyellyn approaching, flashed him a smile, and waited.

He pushed the doorbell and heard the chimes in the hallway.

"Come in. Door's open."

He opened the door and followed the UPS driver inside.

"I'm in here. In the den," he heard LaDonna Mae say.

He poked his head around the corner. She was seated on the couch with her feet tucked under her. She was wearing sneakers. She looked up and saw him, her face brightening into a broad smile.

"Lleyellyn!" she said. "I didn't know you were in town today."

LaDonna Mae spotted the driver. She looked at Lleyellyn, then back at her other visitor.

"You know each other?" LaDonna Mae said.

"No. We just happened to get here at the same time," Lleyellyn said.

"Then I want you to meet Doreen. She's the one I told you about. Found me along the highway after I was attacked. Patched me up and drove me to the hospital. Probably saved my life."

Doreen held out her hand and Lleyellyn shook it.

"I'm Lleyellyn. She told me all about you."

"Just stopped in to see how you're doing," she said to LaDonna Mae. "And to thank you."

"Thank me. For what?" LaDonna Mae said.

"For that nice letter you sent to United Parcel telling how I spotted you and so forth. Company named me Employee of the Month, and I got a write up in the UPS newsletter. I brought you a copy."

LaDonna Mae started thumbing through the booklet when the radio strapped to Doreen's belt let out a beep. Doreen glanced at it.

"Hey! I've got to run," she said. "Great to see you're getting along good," she said to LaDonna Mae. "Nice meeting you, Lleyellyn."

She was gone before they could say anything.

"What a day," LaDonna Mae said. "Didn't expect to see Doreen, and I really didn't expect see you today, either."

"Irene brought me in. Took my driver's test this morning. Got my license. And bought a truck. And here I am."

He handed her the flowers. Then bent down to give her a kiss. She carefully placed the flowers on the end table, then put her arms around him and held him close.

"Sit down. Sure good to see you. Thanks for the flowers. You shouldn't have."

He stepped around the stool and sat next to her.

"You doing okay? You're looking a whole lot better." he said, looking at her feet. "Move okay?"

"Healing pretty good the past three, four days. Swelling's gone way down the doctor says. Infection's almost completely gone. Can put more weight on both feet. Right one's the worst, but I can walk more. I'm doing okay. Feeling ten times better. Sure glad you stopped by. Watched enough Oprah for one day."

"Let's see what they said about Doreen in their little magazine," Lleyellyn said.

"She thumbed through the pages. The inside of the back cover had a smiling picture of Doreen under the words Employee of the Month.

The article mentioned that Doreen McCloud had been with UPS for six years and that this was the second time she had been selected as Employee of the Month. Two years earlier she had pulled the driver from a burning semi and this time she "rescued a young woman left naked, injured and bleeding alongside of the highway." McCloud was an ex-Navy corpsman, and a single mother of a twelve-year-old daughter.

"Sure glad it was Doreen that stopped for you," Lleyellyn said. "She's an expert at rescuing people, don't you think?"

They talked about LaDonna Mae's good fortune and the progress she was making. She was anxious to get back to work at the Big Sky.

"Been cooped up here too long."

"How about we go for a ride? I can carry you out if you can't walk. We could stop and get an ice cream, or something," Lleyellyn said.

"Hey! I'm getting around okay," she said. "I'm all alone until after five when my dad gets back. I'll leave him a note. We'll be back by five. Right.?"

"No problem."

LaDonna wrote her note and had Lleyellyn stick it under a magnet on the refrigerator.

He opened the front door, and held it open for her. She walked to his truck without any problem. Before she got in, she turned and gave him a long kiss.

He settled himself behind the wheel and looked at her.

"Worth the trip already," he said. "I've really missed you. You sure seem to be getting by okay. Hope that bastard didn't mess up any more than your feet."

"Don't worry about me. I'm doing really good. Really feel great, I mean it. Still plan to go back to work Monday after next," she said. "Say, you know, this is really a nice little truck. New?"

"Nine years old. Good shape, though. Runs great"

Lleyellyn backed up and continued the loop in front of the house, and started down the driveway toward the highway. As he approached the road, a sheriff's patrol car coming from the direction of town signaled a left turn and pulled into the driveway. It stopped next to them.

"Mr. Shay," the deputy said. "How you doing?"

Lleyellyn recognized Deputy Thompson. He was the one who had contacted him at the Boyd Ranch to tell him about his mother's murder."

"Catch that s. o. b. yet?" Thompson said, referring to his stepfather.

"Didn't catch him. But his body was found. Run over by a train. Don't know the details. Glad he's gone."

"Yes, I would imagine," Deputy Thompson said. "Reason I'm here is to talk to Miss Ritchie for a moment. That's you, isn't it?" he said, looking past Lleyellyn at LaDonna Mae.

"Yes, sir. Lleyellyn's taking me for a ride. What can I do for you?"

"D.O.T. guy was mowing the grass along the highway south of town. Found some items of clothing. I need to ask if you recognize them. See if you can tell me if they were the items you were wearing at the time of the assault."

The deputy got out of his squad car, took a paper sack out of the back seat area and walked around to the passenger side of Lleyellyn's truck.

"These look familiar?" Thompson said, as he took out a pair of Wrangler jeans, a light blue bra, one Nike tennis shoe, and a leather belt without a buckle.

"Yes, those are mine. Shoe's a size six. That's the belt that had the buckle on it my brother gave me."

"She held up the pair of Wrangler's. These are mine. My size. Recognize that little hole here by the knee. I know the bra is mine, too. Right brand. Vanity Fair. New," LaDonna Mae said. "He find the panties, too? They matched. Same color. Size three."

"No ma'am. But we're going back tomorrow. See if we can find the missing items. Just wanted to make sure we are on the right track."

"There was a tee shirt. Too," Lleyellyn said. '

"Right. Sorry. I forgot. Find it?"

"No, Miss," Anderson said. "Description."

"White. Size small. Almost new."

"Any thing written on it. A logo, or anything?"

LaDonna Mae blushed as she looked first at Lleyellyn, then at the deputy.

"It said Grand Tetons in big red letters across the front."

The deputy made no comment as he noted her answer in his notebook.

"All right, then. Thanks for the information. I'll let you know if we find out anything more."

As the deputy prepared to leave, LaDonna Mae leaned forward and held up her hand, signaling the officer to wait.

"Can I get my jeans and stuff back?"

"Not yet, Miss. Need to keep them in evidence. If we catch the subject, you'll probably get everything back."

After the officer backed out of the driveway and headed off toward Miles City, LaDonna Mae saw a small smile on Lleyellyn's face.

"What's so funny? smart ass," she said, laughing.

"Just wondering what he thought about your shirt," he said. "And if he remembers what it says on your buckle."

o0o

Shay pulled into the lot at the Tastee Freeze.

"What can I get you?" he said.

"I always get the same thing. Single vanilla dipped in chocolate," LaDonna Mae said with a smile. "And plenty of napkins."

Lleyellyn got out and ordered the dipped cone for LaDonna Mae and a double vanilla and chocolate swirl for himself.

"Here you are, Madame," he said, handing the chocolate covered cone to LaDonna Mae, before climbing in behind the wheel.

They took bites from their cones in silence, before LaDonna Mae broke the ice.

"I'm not sure the cops are doing much," she said. "Today's the first day they've been out to talk to me since I was at the ER. Seems like they found some of my stuff by accident."

"How many times have they interviewed you?"

"Just the once far as I remember. After we called and reported the incident. Some female investigator talked to me at the hospital. Told me I was lucky to have escaped. Said they would look for a white Chevy 4X4. Thought my description of the guy would probably fit half the men in the county."

"I know how you feel," Lleyellyn said. "Didn't seem they looked too hard for my step father after he killed my mom. Law enforcement had nothing to do with Mal getting hit by that train. Not like they were trailing him or anything."

"I'd like to think they are at least trying to do something. Think I'll call them tomorrow, LaDonna Mae said. "Investigator gave me her card. It's at home. I want them to know I really want them to catch the bastard."

o0o

When they got back to the Ritchie place, LaDonna Mae insisted on walking on her own. They went inside. Lleyellyn sat at the kitchen table while LaDonna Mae filled two glasses with water and added ice.

"Back already?" LaDonna Mae's brother said, walking into the kitchen from the TV room. "How you doing Lleyellyn?" New truck?"

"Just got it. Feel free to take a look," he said. "In fact, here. Take the keys. Go for a spin."

Jimmy left. They heard him start the truck and head down the driveway. He turned left and was soon out of sight.

"Glad we have a little time," she said. "If I know my brother, he'll be gone a half hour, you'll see."

"No problem. Reason I gave him the keys. Wanted to be here with you. Alone."

"Lleyellyn, I've been thinking. About us. I really do like you," LaDonna Mae said. "Before we get too involved, there's some things about me you should know."

Lleyellyn passed his hands back and forth signaling that he didn't want to hear it.

"Stop right there," she said. "I want you to learn about me from me. Then you can decide."

"I've got skeletons in my past, too. I'd rather we let bygones be bygones."

"Just listen," she said, sitting down across the table from him and taking hold of his hands."

"You don't have to do this," he said.

"I grew up in Starlind, Texas. Did you know that?"

Lleyellyn looked at her, seeing her serious look, small wrinkles between her eyebrows, her blue eyes trained at his.

"My parents met at Ft. Sam Houston. Daddy was in the army. Medic. My Mom worked at an office off base. They got married and they moved up here when he got discharged. They had trouble right from the start. She moved back to Texas about the time she found out she was pregnant. The divorce was final right after I was born. They did try to get back together once. I was here in the ninth grade, but it didn't work out. My Mom and me, we moved back to Texas. She worked in Starlind. Got remarried right after we got back. Never did like my stepfather. I left home as soon as I could. Quit school."

Her eyes never left his.

"Got a job dancing at a go-go club. Little flat-chested ol' me. They called me Little Sister. Most of the time I was on stage in the early afternoon when it wasn't too busy. Made enough money to share an apartment with a girl worked at a bank in town. But there was no future dancing naked in front of a bunch of bozos from the oil fields and such."

He patted her hand, then said, "You don't have to go on. I'm okay with it. Really."

"Well, fact is I got pregnant. Of course I couldn't strip in that condition. Didn't have money for rent. Pretty much hit bottom," she said.

"A social worker found out about me. Since I was only seventeen she had to contact my parents. I wouldn't tell them where my mother was. Not even sure I knew. But my father found out. Came down to see me. Didn't really know him all that well, as you can imagine. My mother never said anything good about him ever. But anyway, he took care of me. Brought me up here and helped me get my head on straight," she said. "I started back at school back here, but didn't have enough credits for my diploma." After a pause, she added, "That's it. I wanted you to know."

Her eyes were tearing up. There was a single tear drop running down her cheek.

"You didn't say anything about the baby," he said.

She didn't let go of his hands, and gripped him tighter.

"Something happened. I had a miscarriage at three months. It was a girl."

He kept silent, aware that she was about to say more.

"It depressed me. Your friend Irene was the social worker I talked to about it. In the end, it was probably for the best. Up until that Montgomery guy came along, I was doing good."

"You are," he said. "You'll be your old self again, soon. Anything you need, I can help."

"I'd been doing pretty good since my daddy brought me up here," she said. "But you sure you want to pal around with a high school drop-out go-go nude dancing slut like me?"

"Told you it doesn't matter. I'm for letting bygones be bygones like I said. Besides, my past isn't so great either."

"Oh yeah, like what?"

"Had a bad step-father, too. Beat me up. Threatened my mom all the time. You know he murdered her. I couldn't stay in regular school. Went to the alternative school with a bunch of delinquents and druggies. Had to steal copper wire to get money to get away," he said. "There was an arrest warrant for me."

"What about now?" she said.

"My public defender got the charges dropped. I paid for what I stole. Starting over with a clean slate. Far as I'm concerned, you're doing the same thing."

She gave his hands a squeeze.

"You're sweet," she said. "Thanks for listening."

He leaned over and hugged her.

"I meant what I said. I really like you. Well, I admit it, more than that. I love you."

She pulled him toward her and they kissed.

"You know, no one around here knows my story," LaDonna Mae said. "Well, I guess Irene does. But she keeps secrets. Has to. And I trust her. I really have been able to make a fresh start. Don't want to screw it up."

"We've got that in common," Lleyellyn said.

"Sitting around like this, I've had a lot of time to just think. About us. And about what I want to do with the rest of my life," she said.

"And?"

"Can't see waitressing forever. Rather do something where I'm doing a real job," she said.

"Like what?"

"Haven't decided. Do know I need more education. Get my GED, for instance. Then maybe vo-tech or even college."

"Costs money, you know."

"My daddy said he'd help me if I'm really serious," she said. "Besides, I can enroll at Miles College. It's pretty cheap."

"You said you were thinking about us, too," he said. "What were you thinking?"

"You could go to school with me. There won't be much for you to do around the ranch this winter," she said. "I'm sure they won't start a new herd until after the spring thaw. We could take classes together during the spring quarter, see how we like it. Nothing to lose."

"You're serious aren't you?"

"I am," she said. "Besides, we'd see each other every day."

"I like that part," Lleyellyn said.

"You think about it. Talk it over with Irene. Bet she'll hire you back when school's out," LaDonna Mae said. "Know I can work part time at the Big Sky if I want."

They heard Jimmy return with Lleyellyn's truck.

"Nice rig," Jimmy said when he entered the house and handed Lleyellyn the keys. "And hey! Nice radio. I set the stations for you."

The three of them chatted for a few minutes, Jimmy monopolizing the conversation about Lleyellyn's new pickup and his own.

After a few minutes, Lleyellyn said his good-byes and headed back to the ranch. He was glad he had spent time with LaDonna Mae. Just the two of them. They had shared a lot of secrets. She was in his thoughts during the long drive home.

Two Shots Quick

CHAPTER 21

TUESDAY AUGUST 18

As usual, the wind was blowing from the northwest. Clouds were bunching across the western horizon. A cold front was moving in. There was a smell of rain in the air.

From the bunkhouse steps they could see the wranglers leading their saddled horses to the cattle pens. Crew members were setting up the cameras. This seemed to be the weather the director had been waiting for.

"Looks like this is the night they move the cattle out," Lleyellyn said. "I know they want to film the herd moving in the rain."

"Could be quite a storm. Might get more than they bargained for," Montoya said. "You sashay over there, see if you can find out for sure if they're moving out. And when. I'll get our stuff organized."

o0o

Lleyellyn walked into the big tent where the film crew ate their meals. Several tables were empty, but he recognized one of the men from the cast party standing at the soft drink dispenser.

"Hey! Lleyellyn, How's it going?" one of them said, by way of greeting.

"Looks like things are happening. This the night?"

"We're getting ready. Cameras supposed to be in place by eight. The cattle start moving out as soon as everything's set up.

Things go right, we'll have everything in the can by the time the sun comes up."

"Where you gonna be?"

"On a boom truck. Maybe a quarter mile out. South of here. Be helping with an elevated camera. Other guys'll be at different levels. Different perspectives. Together we'll have at least a dozen camera set ups. Can't do a rerun. Director says it's important that the grass look undisturbed. You know, no tire tracks, stuff like that messing up the scene."

o0o

Montoya was in his room laying out their gear for the night.

"Told me they're supposed to get the cameras in place by eight. Cattle drive starts at dark. Even earlier if it starts to rain. Got about a dozen or so different crews ready to go. There'll be more than one camera at each location," Lleyellyn said.

"Okay, then. We're about ready," Montoya said, gesturing to the things he had placed on his bed.

Lleyellyn recognized a black Savage automatic handgun like the ones they had used in Wisconsin.

Might be a different caliber, he thought.

There were two flashlights, a clear plastic bag with a half dozen zip ties in it, two pairs of cotton gloves, and a two pairs of cheap looking slip-on canvas shoes.

"You can wear size eleven shoes, right?" Montoya said?

"Sure," Lleyellyn said, not quite sure why he was being asked.

Montoya saw the question on his face.

"We'll slip these on when we get out there. Don't want to leave tracks that can be traced."

Lleyellyn watched as Montoya put everything into a canvas gym bag.

"Grab the rain slickers in the storeroom will you. The black ones," Montoya said, handing Lleyellyn the key.

When he returned with the slickers, Montoya said, "You know what to do. Any questions?"

"No. I'm good."

"All right, let's roll."

o0o

Lleyellyn got the Jeep out of the shed and parked it near the bunk house. As usual Mully jumped in, ready to go.

"Sorry Mully," Lleyellyn said. "Can't come along this time."

The dog reluctantly entered the bunkhouse when Lleyellyn held the door open.

"We'll be back," he said, closing the door and catching up to Montoya who was headed to the motion picture company's compound.

"Stay here 'til you see me in the white pickup with Montgomery. Then you can take off. We'll meet up on the west side, near the water tank."

Montoya moved off between the rows of travel trailers. Montgomery's camper was in the middle of the second row out of eyesight from Lleyellyn's vantage point.

o0o

Through the glass panel in the door Montoya could see Montgomery sitting on a sofa talking on the phone. He waited until he put the phone down, then knocked on the door.

"It's open," Montgomery said.

Montoya opened the door and stepped inside.

"Hate to bother you," Montoya said. "Know this is the big night and everything. But there's something you need to do. Animal safety issue. That's your area, I know."

"My job is to make sure no animals are injured... intentionally injured, in the making of this movie. If you've got something along that line I'd like to hear about it."

Montoya took a half step closer. Montgomery motioned for him to take a seat.

"We were out checking fence today. Making sure the herd can't stray off the property, and so on. Came across a half dozen men watching ten maybe twelve longhorns in a little fenced pen they've set up at the far end of the ranch."

"How's that going to interest me?"

"We kind of snuck up on them. See what they were up to. They didn't see us. Interesting thing is, they're pretty close to a cut bank near the wash that goes through there. Fifteen, maybe twenty foot drop off. When the rest of the herd gets close, they're supposed to drive those animals over the cliff. Might make for a good picture. Sure as hell will injure those animals. Probably kill at least some."

Montgomery didn't say a word at first, but then looked at Montoya.

"If this is true, then they'll be in deep shit. Can you show me where this is?"

o0o

Lleyellyn saw Montoya come out from between the row of campers with Montgomery on his heels. They walked to the parking area. Lleyellyn pulled the Jeep forward so he could see better. Montgomery opened the door to his white Chevy pickup. Montoya stepped up and got in on the passenger side. He waited to make sure which way they would go.

Montoya glanced at the glue spot in the middle of the dashboard. He couldn't help but think of LaDonna Mae's nightmare of an ordeal.

When Montgomery's pick-up reached the dirt track adjacent to the perimeter fence it turned left and started heading counter-clockwise along the boundary of the ranch.

Lleyellyn put the Jeep in gear, and started out along the boundary fence in the opposite direction. It would take over half an hour for Lleyellyn to reach to spot where he was supposed to meet up with Montoya. His instructions were to get there first, and park the Jeep out of sight of the windmill and water tank.

The late afternoon sun was hidden by a bank of clouds on the western horizon. Lleyellyn had driven around the ranch several times before when checking the fence. He kept up a steady pace and was confident he would reach his destination ahead of Montgomery.

o0o

As Montgomery followed the fence line west, Montoya kept an eye on the driver, making sure he wouldn't start to question the story he'd been told.

"Ranch's a full township in size," Montoya said. "Six miles by six miles. Damn near twenty-three thousand acres. There's bigger outfits, but this spread is in the middle of ideal cattle country."

"Yeah. I can see why they chose it for the film. Looks the way it did back in the day," Montgomery said. "Long way from civilization, though, wouldn't you say?"

o0o

They had reached the western boundary and followed the track to the south for two or three miles when the top of the windmill came into view over a small rise to their left.

"See the windmill over there?" Montoya said. "Let me get out and walk ahead. Make sure none of those boys are down by the water tank. I'll motion you forward if it's all clear."

Montgomery got out and stood by the open driver's door as Montoya walked toward the windmill.

When he approached the crest of the rise, he crouched down and inched forward. Except for a Great Blue Heron that was perched on the rim of the water tank, the area was deserted. He moved off to his right so he could see the western boundary fence. Just as planned, the Jeep was parked by the draw that passed under the fence. Lleyellyn was sitting on the hood, waiting.

o0o

"It's clear," Montoya said. As they approached the top of the slope, he added, "Take her slow and head toward the windmill. That's as close as we can get to where they've got that bunch penned up. Have to hoof it the rest of the way."

Montgomery took it easy, crossed over the crest of the rise, and slowly bumped his way down to the windmill and parked next to it.

"Lleyellyn's supposed to meet us here," Montoya said. "He's been riding fence along the south side. Got some supplies we might be able to use."

Montgomery had been silent for most of the trip. Finally he spoke up.

"I'd like to catch those bastards in the act. Like to see if their cameras are set up. Expect they'll want to wait 'til it gets dark so what they've got planned will fit in with the rest of the action. Night sequence. Maybe in the rain. I don't want them to know I'm around. Hate to scare 'em off. Like to catch 'em red handed."

Montoya said he was going to get Lleyellyn. He walked off toward the fence line track to the west where he knew Lleyellyn was waiting.

Lleyellyn climbed off the hood when he saw Montoya approaching.

"So far so good," Montoya said. "He seems to have fallen for our story hook, line and sinker. You set?"

By way of reply, Lleyellyn took the gym bag from the passenger seat and placed it on the hood. Montoya opened it and removed the automatic pistol and a box of cartridges.

Montoya carefully loaded the pistol, put the box of cartridges back in the satchel and smiled at Lleyellyn.

"It's now or never," he said, sticking the gun under his belt in the back of his pants. "You bring the rest of the stuff? Any questions?"

Lleyellyn indicated no with a slight shake of his head.

"Let's do it," Montoya said.

o0o

Montgomery had a camera and binoculars on the hood of his truck. He glanced up when he spotted Montoya and Lleyellyn walking toward him.

"How long you been watching this place," Montgomery said to Lleyellyn by way of greeting.

"Not long. Had to make some fence repairs on the way. Haven't seen anybody, though. I'm sure no one saw me."

"How do you want to do this?" Montoya said.

"I need to catch 'em in the act. Wait 'til it gets dark. Sneak up and keep an eye open. When they start moving the cattle I'd like to follow 'em. Get photographic evidence of them driving cattle over the cliff."

"Wouldn't stopping them before any livestock are harmed be better?" Lleyellyn said.

"If I get the evidence, this movie will be shut down. Serve 'em right. Final cut'll never see the inside of a theater, so to speak. Teach that cocky asshole, DeLong, a lesson he'll never forget."

Lleyellyn glanced at Montoya who pursed his lips, silently telling Lleyellyn to say no more.

Montgomery seemed oblivious to his companions. He reached in the truck and removed a Smith and Wesson 44 Magnum pistol in its holster and placed them on the hood.

They watched as he took the pistol out of the holster and flipped open the cylinder, then reached in the truck for a box of ammunition.

Before Montgomery could start loading the pistol, Montoya removed his automatic from his belt and pointed it at Montgomery.

"Hold it right there," Montoya said. "Put the ammo on the hood and step away from the truck."

Montgomery looked at the black automatic Montoya had aimed at his chest.

"What the hell? What's going on here?"

Neither Montoya nor Lleyellyn said anything. Montoya nodded his hat at Lleyellyn. Without saying anything they both slipped on the canvas shoes they had put in the gym bag. Lleyellyn removed the package of vinyl ties from the bag and took out two of them. He held one between his teeth and moved behind Montgomery.

"Hands behind your back," Montoya said.

Montgomery did as he was told, and Lleyellyn securely fastened his wrists together with the ties.

"Since you asked," Montoya said, "We'll tell you what this is about, won't we?" he added, looking at Lleyellyn.

Lleyellyn stepped around Montgomery and stood next to Montoya facing their captive.

"This is about LaDonna Mae Ritchie," Lleyellyn said. "Remember her?"

"Don't know the fuck you're talking about. Who's she?"

"She's the one you grabbed a few days ago. Held her in your goddamned truck. Had her remove her clothes. Tried to rape her," Lleyellyn said, then paused. "She's my girlfriend."

"Look kid, you've got the wrong guy...."

Montoya interrupted, before Montgomery could continue his denials.

"You're lying. Lleyellyn, see if the keys are in the truck."

Lleyellyn looked inside and saw the set of keys hanging from the ignition switch. He removed them out and held them up for Montoya to see.

"Here's what we know," Montoya said. "Inside the glove compartment you have LaDonna Mae's belt buckle. And her blue panties. Size 3. Vanity Fair brand."

Montgomery watched Montoya warily.

"Here, I'll show you," Lleyellyn said. He took a pair of cotton gloves from the bag and slipped them on, then moved to the passenger side of the Silverado, opened the door, and unlocked the glove box.

"Wait!" Montgomery said. "Found that stuff along the road. Didn't know who it belonged to."

They knew Montgomery was lying.

"One other thing in there," Montoya said. "Your plastic Jesus. LaDonna Mae remembered it on your dashboard that night. You put in in there with her other stuff."

Montgomery didn't say anything. Montoya looked at Lleyellyn, and gave an imperceptible nod.

Two Shots Quick

Lleyellyn reached in the glove box and carefully removed the blue panties and the *Big Cock Country* belt buckle and held them up so Montgomery could see them. He set them on the seat before rummaging around in the back of the glove box. He found the plastic Jesus and held it aloft.

"See this."

"Other thing she identified was that big revolver you've got there," Montoya said, pointing to the hood of the truck. "We expect we'll find other stuff in your room that'll be further proof."

Montgomery started struggling, trying to get his wrists free, but gave up after realizing it was hopeless. He turned around and leaned against the pick-up, aware that he was at their mercy.

"Now you got me here," Montgomery said. "Now what?"

"Stand straight," Montoya said. "Don't lean against the truck. No fancy ideas about getting those ties loose. We'll tell you what we've got in mind."

Montoya looked at Lleyellyn, you want to explain it to him? Or should I?"

Lleyellyn raised his eyebrows as he looked at Montoya, then signaled with an open palm for Montoya to do it.

"You've heard of an eye for and eye, right?" he said, then without waiting for Montgomery to reply continued. "If you'd caused her death, we'd kill you. Punishment to fit the crime. If you had actually raped her before she escaped, we'd cut your balls off. See how that punishment fits?"

Montgomery didn't reply, but stared wide eyed at Montoya, color rising on his cheeks.

"What you did was attempted rape. If she hadn't gotten away, you would have succeeded. Attempted rape is Criminal Sexual Conduct in the Second Degree in the law books. Plus you've got your Assault with a Deadly Weapon. You used a knife and a gun. And you did strip her naked. You forced her to run to get away. Probably kidnapping in there somewhere. Her feet were badly injured. She had other cuts and bruises. Required beau coup medical care," he said, before pausing. "What do you think fits your crime?"

Montgomery remained silent, his eyes focused on Montoya. They could tell he was thinking about how to break loose and get away.

"You ain't going nowhere," Montoya said. "Not yet anyway. Lleyellyn, get his gun. Better load it."

The pistol was as heavy as it looked. Lleyellyn managed to flip the cylinder open. He had no trouble inserting the cartridges. He snapped the cylinder into place and pointed it at Montgomery.

"How's this feel pointed at your head?"

"Need to shoot," Montoya said. "Just pull back on the hammer. When it clicks it's ready. Just pull the trigger and it'll go pop."

Lleyellyn set the hammer and continued pointing the revolver at Montgomery.

"I'll let LaDonna Mae's friend here tell you what we're going to do," Montoya said. "You ready?" he said staring at Montgomery. "Go ahead, Lleyellyn."

Lleyellyn glanced at Montoya to make sure the Savage automatic was pointed at their prisoner. Satisfied, he put the pistol on the hood and removed a pocket knife from the gym bag and stepped behind Montgomery. He cut the vinyl ties, freeing Montgomery's wrists.

Montgomery rubbed his wrists as Lleyellyn picked up the pistol and moved around in front of him.

"Take off your shirt," he said.

When Montgomery was slow to act, he said, "Make it snappy or I'll have to poke you in the chin. Like you did to LaDonna Mae."

Montgomery unbuttoned his shirt and took it off.

"That's better. Now fold it. Neatly."

When the shirt was folded, Lleyellyn said, "Now carefully place in on the seat of your truck. Keep it neat. No tricks."

Montgomery did as he was told.

"Remove your belt."

When the belt was off, Lleyellyn said, "Roll it up nice and neat. Put it next to your shirt."

"Okay, now the boots," Lleyellyn said. "Take 'em off real slow. Put them on the seat next to the belt."

Montgomery had trouble pulling off his right boot while standing.

"Sit on the running board."

Montgomery removed his boots and put them on the seat as instructed.

"Take those jeans off," Lleyellyn said.

Montgomery hesitated. When Montoya raised his automatic a few inches, he unbuttoned his pants and lowered the zipper. He lowered his trousers and stepped out of them one leg at a time, leaving only his black and white low rise undershorts.

"Fold those pants up nice and tidy. Put them on top of the shirt."

Montgomery did as instructed.

Lleyellyn pointed at the underpants with the barrel of the 357 Magnum.

"Take them off," he said. "Slowly."

Montgomery pulled down his undergarment and stepped out of them. Without further instruction he folded them and placed them on top of his jeans in the truck.

"Good job," Lleyellyn said. "Now put your belt on top of the clothes."

Montgomery stood before them trying to hide his privates behind his hands. He was naked except for his socks.

"Better take those socks off, too," Montoya said. "Put them in the boots."

Montgomery had to sit down again to remove his stockings. He did as instructed, rolled them up and stuffed them in one of the boots.

"Okay. Step back from the truck," Montoya said. "Feel anything like LaDonna Mae felt when you did this to her?"

Montgomery glared back at Montoya, opened his mouth to say something, swallowed, then looked at Lleyellyn, then back at Montoya, and said, "Assholes."

"Hear that?" Montoya said. "Now he's calling us names."

Montoya stepped up to Montgomery, and stared up at the much taller man.

"Time for pleasantries is over. We're going to give you a fighting chance. We'll give you a head start. Take off. Try and get away. You might make it back to headquarters. Head due east. You at least have a chance of making it," Montoya said.

"LaDonna Mae made it," Lleyellyn said.

Montgomery looked off toward the east before saying anything.

"Six miles. No shoes. Dark soon. Rain storm. I'm as good as dead. Shoot me now."

Montoya raised the automatic so the barrel was pointing between Montgomery's eyes.

"It's your choice. We'll give you a five-minute head start, starting in three, two, one seconds."

Montgomery hesitated a few seconds, started to open his mouth, reconsidered, then started walking.

Two Shots Quick

He moved slowly, carefully stepping forward, avoiding rocks and stickers. They watched him move off, carefully tiptoeing along for a hundred yards or more.

"How long's he been?" Lleyellyn said.

"I'm not sure. Looks like he's doing the John Colter thing."

They saw Montgomery look back over his shoulder then break into a trot.

"Fire a shot in the air with that thing," Montoya said. "Give the son of a bitch a little more incentive."

Lleyellyn aimed the big pistol in the air and pulled the trigger. There was a loud blast. The recoil nearly made him drop the gun.

"Damn!" he said, as he grabbed the gun with his left hand as he shook his right.

"You okay?" Montoya asked. "Next time use both hands."

The blast from the gun seemed to be doing its job. Montgomery was racing off in the distance oblivious to the terrain.

Satisfied that Montgomery thought he had a chance to get away, they took their time cleaning up the scene.

o0o

Montgomery didn't know if they would come after him or not. The rocky ground made the going tough. Purposely he started moving slowly, hoping they wouldn't come after him right away. He wanted to put as much distance between himself and the crazy greaser and his pal.

He veered a little to one side so he could glance back over his shoulder to see what they were doing. Dusk was starting to set in. He got a glimpse of movement near his pick-up. He could see they hadn't started after him yet.

Suddenly he heard a shot ring out. He recognized the loud report of the .357 magnum. Were they shooting at him? He wasn't sure, but he wasn't taking any chances.

He burst into a run, trying to put as much distance between himself and his pursuers as he could.

His bare feet were cut up and throbbing from stepping on rocks, burrs and stickers, but they were gradually growing numb. He wanted to keep going as long as he could without slowing down.

o0o

"Keep those gloves on. Make sure everything's back in the glove box the way you found it," Montoya said. "Then lock it."

When he was done, Lleyellyn said, "What about the keys?"

"Let's see those?" Montoya said. "I'll take off the two Chevy keys, you keep these other two. Probably for his trailer."

Montoya locked the glove compartment, then the door. He rubbed the truck keys with his handkerchief to remove fingerprints, then got down on is hands and knees and placed them behind the left front tire."

"We ever need these keys, we'll know where they are," Montoya said. "Putting the keys there isn't much different than putting a house key under the door mat. If someone comes looking, they'll probably check there."

"Yes, but who?" Lleyellyn said. "What if Montgomery comes back?"

"He won't," Montoya said. "He'll think we'll still be here waiting for him. He's long gone."

"You think the sheriff's office will send someone out here looking?" Lleyellyn said.

"They will when we get back to the house and call it in. Like we planned, you'll call 911. Tell 'em you came across an abandoned truck and what you saw inside. They'll send somebody."

"Mention the buckle or the panties?" Lleyellyn said.

"We'll let a deputy find them. Should be able to put two and two together, don't you think?"

Lleyellyn nodded.

"What do you think Montgomery will say when they talk to him?"

"He won't mention us. We know where the proof is. He'll probably say he got accidently locked out. Was taking a dip in the tank. Didn't want to bust out a window, so decided to walk back."

Lleyellyn thought about this for a moment.

"Yeah, but he would know where the keys are if he put them there," Lleyellyn said. "Wouldn't he just get the keys and drive back if he accidently locked himself out?"

"Hmm," Montoya said. "You're right. Better put the keys somewhere else. Good thinking. Montgomery will say he lost the keys. Don't want them somewhere obvious."

"I know the place," Lleyellyn said, remembering sitting in the water tank with LaDonna Mae.

Montoya handed him the truck keys. Lleyellyn walked over to the water tank and dropped them in near the edge on the right hand side. He looked in the tank to see if they were visible. They weren't.

"Someone from the sheriff's office comes out here won't find the keys," Montoya said. "Deputy will know how to pop the latch. They'll search the vehicle, inventory the contents. When they find the stuff in the glove box they'll have what they need."

When Lleyellyn went to retrieve the Jeep, Montoya walked up on top of a little rise to see how far Montgomery had gotten. He could see for at least a mile. Montgomery was out of sight.

"Any Jeep tracks will back up your story. You simply drove over to see what was going on with the truck. Found it just like this with no one around. The rain might cover any tracks we made' So much the better," Montoya said. "Let's head back. We can go over the details one more time."

o0o

The light was fading fast. A new moon had arisen in the east. They glimpsed it from time to time when it peeked out between the clouds.

Lleyellyn looked over at Montoya who was deep in thought.

"Back there you mentioned he'd be doing the Colter thing. What's that?"

Montoya glanced at his companion, and continued looking at him as he answered.

"John Colter was one of our greatest explorers. A mountain man. One of the crew that was in the Lewis and Clark expedition. You've heard of that, right?"

"Sure," Lleyellyn said. "I remember their dog. Seaman, I think. And Sacajawea. Don't remember Colter."

Montoya gave him a brief synopsis of what he had learned from books he had studied in prison.

Colter had left the Lewis and Clark expedition before they got back to St. Louis so he could return west and explore on his own. Blackfoot Indians captured him. Stripped him naked. They let him make a run for it so they could give chase for the sport of it. He had started out hobbling away, pretending to be lame. The Indians let him get a pretty good lead before giving chase. He took off barefoot and out ran his pursuers for days. Made it back to civilization. Took more than a week. Only thing he had when he got back was a blanket and a broken spear he had taken from one of his pursuers.

"He recover?" Lleyellyn asked.

"Pretty much. Fought in the war of 1812. Daniel Boone's son was his commanding officer. Think he died of natural causes a few years later. In Missouri."

"Think Montgomery will make it?"

"Don't see why not. No one's actually chasing him. He'll figure it out eventually. Maybe take him all night, but basically the terrain isn't too bad," Montoya said.

"You sure he won't tell what happened?"

"If he says anything, he'll be setting himself up for several felony charges," Montoya said.

They rode along over the rutted track, each lost in their own thoughts. Half way to the buildings, Montoya spoke up.

"We get back, you put the Jeep away. Then I'll visit Montgomery's trailer. See if there's anything else connecting him to LaDonna Mae," Montoya said. "You okay with that?"

o0o

It was hard for Montgomery to see where he was going in the dark. He caught an occasional glimpse of the North Star when there was a break in the clouds. He headed east, hoping to see lights from the building site or even some sign of the wranglers and members of the camera crews. He knew anyone following him couldn't see any better. He was gaining confidence that he would make it back to the movie compound and the safety of his trailer.

o0o

Lleyellyn was able to make better time than Montgomery had in the the Silverado. They continued along the twin rutted drive, each lost in their own thoughts. The headlights picked up a pair of red reflections. Lleyellyn slowed as a skunk shambled off into the grass.

Finally, Montoya spoke again.

"When we get back to the place I want you to call the sheriff's office first thing. Use 911 if you want. Tell about coming across the pick-up and what you saw inside. Looked weird to you. Decided to call. Don't have to say anymore."

"They might have questions."

"Say you were out checking the fences. Didn't want any issues with tonight's cattle drive. Hell, tell 'em you recognized the truck. Belongs to a guy named Montgomery with the movie. He's the one makes sure no animals get injured during the filming. You know this because you helped me change his flat tire a few days ago. You know. Stuff like that."

"What do I say when they ask me why I waited so long to call it in?"

"Tell 'em it took a while to get back. Had chores to do. Slipped your mind."

o0o

They reached the east end of the property line and turned right, heading south on the final stretch toward the buildings.

"One more thing I need you to do when we get back," Montoya said. "Take my new pistol. Cover it with axel grease you'll find in the shop, then wrap it in plastic or something and then hide it. Bury it."

Lleyellyn looked at him, not sure why he wanted this done.

"Gun wasn't used," Lleyellyn said. "So why?"

"Well, I can't be found with a firearm of any kind. Felon in possession, you know. If you put it in your locker you wouldn't be able to explain where you got it. Just better to hide it."

"Put it somewhere where you can find it if you ever need it. But where it can't be found. I don't want to know. Okay?"

"Sure, Lleyellyn said. "I can see your point. I should hide the shells, too. Right."

"You got it."

oOo

The wranglers were saddled up and waiting for the signal. Earlier that afternoon they had been briefed about the drive. The general direction they were to go. Signals to follow. What to do when it started to rain. It had all seemed straight forward. Routine. Camera crews were set up along the route.

"Look for the blue lights," the unit director had told them. "Keep on the right or westerly side. Each light represents a camera location. Take her nice and slow. We want this to look like a legitimate drive. Keep the herd moving at an easy pace. Remember, that god damned humane association officer will black ball us if we injure any livestock. I don't know where Montgomery is, but he'll be around somewhere. Ignore him. Do your jobs. Any questions?"

oOo

Lleyellyn dropped Montoya off at the bunkhouse. Before Montoya got out of the Jeep, he removed the clip, ejected the cartridge, and handed them to Lleyellyn. He picked up the gym bag, removed the rest of the bullets, and gave them to him.

"I'll get rid of this stuff," Montoya said, checking to make sure he had both pairs of canvas shoes, the cotton gloves, and the vinyl ties. "You make your call first. Then take care of the gun. I'm going to take a look at Montgomery's camper. It's dark enough, everyone's busy with the cattle drive. You don't have to keep a look out. I'll be in and out in no time."

He parked the Jeep in the shed, and carried the gun and ammunition to the bunkhouse.

I'm not sure finding the pick-up abandoned is a real emergency, he thought.

He found the general office number of the sheriff's office in the front of the phonebook, and placed the call from the wall phone outside Montoya's room.

A male voice answered on the third ring.

Lleyellyn identified himself, told what he had found that afternoon, and explained where the pick-up was parked.

"Seemed kinda funny," he said. "Thought I'd better report it."

The person on the other end thanked him, took his name and phone number, and concluded the call.

o0o

No one was around when Montoya approached Montgomery's camper. He slipped on the cotton gloves. One of the keys he had taken from Montgomery's key ring slipped into the lock easily and he opened the door. He stepped inside and silently closed the door behind him. The whole area seemed deserted. He figured all hands were busy with tonight's cattle drive. To be doubly cautious he didn't turn on the light, but used his flashlight instead.

He found what he was looking for in the bottom drawer of the dresser. An LL Bean box containing a HeadLamp. A handy device, the box said, for working in the dark. Fully adjustable. The illustration showed a pretty blonde with a strap around her head securely holding a light on her forehead, the beam illuminating a tackle box. He knew it was the light LaDonna Mae had described.

In the desk drawer he found a leather sheath holding a knife. At first he thought it might be a letter opener, but upon close inspection he discovered that it was honed to a sharp point and extremely sharp.

A stiletto, he thought. *Fits the one LaDonna Mae described.*

He put the light and the stiletto back where he had found them and continued his search. In a compartment under the built in bed he discovered a half dozen pairs of women's panties.

LaDonna Mae wasn't his only victim.

He put the box back in the compartment, peeked out the door to make sure the coast was clear, then stepped outside. He locked the door, put the key on a ledge over the door, and left, confident he hadn't been seen.

o0o

There was a tin of axle grease under the work bench in the work shop. Lleyellyn unrolled two feet of vinyl sheeting he found sticking out of a box in the corner and put it on the work bench. He used part of a wood shingle to spread a half inch coating of the grease in the center of the vinyl. He placed the gun in the center of the grease, folded the vinyl sheet once and applied more grease. He spread out the clip and the cartridges and bundled up the vinyl so everything inside was grease coated and sealed. He tied the bundle with string and put it in a paper bag along with the grease covered shingle.

Montoya wanted the gun hidden, and he didn't want to know the location of the hiding place. He wanted Lleyellyn to be able to find the pistol if he had to.

Lleyellyn didn't think the hiding place should be too close to the house. The gun should be hidden somewhere not too obvious, but somewhere easy to locate. He thought about it for a few minutes before deciding where to put it.

He took the bag to the shed, put it in the back of the Jeep, and drove out toward the road. It was dark and he drove slowly. He turned left and followed the dirt track that ran parallel just inside the boundary fence next to the county road. At the corner where the track turned west he counted off ten fence posts and stopped. Three feet inside the tenth fence post he used the short handled trenching tool from the back of the vehicle to dig a hole. He buried the bundle and filled in the hole, then carefully drove back and forth over the filled-in hole several times to tamp it down good and solid. He raked the disturbed ground with his hands and admired his handiwork. There was nothing that would give the hiding place away if you didn't know exactly where to look.

Three feet in from the tenth post, he thought. *Should be easy to remember.*

When he put the Jeep in the barn he took a pencil from a can on top of the workbench and wrote '10 – 3' next to the window frame above the workbench.

Just in case I forget.

o0o

The unit director called the head honcho of the cattle drive crew over and told him to be ready to move the cattle out in ten minutes.

"When you hear me shout 'Move 'em out!' get going. Remember, easy does it, just like we said at the meeting."

o0o

SHERIFF'S DEPARTMENT

Memo to Duty Officer
Re: Abandoned vehicle
Date: Aug. 18
Time: 2141 hrs

A non- emergency call was received from Lleyellyn Shay an employee of the Boyd Ranch. (Current site of filming of a motion picture.)

Shay said he was checking out the perimeter fence surrounding the ranch and came upon a white Chevrolet C/K 4X4 (Silverado edition) pick-up parked near the west boundary of the ranch close to a windmill and stock tank. The vehicle was locked. Visible inside were a pile of neatly folded clothes, boots and a revolver. No one was around.

Shay did not have the license number but reports it had California plates. Shay said the owner is associated with the motion picture and that his surname in Montgomery. (He met Montgomery when he helped change a flat on the same vehicle a few days ago.)

Shay can be reached at the ranch, number (406) 555-7134.

<u>Assignment:</u> Have deputy on patrol check out the vehicle at earliest convenience.

GPK
Communications/SO

o0o

The shift commander met with the five deputies who would be on routine patrol at the beginning of their eleven o'clock night shift.

"I'll pass out a few non-emergency items for you to follow up. There's several subpoenas need to be served, couple civil suits needing personal service. Hoping for an easy shift. I've assigned the same sectors as last night. Keep your eyes open. Be careful out there."

Deputy Robert Thompson stood up and was handed two documents that would be his responsibility. He took a quick glance at them. A pair of subpoenas in a civil suit. Both subjects at the same address. He looked at the case caption, recognizing the names of the parties from an auto accident that had made the paper several months back.

As Anderson was preparing to leave, the night receptionist entered the room and handed a paper to the duty officer. The duty officer held up his hand.

"Hang on a second," he said.

After reading over the document, he looked at Thompson.

"This'll be for you, Bob."

Thompson took the memo and read it through. As so often happens in ranch country, he was familiar with both the ranch and the reporter. He remembered meeting Lleyellyn Shay the day he had to go to the Boyd Ranch to tell the young man his mother had been murdered. And he had seen him again recently when he had stopped to talk to the Ritchie girl. He was not familiar with Montgomery.

o0o

Some nights were slow. Thompson got lucky. He served the two witness subpoenas at the start of his shift. The witnesses lived a mile or two out of town. Luckily they were up watching

Letterman when he pulled into the driveway. Besides routine patrol, the only other thing he had to do was take a look at the abandoned pick-up out at the Boyd ranch. For that he would wait until sun up. Easier to look around the scene when there was daylight.

CHAPTER 22

WEDNESDAY AUGUST 19

He filled in his time until his meal break by checking out the implement dealer. He was making sure the gates were locked and no strange vehicles were around. A little later he came across a car parked on the shoulder with its flashers blinking about ten miles southwest of town. The back passenger door was open and a young woman was bent over changing a baby's diaper.

He pulled in behind the car and approached the car from the rear. The woman was just finishing up. She said everything was fine and he sent her on her way. He watched her get behind the wheel and head toward town.

He was going toward Miles City to get something to eat, when a call came in over the police band on his radio.

"Thompson, you copy?"

"Ten four," Thompson said into his transceiver. "Loud and clear."

"What's your twenty?"

"Nine miles southwest of MC. On patrol."

"Need you to get out to the Boyd Ranch pronto. Movie company headquarters. They'll direct you to the scene. Accident, apparently, Fatality. Do the usual. Protect the scene. Take statements. Coroner being notified."

Thompson made a quick U-turn, activated his flashing lights, and headed for the ranch. There were no cars on the highway. He rocketed along at over a hundred, slowed for the turn to the ranch and continued at the same speed until the yard lights at the Boyd ranch came into view.

Many of the lights at the motion picture headquarters seemed to be on. He recognized the ranch foreman, Montoya, standing with a group that included his number two man, Shay, and others that he guessed were movie people.

He stopped next to the group, turned off his flashing lights, and got out.

"Can one of you fill me in?" he said.

Several of the people dressed like cowboys, movie extras, or maybe wranglers, he surmised, looked from one to another.

Finally, a tall man in his mid-thirties stepped forward.

"We were filming the cattle drive tonight. Raining just like we've been waiting for. Things…" he said, before Thompson held up his hands to stop him for a moment.

"I need to take some notes," Thompson said. "Your name."

"I'm Rene Auriere," he said, extending his hand. They shook hands and Auriere continued, "Unit director of film crew six."

"Anywhere where we can get some privacy?" Thompson said. "Easier to take notes at a table or desk."

Auriere turned and walked over to one of the motor homes parked adjacent to the headquarters tent. A sign on the door said *Cinematography (Restricted)*. Auriere punched in a code to unlock the door and stepped inside, motioning for the deputy to follow.

The motor home was filled with modern electronic equipment, television monitors, and electronic things Thompson didn't recognize. There were several desks and a conference table.

They sat down. Thompson placed his notebook on the table, clicked his ball point, and looked at Auriere.

"Okay, as I said before, we were filming the herd moving across the prairie getting nighttime shots for the picture, hoping for rain to make the action more realistic. It started to rain.

Things were going just as planned. Perfect in fact. A dozen or so different units were set up. We were getting exactly what we needed. I was in charge of a back-up crew. Ready to help out if there was a breakdown anywhere."

Auriere stood up, then removed two bottles of water from the refrigerator, and handed one to Thompson. They both took a drink before Auriere continued.

"While this was going on, one of the crew looked up and saw someone up ahead of us walking our way. Middle of nowhere. Hard to make out who it was. We knew he wasn't supposed to be there. We couldn't figure out why he was there. He signaled us with a wave, probably saw the blue lights on top of our rig. Then he started really waving with both hands overhead, trying to get our attention. My boss saw this and told me to use the backup gear to film the guy. We did. I've got the film. Made a digital CD. I'll dub you a copy. Show it to you in a sec. You'll be able to see everything that happened. Right after we started filming, there was a lightning flash and a big clap of thunder. Damned herd started to stampede, and that poor sucker was trampled to death. I'll take you out to the body. Or what's left of it. But first you have to watch the CD. Okay?"

Thompson was still writing his notes, having had trouble keeping up with Auriere's narration.

"Just a moment," he said, reading over his notes. "What time was this?"

"Close to one. Maybe closer to one thirty. Precise time, not really sure."

"Know who the victim is?"

"Couldn't tell when we were filming. Used ambient light. Could get some clarity when there were lightning flashes or the moon peeked out, but could just tell it was a he. Adult male. White," Auriere said. "And he was naked as a jaybird."

Thompson looked at Auriere, remembering the memo he had been given at the beginning of his shift.

"Name Montgomery mean anything to you?"

"Humane association rep," Auriere said. "Supposed to make sure no animals are injured during filming. Kind of a hard ass."

"Think it was him you saw?" the deputy asked.

"Suppose it could be. Not sure. Pretty hard to tell. Didn't think of him when I saw the guy coming our way."

Auriere reached for the play button. Thompson nodded. Without any preliminaries the monitor flashed on and they could see the forms of cattle slowly moving along a draw in the rain. The camera moved up and in the distance a person could be seen walking toward the camera at a distance of two or three hundred yards beyond the moving heard and at a slightly higher elevation.

The camera moved in for a close up of the approaching figure, but the image grew grainy, hampered by the falling rain and the darkness.

As they watched, an obvious flash of lightning illuminated the landscape, followed by a loud reverberating clap of thunder. The screen returned to near darkness. But it was clear the cattle were moving faster, scared into a stampede by the flash of bright light and the thunderous roar. At first it was hard to tell what was happening, but it became apparent that the herd turned to the right and were moving up the slope directly at the approaching man.

The cameraman concentrated on the approaching figure. He kept moving forward, oblivious to the herd heading his way.

Then the figure stopped, raised his hands and turned to make a run for it. The cattle closed in and the human figure disappeared, finally displaced by several mounted cowboys desperately trying to turn the herd back into itself. Their efforts were successful. The stampede came to a halt and the cattle milled around, bumping into each other, and coming to a halt. The wranglers were able to get them calmed down, before finally herding them back to the holding area.

Thompson sat there for a moment after the video ended.

"Body been found?" he finally said.

"Yes, like I said. At least I guess you could call it that. What's left of it. All those cattle milling around there at the end. That's right where he was."

Thompson looked at Auriere and shook his head.

"Glad you had the camera rolling. Not much doubt about what happened," he said. "Wonder what the hell he was up to."

Auriere didn't have an answer. He had been wondering the same thing.

"Want me to take you out where the remains are," he said.

"Let's wait for the coroner. We'd better show this video to him first. Help him with the cause of death. Thompson said, then added, "I hate to report in over the radio. Too many ears. Cell phone's out of range. You have a land line here?"

Auriere nodded. "You're welcome to use it. Want me to step outside?"

"No. Stay put. You know more than I do, anyway."

o0o

Thompson called the Sheriff's office on the land line and talked to the duty officer. He'd already notified the coroner.

"ETA's about twenty minutes. He lives out that way. Told him to stay off the horn," the duty officer said. "Anything else you need now?"

"I'm good," Thompson said. "Can't do anything more until the coroner gets here."

He thanked Auriere for the use of the phone.

Two Shots Quick

"Coroner should be here in fifteen, twenty minutes. You can take us out and show us the remains then, Okay?"

"Sure," Auriere said. "Say, I know you'll have to retrieve the body. I worked graves registration in the service. Suggest you take some shovels, maybe a rake. And a couple buckets. There's not much left."

Thompson gave him a look, but made no comment. Auriere started moving away before Thompson said, 'I've got buckets and stuff in my squad. Ready for most anything."

"Okay then, officer, I'll be right outside. Holler when you're ready," Auriere said. "Stay in here as long as you like. Feel free to use the phone."

o0o

The coroner located Thompson's squad car without difficulty, and walked towards it. Auriere motioned him over and introduced himself, then led him to his office trailer where deputy Thompson was waiting.

"I want you to watch some film. The victim's death was caught in Technicolor. You won't believe it," Thompson said.

Auriere dimmed the lights and started the video without delay.

They watched intently as the scene unfolded, alert from start to finish. When it was over the coroner was the first to speak.

"Cause of death. Misadventure with livestock. No doubt about that," he said. "Let's go take a look at the remains."

The coroner took a leather satchel out of the trunk of his car and climbed in the backseat of Thompson's squad. Auriere rode shotgun and gave directions.

They drove cross country over the prairie grass toward several lights in the distance.

"Had the crew set up those lights," Auriere said. "So we could go the right way. Lights up the scene, too. It's about two miles, give or take."

Thompson's vehicle was a four-wheel SUV. It made good time across the grass, slowing down several times for low spots and boulders.

As they got closer they could see that the lights were mounted on boom towers jutting from the back of two camera trucks. All the crew members were huddled around the front of one of the trucks, waiting for their arrival.

They looked at the illuminated circle of grass for signs of the corpse, but they didn't see anything that stood out in the harsh artificial light.

"Body's near the center of the lighted area," Auriere said. "In a little depression. Flat as a god damned pancake. You'll see."

They stopped near the waiting camera crew and got out.

"Evening gents," Thompson said. "And ladies," he added, noticing that at least two of the dozen or so crew members were female. "I'm Deputy Thompson. This gentleman is the County Coroner. Appreciate all your assistance. We'll go take a look. You all stay here. We might have some questions."

The coroner picked up his satchel. Thompson looked at Auriere,

"After you, if you don't mind."

Auriere started off with Thompson and the coroner following. Their shadows preceded them as they walked to the bright center of the lighted area.

In a slight dip in the terrain, the flattened remains of the body were spread out over a nine or ten square foot area in roughly the shape of an investigator's chalk outline of a shooting victim. At first glance, it appeared that every inch of the body had been trampled.

The bright lights from the camera trucks cast dark shadows between the parts of flesh imbedded in the grass. The coroner used his flashlight to get a better look.

"Get some evidence bags out of my case, will you?" he said, glancing at Thompson. Then he donned rubber gloves before picking up a long pair of forceps.

"He held up a body part and moved it toward the deputy. Thompson opened the bag and the coroner dropped it inside.

"A finger," he said. "Or at least part of one. Might help with fingerprint identification."

The coroner placed a part of a mandible in another bag and explained it could help with identification through dental records.

He continued examining the remains, picking up pieces and looking at them, before putting them down and moving on. He continued his examination for twenty minutes, if not longer, before standing up and removing his gloves.

He moved over toward Thompson, motioned him forward several feet out of Auriere's earshot, before leaning toward the deputy.

"Damnedest thing I've ever seen," he said. "Like looking at ground hamburger. Maybe that finger will help. Good thing we have the film."

"What should we do about the remains?"

Well, I don't think we should call the funeral home. This is out of their ... whatever," the coroner said. "Any suggestions?"

"They told me there wasn't much left. Said to bring scoop shovels and a rake. I've got them, and a couple pails. I'll do the deed, if you want to help."

The coroner looked at him and gave a grim nod.

They scooped up the remains as best they could and put them in plastic trash bags and placed the bags in the five gallon pails to make handling easier.

After the buckets were placed in the back of Thompson's SUV they looked at what was left – red stained grass still resembling the shape of a spread-eagled human figure.

Without a word Thompson started digging with one of the shovels, turning the earth over and hiding the gore. The coroner used the back of the rake to break up the dirt clods, then turned the rake over and used the tines to smooth over the disturbed earth.

When they were done they silently put the tools back in the vehicle.

"We're done here," Thompson said. "Thanks for your help."

o0o

Lleyellyn and Montoya were in the bunk house when Thompson's vehicle pulled up in front pf the porch. They heard the crunch of gravel and saw the coroner getting out of the passenger side as they came outside.

"I better take the remains into town," the coroner said to Thompson. "I'll get my car."

"Mr. Shay, you reported an abandoned pick-up. I'll be ready to go take a look at it in just a sec. You ready?"

"Yes, sir."

They watched as the deputy removed three five gallon buckets from the back of the SUV. He was finishing unloading the third one as the corner drove up. They watched as the two men wordlessly put the buckets in the trunk of the coroner's car.

When they were done, Thompson slammed the trunk lid shut, and the deputy and the coroner stood there for a moment, silently looking at each other.

"Hell of a deal," Thompson finally said. "Thanks for your help. And for getting here so fast."

The two shook hands. The coroner opened the door, looked at Thompson again.

"We've got to stop meeting like this," he said, then started the car and slowly made a turn and headed for town.

"Before we go," Thompson said, addressing Lleyellyn. "Mind if I use your facility? Have to clean up a little.

o0o

Montoya and Lleyellyn waited on the porch while Thompson went inside to use the rest room.

"Those buckets," Lleyellyn said. "Think that's what's left of Montgomery?"

Montoya put his hand on Lleyellyn's shoulder and made eye contact.

"Remember this. Whatever happened to that bastard was an act of God. Got that? Not our doing."

Lleyellyn looked down and mumbled something Montoya couldn't hear.

He was about to question Lleyellyn, find out what he had said, but they heard Thompson open the door and step outside.

"I'm all set, Mr. Shay. Hop in."

Shay told the deputy to follow the track that paralleled the line fence, and they set off.

"Takes me about forty-five minutes, or so to get there in our old Jeep," he said. "Must be something like seven miles altogether."

"Perfect. Sun should be up by then," the deputy said.

Thompson checked in with his dispatcher on the police band before glancing over at his passenger.

"How you getting along?" he asked. "It's been only a few months since you lost your mother, isn't that right?"

"I'm doing okay. Irene and Mr. Montoya keep me pretty busy."

"Must have been a relief when they caught up with her murderer."

Lleyellyn remained silent, thinking Thompson's statement didn't need a reply.

"Say anything about how they got him?"

"Told me he was hit by a train. Killed," Lleyellyn said. "No idea how it happened. My grandma said she thought it might've been suicide."

Thompson was lost in his own thoughts for a few moments. "At least he's dead," he said. "Must be a relief to everybody."

o0o

The shocks on the SUV were better than those on the Jeep. They were making better time than LaDonna Mae had the day they'd driven out to skinny dip in the water tank.

"I've got a question," Lleyellyn said. "Those buckets back there. That what's left of the guy got trampled?"

"Unfortunately. We could hardly tell it had been a human body. Never saw anything like it," Thompson said. "Sure as hell hope I never do again."

"Then you couldn't tell who it was."

"We don't know. Not yet. Coroner will do some testing. Have it figured out before too long, I'm sure."

o0o

The sun wasn't fully up, but full daylight was fast approaching. As they drove along the western boundary of the ranch, Lleyellyn pointed out the windmill sticking its head over a rise off to their left.

"Truck's parked over by the windmill," Lleyellyn said. "You can follow a track to the water tank just up a little ways."

Thompson followed Shaw's instructions, followed the track, and pulled up and stopped some fifty feet behind the pickup.

"You recognized this truck, right?"

"Yes, sir," Lleyellyn said. "Mr. Montoya and I changed a flat on it a few days ago. Belongs to a guy named Montgomery."

"With the movie outfit?"

"Yes. He's got a trailer back at their compound."

"You wait here a minute," Thompson said. "Need to document the scene. Make a few notes."

Lleyellyn watched as the deputy got out. He took a series of photos with a digital camera, then wrote down the license plate number and made other jottings. Then he moved closer to the truck and looked through the window from the passenger side.

He took pictures of the interior through the window, then moved around to the driver's side and repeated his actions.

He motioned for Lleyellyn to join him.

"You try the doors when you found the vehicle?"

"Yes, sir. I did," Lleyellyn said. "Both doors were locked."

Thompson made a note.

"I suppose I shouldn't have," Lleyellyn said. "What if there were fingerprints?"

"No problem. Anybody would have done the same."

Deputy Thompson bent down by the left front tire and felt behind it, trying to locate a key.

"Lot of people hide their keys behind the front tire," he said. "Not this time, though."

He stood up and looked at Lleyellyn.

"Looks like he folded his clothes and piled them there on the seat. Put his gun there, too. He probably hid the keys somewhere. You look around. See if you have any luck finding them. I'll get a Slim Jim from the squad."

Lleyellyn knew where the keys were; he'd put them there. He made a show of getting down on his hands and knees and looked behind the other three tires, around the trailer hitch, in back of the license plates, and behind the gas cap cover. When he stood up he had mud on his pants and on both hands.

He waited until Thompson started walking back from his vehicle, then moved toward the water tank.

"Gotta wash off this mud," he shouted in the direction of the deputy, as he approached the tank.

He couldn't see the set of keys in the bottom of the tank, but he knew they were there. He bent down pretending to study the murky bottom of the tank.

"They're in here!" he shouted to the deputy.

Without waiting for a reply, he peeled off his shirt and leaned over to retrieve the keys from the bottom of the tank. It was deep enough that he had to bend over and get his head and shoulders wet. The cold water caught him by surprise. He touched bottom and felt the keys immediately. He stood up, holding the keys out toward the deputy.

"Saw 'em when I went to wash up," he said.

Lleyellyn used his tee shirt to dry off as the officer walked over to the Silverado and unlocked the passenger side door. He took several photographs and repeated the process from the other side.

Thompson examined the pistol, removed the cartridges from the cylinder and placed the gun in one plastic evidence bag and the shells in another. Then he bagged the clothing, belt and boots and stowed them in his SUV. He carefully labeled each bag.

Lleyellyn stood aside as the truck was searched. When the deputy came back, Lleyellyn looked at Thompson and said, "What do you think happened here?"

'Sure seems he got undressed and put everything in his truck for safe keeping. Wonder if he took a soak in that tank? Maybe he dropped the keys and couldn't find 'em. Decided to hike back. Who the hell knows? What do you think?"

"I'm not sure," the deputy said. "Makes some sense, though."

'Yeah. But then why fold everything up. Lock the truck. Sure as heck isn't anybody out here in the boonies."

"Good point," Thompson said, then held up the set of two keys. "This one must be for the glove compartment. Best check it out. Need to make an inventory."

Lleyellyn followed the deputy around to the passenger side and watched as he unlocked the glove compartment. Thompson placed several new evidence bags on the seat and put on a pair of latex gloves.

"Could be some fingerprints."

The first thing he removed was a black vinyl covered owner's manual. The deputy opened it and looked over some loose papers stuck in the front.

"Registered to Cass R Montgomery," he said. "Culver City, California. U.S.A."

He put the owner's manual in a plastic bag, and continued examining the rest of the glove box. He removed a pair of light blue women's panties, and looked at the label.

"Size three. Vanity Fair brand."

Lleyellyn knew who the panties belonged to. He remembered LaDonna Mae telling the deputy about them when he stopped by her place with the things the highway department guy found along the road.

Thompson next took out a cylinder about the size of a ball point pen.

"Touch up paint," he said by way of explanation, before putting it into a separate bag.

He removed and bagged a two cell flashlight and two books of matches and put them in another evidence bag.

"Couple things left," Thompson said, as he removed a brass embossed belt buckle. The words *Big Cock Country* were spelled out next to an image in relief of a Ring-necked Pheasant and the words *SO DAK*.

"That's LaDonna Mae's buckle!" Lleyellyn said. "Bet those are her underpants, too."

Thompson placed all of the evidence bags into a larger sack before he said anything.

"If you're right, and I think you are, then Montgomery may be our guy."

"Those are her panties. Her belt buckle. It's gotta be him."

"Think you're right. Need the lab to verify. Sure looks like he's good for it. Odds of finding these things belonging to someone else seem remote. Damned unlikely."

"You going to arrest him?" Lleyellyn said.

"If we find him, sure," Thompson said, before taking a final look in the glove compartment.

"Lookey here," Thompson said, showing Lleyellyn a plastic Jesus he found back in the far corner. More proof, wouldn't you say?"

The deputy examined the statuette and noted greenish felt or something on the bottom. He carefully looked over the surface of the dash board and found a small semicircle of a similar material dead square in the center. He held the plastic Jesus over the spot matching them up, then laid it down before taking a photo showing the bottom of the statute and the spot on the dash.

Before locking up the pickup, he checked under and behind the seats. In a pocket on the back of the driver's seat he found a thin billfold with Montgomery's driver's license, a Visa card and exactly one hundred sixteen dollars in U.S. currency. He placed them all in another plastic evidence bag and looked at Shay.

"I'm done here. What say we head back?"

He locked the truck, then led the way back to his official vehicle.

"Need to search his trailer. See what else we can find."

o0o

As they pulled up to the bunkhouse, Mully came bounding down the steps and stood waiting for Lleyellyn to get out.

"May I use your phone?" Thompson said. "Need to get a search warrant authorizing a search of his motor home. Hang here, will you? Need you to show me which one it is. Won't take long, if the judge is near a phone, that is."

o0o

He sat on the steps rubbing Mully's ears wondering what the deputy was thinking. *Must figure the body belongs to Montgomery. Who else could it be?*

It took fifteen minutes before Thompson returned.

"Good to go on the search," he said. "Talked to the coroner, too. Gave him a heads up on the name, Cass R Montgomery of Culver City. I gave him the full details from the driver's license. Might speed up the positive ID process."

Shay gave directions and the deputy pulled up in front of Montgomery's trailer.

"How do you know this is his trailer?" the deputy said.

"Told us when we fixed his tire. They're all numbered."

Thompson approached the front door of Montgomery's travel trailer and tried the door.

The door was locked. Thompson felt around on a drip channel over the front door and found the key almost immediately. He slipped on a new pair of rubber gloves, unlocked the door and stepped inside. Lleyellyn saw the lights go on.

"I'll have to do this alone," he said, looking back from just inside the entryway. "I'll let you know if I find anything interesting."

The deputy was back in a couple minutes.

"Need some evidence bags," he said. "Won't take too long."

When Thompson came back outside after spending at least a half hour searching the place, he was carrying several clear plastic bags. He put them in the rear of the SUV. Lleyellyn couldn't see what he had found.

After turning off the lights in the trailer and locking the door, the deputy placed a yellow vinyl strip across the door. It read *SHERIFF'S LINE – DO NOT CROSS*. The trailer was officially sealed.

"Pretty certain he's our rapist," Thompson said. "Found a light the guy could wear on his forehead. Called a HeadLamp. Sort of like miner's use. Like Miss Ritchie described. Plus, several pair of woman's panties. Doubt if your girlfriend was his only victim."

He slammed the back of his SUV shut, and moved closer to Lleyellyn.

"Need to use your telephone. Okay?"

"Sure. No problem."

They drove back to the bunkhouse. As the deputy headed up the steps to use the phone, Montoya stuck his head out the back door of the house, gave a whistle and motioned Lleyellyn over.

"I'll be over at the house," he said to Thompson's back, as the deputy opened the bunkhouse door to make his call while Lleyellyn went to the house.

Montoya looked like he wanted to say something, but silently held the door open instead.

Irene was standing at the stove.

"Coffee?"

She poured two cups and took a Mountain Dew out of the fridge.

"Don't keep us in suspense," she said. "What did you and the deputy find out?"

"He searched the abandoned truck. Found LaDonna Mae's belt buckle, her underwear and that plastic Jesus she talked about. Montgomery has to be the guy attacked her. Looked like he took off his clothes. They were on the seat of the truck. A pistol, too. But he wasn't around," Lleyellyn said, before taking a sip of his soda.

Montoya didn't comment, but Irene said, "He must be the guy got trampled. Wandering around out in the middle of nowhere buck naked. Why would he do that?"

"Deputy thinks he might've accidently locked himself out of his truck. Maybe he got out to take a dip in the stock tank to cool off. Could've decided to walk back, rather that break any windows. Found his damned keys in the bottom of the tank."

Irene looked first at Lleyellyn, then at Montoya.

"That make any sense to you?"

Montoya was slow to reply. He sipped coffee before talking.

"Well, he couldn't find the keys, apparently. Wouldn't do any good to break into the truck without 'em. Wouldn't be able to start it. Nobody around. Isolated out there. Walking back might have been his best option."

"What else did you learn?" Irene said.

"Coroner's supposed to do some testing on the body. What's left of it, at least," Lleyellyn said. "Thompson just finished searching Montgomery's trailer. He found a light like LaDonna Mae talked about. Deputy called it a HeadLight. And, he found some more women's underwear. He suspects there could be more rape victims."

"Where's he now?" Montoya said.

"Making a phone call. Doesn't want to use the radio, I guess. Too many listening on their scanners."

o0o

Deputy Thompson knocked on the back door and Montoya invited him in.

"Fresh coffee," Irene said. "Can I pour you some?"

He joined them at the kitchen table and seemed to relax as he warmed up with the hot liquid.

"I suppose Lleyellyn filled you in," he said.

Irene nodded, then said, "Just imagine, that guy was out here at the ranch the whole time. Gives me the willies when I think about it. And poor LaDonna Mae."

"Remember, some of what I suspect is just that, a suspicion. Need to get some confirmation from the coroner. And the crime lab."

"Maybe so," Montoya said. "But the buckle, the plastic Jesus, and so forth, seems to point in just one direction."

They changed topics and made small talk until Thompson finished a second cup.

"Wonder if I can get one of you gents to go back out to the windmill with me. Drive Montgomery's truck back here. Keep it safe. Maybe park it in one of your buildings until I can get somebody to take it back to our impound lot. Should've asked you earlier," he said. "When we were out there."

Montoya volunteered to do it, and left with the deputy.

oOo

Thompson was deep in thought as they started out. Montoya figured the deputy was going over the things he had learned so far about Montgomery. When the deputy started talking he knew he was right.

"It's pretty clear that that Montgomery fella is the one that attacked Lleyellyn's girlfriend," he said. "That's right, isn't it? She is his girlfriend, correct?"

"They've got together a few times. He likes her, no doubt. Not sure just how close they consider themselves to be."

"Well, whatever. She was damned lucky to have gotten away. Good chance she wasn't his first victim with what I found searching his trailer."

"Lleyellyn, told me. I'd say you've got an air tight case. Don't you agree?"

"I think he's good for it. Also pretty sure he's the guy run over and trampled to death during the stampede," the deputy said. "You see the film of him out there?"

"No," Montoya said. "Didn't know there was one."

"They were filming the cattle drive last night when it started raining. Someone saw a guy coming toward them across the prairie. Trained a back-up camera on him and started filming. There was a bright flash of lightning. Could see it real clear in the film. A loud clap of thunder spooked the herd. They took off. Changed direction and started heading for our pedestrian. Camera man lost sight of him then. They got the herd turned in on itself so the stampede was aborted and the cattle were stomping around in a confused mess. When the camera crews checked, they found fresh human remains, damned near unrecognizable. Coroner's hoping to identify the vic with a finger he found.

Maybe match known fingerprints. Needs to make a positive identification."

Montoya made eye contact with the deputy when he glanced his way, but remained silent.

"Why the son of a bitch would strip down, lock everything in his truck, and start hoofing it is beyond me," Thompson said. "Any ideas?"

Montoya didn't reply. Finally he shrugged.

"Your pal, Mr. Shay found Montgomery's truck keys in the bottom of the stock tank out there. Thinks they must've got lost. Not sure I can see how that happened, Can you?" Thompson said. "If he took off all his clothes and locked everything in his truck, how the hell did he just happen to drop the keys in the tank?"

When the deputy looked at him for an answer, Montoya shrugged again and said, "Good question."

o0o

They pulled up so the two vehicles were nose to nose.

"You drive the Chevy," the deputy said. "I'll be right along. Couple things I need to do first."

"Need any help?" Montoya said. "I can always hold the dummy end if you plan to take measurements."

"No. Just need to take a look at the water tank."

Montoya got in Montgomery's truck, adjusted the seat and mirrors out of habit, but kept an eye on Thompson.

Thompson stood looking into the water tank, then removed some coins from his pants pocket and dropped them inside. He stood there for a moment, then removed his digital camera and took several pictures of the bottom of the tank.

Wants to see if the keys would have been easy to spot, he thought. *See if what Lleyellyn said about spotting the keys makes sense.*

Thompson got in the sheriff department's SUV and started back to the bunk house, retracing the way they had come. Montoya followed in Montgomery's pick-up.

When they got back to the buildings, Montoya parked the Chevy in one of the sheds, locked it, then met Thompson near the bunkhouse.

"Here's the keys. Got her locked. Happy to keep it in the shed for a few days," Montoya said, as the deputy pocketed the keys.

"We'll get her hauled to impound as soon as possible. Probably tomorrow. We'll take his trailer in at the same time. Thanks for your help."

The deputy drove out to the road and turned left to head to town. Lleyellyn came out and sat next to Montoya on the steps. Mully came out from under the porch and joined them.

"What do you think?" Lleyellyn said.

"I think we're okay. He was suspicious about how you found the keys. Checked out the water tank. Looked like he dropped a couple coins in there to see if they were easy to spot. Seemed to be satisfied. He has a hard time understanding why Montgomery would lock his truck if he was just going to take a quick dip in the trough."

"You worried about it?" Lleyellyn said.

Montoya thought about it for a while before answering.

"Not really. It'll just be one of those little mysteries that won't get answered."

Lleyellyn nodded, and added, "As long as we keep quiet."

o0o

Thompson entered the sheriff's office toting a card board box containing the bags of evidence he had collected during his search of Montgomery's truck and camper.

"Sheriff wants to see you," the duty officer said.

The deputy locked the evidence bags in his storage locker, and went up the stairs to the sheriff's private office.

"Good job out there," the sheriff said. "Got a positive identification on your trampalee. Coroner had us make a print from the finger he found. Used the info you gave us to contact the Culver City PD and LA County where Montgomery resided per his DL. Faxed them a copy of the print. You won't believe what we've learned about him. Take a look at this report they sent us."

Thompson sat down across the desk from the sheriff. The sheriff slid the report across the desk. Thompson read it.

FAX

FAX FROM: Culver City Police Department
County of Los Angeles
California

FAX TO: Custer County Sheriff
Miles City
Montana

ATTN: Thompson (deputy sheriff)

IN RE: Name: Cass R (only) Montgomery
Aliases: None known
Male Height: 74 in.
Cauc. Weight: 205 #
d/o/b 21 June 1954
Last known address:
Apt. 37C

Two Shots Quick

729 W. Adamson Lane
Culver City CA

Tattoos/Distinguishing marks: None known

Subject's Background:
Montgomery was born in Pismo Beach CA. Later moved to Mojave CA where his father was stationed at Edwards Air Force Base. Attended local public schools and graduated from Desert High School in Mojave. Salutatorian. Attended college at Cornell College in Iowa (liberal arts), and graduate school at Iowa State University in Ames.

Successfully completed his studies and obtained a Doctor of Veterinary Medicine degree. [Note: HAS NEVER BEEN LICENSED AS A VETERINARIAN.] (See below.)

Marital Status: Single, never married.

Military: None

Criminal Record:
During his final year at ISU, Montgomery was suspected in a series of sexual assaults of female students. The victims all claimed they were blinded by a bright light, forced to disrobe at gun point, and assaulted. One of the victims obtained a license plate number which led to Montgomery. There were problems with some of the cases. Montgomery reached a plea agreement resolving all matters and pled guilty to one count of Criminal Sexual Assault in the Fourth Degree. He was placed on probation for three years and required to complete a psychosexual evaluation and follow recommended counseling. (Which he apparently did satisfactorily.) He completed probation successfully. He was required

to register as a sex offender for a period of ten years. (Ten years has expired.) His criminal record makes him ineligible for a Veterinary license in California (and other states).

[Note: The criminal charges and resulting conviction did not come to light until after Montgomery had graduated and had obtained his degree.]

Recent arrests: None, since his conviction for Crim. Sex. 4. (1975)

Direct further inquiries to: Maria Lopez, records #ML249

Culver City P. D.

AN EQUAL OPPORTUNITY EMPLOYER
SERVICE IS OUR AIM
BUCKLE UP!
SE HABLA ESPANOL

o0o

Irene went upstairs. Montoya was feeding the dog while Lleyellyn went to the bunkhouse to use the phone.
"Ritchie's," LaDonna Mae said after three rings.
"How you doing today?" Lleyellyn said. "Feeling better? Feet still hurt?"
"Told the doctor they're about a three. Other words, not too bad. Better," she said. "What's going on at the ranch?"
"Deputy found out who attacked you. Guy with the movie, name's Montgomery."
"How'd he find him? They arrest him?"
"Searched his pick-up. A Silverado, just like you said. Guess what he found in the locked glove compartment."
"No clue," LaDonna Mae said. "What was it? My driver's license?"

"Three things were in there. Your favorite belt buckle. A plastic Jesus. And a pair of size three women's panties. Blue."

She didn't say anything.

"Vanity Fair brand. With lacey trim," he said. "Just like you were wearing out at the water tank that day."

"They got him locked up, right?"

"Hold your horses. Searched his trailer and found that head lamp thing he wore. Bunch of other panties, too."

"Other panties?"

"Yeah. They think he had other victims. Kept souvenirs."

"Oh my God," she said. "Where is he now?"

"The son of a bitch got caught in a stampede. Trampled to death."

"What? How could that happen? Tell me."

Lleyellyn explained what the film crew had seen. How the thunderstorm had frightened the herd, started the stampede which headed straight for Montgomery, and trampled him to death.

It was quiet at the other end of thine. LaDonna Mae was at a loss for words.

"You still there?" he asked.

"Can't hardly believe it," she said. "I feel relieved, I guess," then paused and continued. "When you coming into town so I can see you?"

"Now, if that's okay with you. Be there in a couple hours."

"Great," she said. "Thanks for telling me. Haven't heard a thing from the sheriff's office. And, Lleyellyn, honey. Love you."

"Me, too. See you soon."

o0o

"Culver City PD got back to us quickly," the sheriff said.

"Looks like we identified the perp, doesn't it?" Thompson said. "Montgomery is, or rather was, a serial rapist. With a little luck those other pairs of under garments might help someone solve other attacks."

"I'm holding a press conference in about an hour. Like you to be there. Need to inform the public about solving the crime and the leads we got on other possible vics. I'll have you discuss what you discovered in your searches."

The sheriff stood up and extended his hand. As they were shaking hands, he said, "Good job. Excellent detective work. You can close the file on the Ritchie assault. Mark it *CASE CLOSED*"

"I will. I'm going to notify the FBI about what we found. Might be the fastest way to spread the word. Maybe it'll help other departments somewhere solve a case or two."

"Might as well close your own file on Montgomery's death, too. *Accidently stampeded to death*. Makes a pretty good headline."

"There's a few loose ends about that," Thompson said. "I'm still trying to figure out why he was walking around out in the middle of nowhere buck naked. I'll get a report to you in a day or two."

"Far as I'm concerned we've got two solved cases. Attempted rape, kidnapping and what not with the Ritchie gal, and the accidental demise of her attacker. Great way to end the day. I'll sleep like a baby tonight," the sheriff said.

o0o

Thompson went to his own desk, put his feet up and called his wife.

"I'll be home soon, Honey" he said. "Just finishing up my report."

He continued sitting for a while, lost in thought. Then he reached for a legal pad and a ballpoint.

Questions:

1. Why was Montgomery walking around naked?
2. Why didn't he break the truck window to get his boots?
3. How did Shay spot the keys in the water tank?

He didn't have an answer to any of his questions, but they continued to bother him. He decided to head home, enjoy dinner. Sleep on it overnight.

CHAPTER 23

FRIDAY AUGUST 21

Benedict Stephenson had spent thirty-five years in law enforcement, 20 years as an investigator with the Custer County Sheriff's department, followed by fifteen years as chief investigator with the Montana State Police. He had been the go to guy when there was a major crime to be solved.

Thompson's dad had been a hunting buddy of Stephenson. Growing up, Thompson had looked up to Stephenson and relied on him as a mentor in his early days in law enforcement. He was looking forward to getting together with his old friend.

Stephenson had beaten him to the Big Sky. He was seated at his usual table in the back of the room chatting with one of the waitresses when Thompson walked in.

"Ben, glad you could make it in today. Lunch is on me," Thompson said.

"You're looking good," he said. "But, if I recall correctly, it's my turn to buy."

Thompson sat down opposite his friend, checked the *Specials Board* behind the counter, and got right to the point.

"Got something I want to run by you, if you've got the time."

"That's why I'm here. Better than sitting around at home watching the tube or rereading the paper," Stephenson said.

He nodded when Thompson asked if he'd heard about the guy getting trampled to death during the filming going on out at the Boyd ranch. He hadn't heard about the Ritchie girl getting assaulted out on the highway.

"She was out at the ranch, visiting her boyfriend. Started back around ten, ten-thirty or so. Her car conked out. Guy stopped to give her a lift almost immediately. As soon as she got in his vehicle he pulled a gun, had her take off her clothes, and was getting ready to rape her."

"She describe him?"

"Oh yeah, she did. When she opened the car to get in the interior lights were out. Guy said they weren't working. She got in anyway and the doors locked immediately. He turned on one of those lamps you wear on a strap around you head. Called a HeadLamp, I think," Thompson said. "She caught a glimpse of him when a vehicle passed. He was wearing a kerchief over his face. She guessed he was mid-forties, give or take."

He continued with his narrative, telling Stephenson how she managed to escape, the injuries she suffered, and what she said she could remember.

"Knew it was a Chevy Silverado. Saw a glow in the dark plastic Jesus on the dash. Guy kept her clothes. She described them. Had on a brand new pair of light blue panties. Size 3. Vanity Fair brand," Thompson said. "That turned out to be important."

He explained how the department got a call about a Chevy Silverado seemingly abandoned on the far west edge of the Boyd Ranch, six or seven miles from the building site and movie headquarters.

"I went out to take a look at the truck. Neatly piled on the front seat were clothes, a revolver and so forth. A pair of boots were on the floor. The doors were locked."

"You do a search?" Stephenson said.

"Thompson nodded. "Found a plastic Jesus and a pair of blue women's panties fitting the description."

"In other words, you got evidence that your stampede victim was the assailant."

"Yes. But that's not half of the story."

Thompson went on to explain how he had gone back to the scene to retrieve the pick-up.

"Guy went with me works at the ranch. New man. Comes from Minnesota. Met him a few weeks ago. Had to go out and tell him as the next of kin that his mother had been murdered back in Winona, Minnesota," Thompson said. "And another thing, he's Miss Ritchie's boyfriend."

Stephenson looked at him, motioning for him to continue.

"I was trying to figure out how to get the truck started when the kid reached into the bottom of the cattle trough out there and pulled out a set of keys. They fit the truck. Used them so I could search the vehicle. Get it driven back to ranch headquarters."

"How'd he happen to locate the keys?"

"That's just it. No way he could've, unless he knew they were there. I dropped some coins in. Damn things were damned near invisible when I looked in the tank," Thompson said.

"What're you thinking? Kid put the keys there?"

Thompson sat there, looking at his friend. He shrugged, wondering what he should say next.

"Intuition. Hunches," Stephenson said. "Just other names for suspicion. That's what's eating at you?"

"Okay. Why was Montgomery locked out of his pickup? Why was he walking cross country bare-ass naked? Why didn't he break a window in the vehicle, get his boots and clothes? How'd he lose his keys? Why'd he take his clothes off in the first place anyway?" Thompson said.

"All good questions," Stephenson said.

"Oh, there's more, I haven't mentioned yet," Thompson said. "Searched his camper. Found a HeadLamp like was used in the attack. And several more female panties. Probably from other victims. Looking into it."

"So, more indications that Montgomery is good for the attack."

"Here's what's bothering me. Miss Ritchie gets assaulted, then gets away. Fucks up her feet running down the road embankment and in the ditch. Needs surgery and hospitalization. Her attacker, who we now know is Montgomery, for some reason walks bare foot several miles back to where the movie crew is situated. If he made it, his feet would have been screwed up, too."

"Does seem like more than just coincidence," Stephenson said. "What else you got?"

"Sheriff likes it that we solved the attempted rape, and maybe several more, if the other undergarments match up. Kinda thinks Montgomery got what he had coming. Saved the county the time and expense of a jury trial."

"He may be right," Stephenson said. "But I think you have to follow your instincts. Look into that Minnesota kid a little. He's probably not liable for Montgomery's death. Stampede was more of an accident than anything. But something doesn't seem right to you. And I agree. Do some more checking. See if anything pops up."

The waitress must have noticed that their conversation was winding down.

"Can I get you gentlemen the special?" she asked.

o0o

Back at the office, Thompson checked the notes he had made a few weeks earlier regarding an assignment to go out to notify Lleyellyn Shay of his mother's murder. The investigator in Winona was named Williams.

The receptionist at the Winona PD put him through to Investigator Williams immediately.

Thompson identified himself. He got down to business right away.

"You might remember several weeks ago you asked me to notify a young man named Lleyellyn Shay that his mother had been murdered," Thompson said.

"I remember. How can I help you?"

"Shay's girlfriend here in Miles City was recently assaulted. She managed to get away but injured her feet in the process. Hospitalized. In a wheel chair for a spell. Found out who did it. Son of a bitch went and got himself killed. Caught in a cattle stampede, believe it or not."

"Weird. What can I do you for?"

"The perp was walking across open country buck naked and barefoot. Just like Shay's girlfriend had to after she escaped. Don't know if Shay was involved, but seems like a coincidence worth following up," Thompson said.

"You got anything pointing his way?"

"Just suspicion. Need to talk to somebody out there. Just exactly what happened to the guy killed Shay's mother is what I'd like to find out."

"Here's the deal on that. Maybe you know, Winona's right here on the Mississippi River. The killer, Dotwich, crossed the river and hid out in Trempealeau County, Wisconsin. His body was found over there. Guy who handled the investigation was Ralph Good Thunder. Works for the Trempealeau County Sheriff's Office. Good man. We coordinated some. But he's the guy was in charge of the investigation into Dotwich's death," Thompson said.

Thompson was taking notes.

"You got Good Thunder's number?"

Williams read off the number, then said, "We closed our investigation here in Winona. Know Dotwich murdered his wife. He's dead. Our file is closed on that case."

Thompson thought Williams was about to end the call, but he started talking again.

"You'll find out Trempealeau County's closed their file, too. A fugitive murder suspect was hit and mangled by a train. Didn't want to delve any farther," he said. "But I know Ralph thought there were some loose ends. I'm sure he'll fill you in."

o0o

Thompson decided it was probably lunch time in Wisconsin.

He waited until two fifteen their time, and placed a call to the number Williams had given him.

"Deputy Good Thunder is on another line," a receptionist said. "Care to hold?"

"Okay. No problem."

Almost immediately Good Thunder picked up the phone.

"Ralph," is all he said by way of greeting.

"Good afternoon. This is Bob Thompson, deputy with the Custer County Sheriff's Office in Montana. Miles City. Williams at the Winona PD gave me your number."

"What can I do for you?"

"It is a long story, but I'll try and condense it. Really, though I'm just trying to tie up some loose ends," Williams said.

"I'm all ears," Good Thunder said. "Shoot."

Thompson summarized everything he'd told Williams.

"I guess what I'm wondering is whether or not Shay had anything to do with Montgomery ending naked and barefoot. Same as his girlfriend. Tit for tat – or an eye for an eye kind of thing," Thompson said. "See what I'm wondering about?"

"Your department's happy with the result?" Good Thunder said. "You found out who attacked your vic and some other women as well, apparently. I expect your boss doesn't want to stir anything up more than usual. Let sleeping dogs lie. Am I right?"

"I hear you, and you're right," Thompson said. "What about your case?" Williams told me his department was satisfied with their killer caught and dead."

There was static on the line, and Good Thunder kept quiet for a minute.

"Just a sec," he finally said. "Need to close the door."

Thompson heard Good Thunder's muffled voice tell someone he didn't want to be disturbed.

"Okay. Just need some privacy," Good Thunder said. "This is between you and me, okay?"

"Of course."

"I thought there might have been something funny with the death of Dotwich. I'll run through what we found."

He gave Thompson the condensed version. Told him how some kids found a foot floating in the river next to the rail road tracks, and how the body was found in two separate parts some distance from the tracks.

"The body sure as hell didn't get there by itself," Good Thunder said.

He explained to Thompson how the investigation established that Dotwich had lost a foot when it was severed by a fast moving freight train heading up stream along the Mississippi River. The body had then been placed on a track of an adjoining siding and run over at slow speed by a train heading the other direction.

He went on the say that the body was found several hours post mortem. There is a video camera recording everything mounted on the front of every train engine. By the time they went looking for it, it was recorded over. We interviewed the crews of every train passing through. Nobody saw anything helpful.

"I checked over the scene personally," Good Thunder said. "Maybe not the most thorough job. It was raining like a son of a bitch. Did find a spent cartridge. Thirty-eight caliber. Don't know if it had anything to do with Dotwich. Medical examiner removed a slug from the deceased's shoulder. Thirty-two caliber. Non-fatal injury. Rest of the body was too mangled to determine if some metal particles found were from a thirty-eight or a thirty-two. Really couldn't tell me if he was hit by the train before or after death."

Thompson waited for Good Thunder to go on, but he remained quiet.

"You thinking it was a homicide?"

"Had me wondering. Person most interested in avenging his mother's death would have been your Mr. Shay, wouldn't you say?"

"That's what they say," Thompson said.

"Well, I thought that could be the case. Did some checking. Apparently Shay never left that ranch where he was working. Talked to the boss lady. Boyd, I think. Irene Boyd. And her foreman. Also checked all public transportation out of your neck of the woods. Shay didn't rent a car, take a plane. Or the train. Or the bus, either. Complete dead end."

"Sounds like there was nothing there," Thompson said.

"If there was, I never found it. Sheriff told me to close the file. Haven't lost any sleep over it. No one was worried about the death of a murder suspect."

Thompson couldn't think of any more questions.

"Well, thanks for your assistance. Not sure it helps me any. Seems like we both have similar cases."

"Before you go, there is one thing. You know about that foreman at the ranch, right?"

"Manual Montoya. What about him?"

"Williams told me he was a parolee. Spent a few years in prison. Assault, I think. Must have a parole agent back there somewhere if he's still on paper," Good Thunder said. "Might be worth checking out."

"You know what state?"

"Don't. Not sure I ever knew. Check with Williams at Winona PD. He's the one told me."

o0o

Investigator Williams wasn't in when he made his second call to the Winona Police Department. The receptionist said she would leave him a call back message.

"Not sure how long he'll be out," she said. "He's at career day at the high school."

o0o

His phone started to ring when he returned from the lavatory. It was Williams from the Winona PD.

"What can I do you out of?" Williams said.

"Talked to Good Thunder. Nice guy. Very helpful. Told me that Shay's foreman, Manual Montoya, is a convicted felon. Did a stretch. You know anything about that?"

"Not that I remember,' Williams said. "Hang on a sec. I'll get the file. Should be in my notes."

Thompson waited, straightening his desk top and glancing through an equipment catalog.

"Got what you want," Williams said. "Sorry to keep you waiting."

"No, it's okay. What can you tell me?" Thompson said.

"You're in Miles City, right?" he said. "Montoya's on felony parole. His agent there in your town is Maggie Cremer. I guess that's Margaret. You know her?"

"Sure. Offices in this building."

"Montoya was convicted of first degree assault. South Dakota conviction. Did his time there. Really don't know the details. Margaret did tell me he was a model parolee. Plans to recommend him for discharge pretty soon. If she hasn't already."

Thompson thanked Williams for his assistance, and immediately placed a call to the parole agent.

oOo

"You didn't have to come here," Thompson said, when corrections agent, Cremer, walked into his office a few minutes after hanging up the phone.

"It's okay. I have to see a client in the jail anyway," she said, sitting opposite the deputy and putting her brief case on a chair next to her.

"I've got Manuel Montoya's file right here."

"Tell me about his conviction. What did he do?" Thompson said.

"He castrated a guy back in South Dakota. Then he took the guy to the ER. Admitted everything. Convicted. Sentenced. Served his time. Released early on good behavior. Been a model parolee as long as he's been assigned to me. Before, too. Seems like a nice guy, really. Can't say that about most of my clients."

"Interesting short hand account," Thompson said. "Tell me the details. Why? Who? That sort of thing."

"It was big news some thirty-five years ago. Montoya went to high school here in Miles City. Girl in his class got raped. Rapist was charged and was acquitted after a jury trial. Lot of folks thought he was guilty. Some of his friends lied on the witness stand and gave him an alibi. This was way before DNA of course. Whole town knew he was guilty, it seems."

She watched as Thompson finished writing on a legal pad, then continued.

"Perp was the son of a ranch owner north of town. In fact Montoya's dad was his foreman. At any rate, there was too much talk in town and his dad sent the perp away to college. Montoya found out where he was, tracked him down in South Dakota, and committed the crime. Took the law into his own hands, you might say."

Thompson sat there staring at her for a few moments, lost in thought.

"Victim still around here?" he said.

"Yes, she is. Not sure if I'm supposed to release the victim's name, but I think it's common knowledge among people around the area of a certain age, if you know what I mean. Name's Irene Boyd. Owns the Boyd Ranch. Place they're filming that western," she said. "You know her?"

"Yes. I've talked to her a time or two. Nice lady. She's the county's sexual abuse counselor, am I right?"

"Yes. Part time position. She's very good at her job," Cremer said.

"You find it strange Montoya's her right hand man now?"

"A little. Far as I can figure out, they didn't really know each other very well in high school. Apparently Montoya didn't like it when one of his class mates was raped and humiliated. She told me she sent Montoya a letter after he had been in prison for several years. That developed into a long range friendship. She offered him a job when he got out. I know he grew up on a cattle outfit. It was a good fit. Seems to be good at his job."

Thompson scratched his head and smiled at Cremer.

"Can I get you a coffee? Soda? Anything?"

"I have to get going. Maybe next time. Anything else you need from me?"

"I don't know. Ever meet Montoya's new hired help? Hard first name to pronounce. I'll spell it. L-L-E-Y-E-L-L-Y-N. Lleyellyn, I think. Last name Shay."

Cremer seemed to think about it for a minute as she packed up her brief case and prepared to leave.

"No. I'm afraid I haven't. Sorry."

o0o

Thompson needed to talk to Investigator Williams again.

He left a message for Williams, and received a call back a half hour later.

"Sorry to bother you again," he said. "This time I'm calling about Shay."

"Find out what you needed about that Montoya guy?" Williams said.

"Right. His first degree assault was a new one for me. Castrated a guy, then took him to the emergency room. Admitted everything. Apparently his assault victim had beaten a rap for rape of one of his class mates. Thought he was doling out a just punishment, trying to make things even," Thompson said. "When you think about it, maybe he did."

"New one for me, too," Williams said.

"Another thing, Montoya is now the foreman on the ranch owned by the rape victim."

Williams didn't reply at first. Finally he said, "You learn something new in this job every day. Am I right?"

"You can say that again," Thompson said. "Truth is stranger than fiction," he added. "Now I'm looking into Shay. He's working on that same ranch."

"Shay's story is simple," Williams said. "Pretty good kid. Smart. Lived with an abusive step-father. That was Dotwich. Missed some school, then started at the alternative high school. Did well. Even graduated a little early. Mainly to get away from home. Stole a bunch of copper wire from the abandoned telegraph poles along the railroad tracks, then headed west. To Miles City, in fact. There were charges brought concerning the theft. Judge limited the arrest warrant to Minnesota only. Judge knew the kid from his elementary school days. Went to school with her kids, I guess. At any rate, after his mother was murdered we agreed to drop the theft charges. He paid restitution. Part of the deal. He has absolutely no criminal record in Minnesota. Last I heard he had a good job on that ranch," Williams said. "That's about it. Need anything more?"

"Was he ever a person of interest in his mother's death, or his step-father's?"

"Maybe at first. Found out almost immediately Dotwich murdered the mother. Dotwich's death wasn't in my jurisdiction. You've talked to Good Thunder, right?"

"I have," Williams said. "Thanks for your help. Just had to do my due diligence. Think I have what I need. Thanks."

Two Shots Quick

CHAPTER 24

MONDAY AUGUST 24

Deputy Robert Thompson had a restless night's sleep.

"Honey, what's bothering you?" his wife said when his tossing and turning woke her up a little after three.

"Nothing," he said, mumbling. "Just thinking about that incident out south of town. Guy killed by the stampede."

He didn't think his wife heard his response. She was breathing heavily, apparently asleep.

Several things raced through his mind most of the night. When he got to the office, he closed the office door, told the receptionist to hold his calls, and did as he often did. He made a list.

LIST

1. Montoya went to HS with Irene Boyd
2. A HS schoolmate raped Boyd
3. Classmate was acquitted of rape charge (based on perjured testimony of friends)
4. Montoya tracked down rapist and castrated him
5. Montoya took schoolmate/rapist to emergency room
6. Montoya admitted castrating (assaulting) schoolmate and pled guilty
7. Montoya served time in prison in South Dakota (model prisoner)
8. Montoya released from prison, placed on parole, parole transferred to Montana
9. Montoya hired by Boyd (foreman at Boyd Ranch)
10. Montoya is a model parolee about to be discharged from parole early

Two Shots Quick

1. Shay was not a troublemaker
2. Shay's step-father was abusive to him
3. Shay was a good student (graduated early)
4. Shay decided to leave home after completing school
5. Shay stole copper wire from abandoned telegraph poles along railroad right of way to raise get away money
6. Shay took the train west and ended up in Miles City
7. Shay was charged in Minnesota (Winona County) with theft of copper wire
8. Irene hired Shay
9. Irene Boyd owns the Boyd Ranch
10. Shay was hired to assist Montoya at the Boyd ranch
11. Shay's step-father (Dotwich) was found dead along the railroad tracks in Tremplo Co. (sp???) WI
12. Dotwich manner of death not determined (Gun shot to shoulder, body moved from main track to siding, run over, then body tossed in weeds)
13. Medical examiner did not determine cause of death
14. Winona Co. MN no longer investigating death of Shay's mother (or step-father)
15. Tremplo Co. WI no longer investigating death of Shay's step-father
16. Dep. Good Thunder (Tremplo Co.) found no evidence that Shay (or Montoya) were ever in the area when Dotwich was killed
17. Winona Co. and Tremplo Co. had no incentive to continue their investigations of Dotwich death (he was a known murderer)
18. Shay and LaDonna Mae Ritchie met at a café in Miles City
19. Ritchie is (now) Shay's girlfriend
20. Ritchie was assaulted on her way back from the Boyd ranch by a person in his mid-40's driving a Chev Pick-

up (full size; deluxe, Slvdo.). With a plastic Jesus on the dashboard
21. Ritchie managed to escape her attacker but badly injured her feet in getting away
22. Cass Montgomery owed a Chev C/K 4X4 (Slvdo.)
23. Montgomery's glove box contained a plastic Jesus and Ritchie's panties etc. etc.
24. Montgomery's camper-trailer contained a "head lamp," other panties etc. & etc.
25. Montgomery was Ritchie's attacker (evidence indisputable)
26. Montgomery's locked pick-up was abandoned in boonies
27. Montgomery was spotted walking naked and barefoot across the Boyd Ranch
28. (Montgomery's feet would have been cut up while walking)
29. Montgomery was killed by stampeding cattle
30. Shay spotted the keys to Montgomery's vehicle in bottom of water trough. (How'd he know where to find them?????)

ISSUES

(It is a known fact that Montoya castrated Boyd's rapist.)
Did Montoya/Shay kill Dotwich?
Did Montoya/Shay force Montgomery to walk barefoot from pick-up to his trailer (6 -7 mi)? If so, can they be blamed for Montgomery's death
Does it really matter anyway??????

o0o

Two Shots Quick

Thompson finished his list, got up and stretched, then sat back down behind his desk, and went over the list several times. He knew Montoya had castrated one man.

Did he, alone, or with Shay, avenge Shay's mother's murder? He thought. *And did they have Montgomery disrobe and start walking across the prairie to get even for Ritchie's attack and injuries? Can't be just a coincidence, can it?*

The intercom buzzed and the receptionist reminded him that he had a talk to give at the elementary school. He put away his notes, and prepared for his presentation to the class.

o0o

Thompson had lunch after his duties at the school. As he drove back to the office he decided to talk to Benedict Stephenson again, see what he might have to say about the things that were troubling him.

Rather than go all the way to the office, he took a detour to Stephenson's house on the edge of town. He spotted Stephenson and his wife working in their vegetable garden as he pulled into their driveway.

Stephenson looked up and smiled. His wife walked up to the squad car and waited for Thompson to open the door.

"I know you probably want to shoot the bull with my husband," she said. "But come and sit inside where it's cool. I was just going in to get a pitcher of ice tea. You can talk to him after. I have to run to the store anyway."

With the tea finished, and Mrs. Stephenson on her way to the store, the two men continued sitting at the kitchen table.

"Hate to bother you," Thompson said. "But I'd like to see what you have to say about some things that are bothering me."

He unfolded his notes, and handed them to Stephenson.

"Take a look at this. See if you think I'm seeing things in my imagination, or not."

Stephenson put the notes on the table, poured another glass of tea for himself, and offered a refill to Thompson.

He studied the list for several minutes, carefully reading it from top to bottom.

"You got another copy of this?" he asked, nodding toward Thompson's notes.

"Back at the office. Yes."

"Tell you what. Give me a chance to think about these things a little. Maybe we could meet in town tomorrow."

"Sure. At the office," he said. "Or, how about I treat lunch? Say eleven thirty at the usual place."

"Fine. But I think it's my turn to buy. Am I right?"

"No. Remember. You picked up the tab the last time. My turn."

Two Shots Quick

CHAPTER 25

TUESDAY AUGUST 25

The Big Sky Café was starting to fill up. The back corner "law enforcement table" was empty.

"Ben, haven't seen you for a long time," the waitress said to Stephenson. "You still drinking Arnold Palmers?"

"Good memory. Yes, please," he said.

"I'll have an iced tea, Becky," Thompson said. "Few things we have to discuss before we place our orders."

When the waitress went to fetch their drinks, Stephenson removed the notes Thompson had given him from his shirt pocket, unfolded them, and smiled.

"Good detective work," he said. "I agree with you. There seems to be a connection. People known to Montoya, and I guess Shay now, too, get killed, raped or attacked and, how shall I put this?"

"Just let's say, they receive extra-judicial punishment. Punishment that fits the crime," Thompson said.

Stephenson nodded his agreement.

"There's not much more to say. Montoya went to prison for what he did to Irene Boyd's attacker. Paid his debt to society. Those other guys, both Dotwich and Montgomery, got retribution that fit their crimes. Law enforcement in those instances never really pursued the matters."

"But, there seems to be something there. Dotwich was probably murdered. Montgomery, at the very least, was assaulted. Probably can't blame the stampede on anybody, I know that," Thompson said.

"Wait a minute. I know we are sworn law officers, sworn to uphold the law," Stephenson said. "But consider this. Justice is what matters. Seems like that's what happened here."

Thompson considered what his friend and mentor had just said, while pretending to read the menu.

"What do you think I should do then?" he said meeting Stephenson's eyes.

"Let sleeping dogs lie," Stephenson said. "You've got plenty of other things to look into that might not turn out near as well."

They were interrupted by the waitress bringing their drinks. "Ready to order yet?" she said.

CHAPTER 26

WEDNESDAY AUGUST 26

Thompson woke up at twenty minutes past three. His wife was sleeping soundly by his side. His thoughts kept returning to what Stephenson had said. The same thoughts had been bothering him almost every night.

I am a peace officer sworn to uphold the law, he thought. *I have suspicions about Montoya and Shay. Could they have caused Dotwich's death? Made Montgomery strip and walk miles barefoot? But if they did, so what? I can't prove it. Besides, they both got what they had coming, didn't they? 'Let sleeping dogs lie,' Stephenson told me.*

When he finally managed to fall asleep, he had pretty much made up his mind to heed Stephenson's advice.

o0o

The call came in at nine fifteen, just before he planned to leave on patrol. He hadn't expected to hear from Stephenson again so soon.

"Ben here," the caller said. "You free around lunch time? Something new I want to talk to you about."

They agreed to meet at the Big Sky again. At one thirty.

"Crowd should be thinned out by then," Thompson said.

Thompson recognized Stephenson's car in the parking lot when he arrived at the café.

Stephenson was sitting at the same corner law enforcement table talking to two officers from the Miles City PD.

He joined them at the table just as the policemen were getting ready to leave.

"Hey, don't leave on my account," Thompson said. "How's it going?"

"Same O, same O," the younger of the two cops said. "We're just leaving. Time to go back to protecting the public."

When they left, the waitress came over. They placed their orders.

"Reason I called. Thought I'd tell you about what turned out to be one of my worst cases. Homicide. Didn't turn out the way I'd hoped. Thought maybe you might benefit from my experience. Then maybe not," Stephenson said. "You told me about those two cases that were bothering you. I thought I'd tell you about one that's bothered me ever since I turned in my badge. Eight years, I guess. Hell, it's bothered me ever since it first happened,"

Thompson didn't get a chance to say anything as the waitress was back sooner than they had expected with their orders.

"Two commercials," she said. "Did you want coffee?"

They both declined the coffee.

"Water's good," Stephenson said.

"Me, too," Thompson said.

When they were alone, Stephenson pulled out a folded sheet of paper from his shirt pocket. As he unfolded it, he said, "This article pretty much says it all."

He handed the photocopied newspaper clipping to Thompson.

"I'd like you to read this. Take your time."

Thompson looked at his mentor for a moment. Stephenson had a serious look on his face. He motioned for Thompson to start reading.

o0o

MURDER CHARGES DISMISSED
CONFESSED KILLER TO GO FREE

Miles City MT (AP) Judge Wallace S. Peabody has dismissed first degree murder charges pending against Terrence Spencer Walker following a pretrial hearing Tuesday.

Earlier police reports indicated Walker, 22, of Miles City confessed to the slaying of Pamela Whitedeer, address unknown, by strangulation last November.

Judge Peabody granted the motion of Walker's public defender to declare Walker's confession inadmissible because of a denial of the accused's constitutional rights.

Walker's confession, set out in full in an accompanying box, was extensively quoted in the press, and a recording of his statement was broadcast by local radio and television stations.

The Court determined that Walker was not given a Miranda warning after his arrest and before he was questioned, and that not only was his confession inadmissible, so was the evidence found as a result thereof, including the murder weapon found during a search of his storage unit, which the court referred to as the "fruit of a poisonous tree."

The county prosecutor, Carl Kanear, had no comment, but said through an assistant they were studying appeal possibilities.

Walker's public defender, Davis Lee Thaymes, expressed his gratitude to the court for following the clear mandate of the Constitution and the "black letter law" of the Miranda decision.

Walker was released from custody immediately following the court's ruling. His present whereabouts are unknown. He is not currently subject to any release conditions of the court.

Attempts to contact next of kin of Ms. Whitedeer have continued to be unsuccessful.

Two Shots Quick

oOo

A KILLER'S CONFESSION

My name is Terrence S. Walker. My middle name is Spencer. People usually call me Terry.

I am 23 years old and have an associate degree in accounting from Miles College. I am a book-keeper at Spencer Realty. (Spencer Realty is a family business started by my grandfather.) Actually I turn 23 tomorrow.

I met Pamela Whitedeer when she stopped to give me a ride after I ran out of gas on my way to town Wednesday night. I had never seen her before. She told me her name was Tammy. I never suspected she was Indian. She did not tell me her last name.

She pulled over at a wide spot, and we started fooling around. Suddenly she told me to get out of the car. We argued. Said I wasn't showing her any respect.

I'm not sure exactly why, but I lost it. Pulled out my hunting knife and stabbed her in the neck. Left her by the side of the road.

I got back in the car and took off. Didn't know she was dead until I heard about it on the radio.

Her car is the one caught fire behind the sewage plant.

I'm sorry it happened.

Tell you the truth, she's the one disrespected me. And I swear, I never knew she was Indian.

That's all I remember.

Might as well tell you, the knife and my clothes are in a storage unit I have at Prairie Safe Storage, unit 19.

Yes. I lit the car on fire.

Signed: s/ T. S. Walker ("Terry")
Terrence Spencer Walker

o0o

"Holy shit! This Spencer guy got away with murder," Thompson said. "Where's he now?"

"Still in town. Still working for his old man. Goes by Spencer Walker now. Old timers know who he is, what he did. People pretty much stay away from him," Stephenson said.

Thompson started to hand the article back, but Stephenson held up his hand to stop him.

"You keep it," he said. "Just wanted you to know what's been keeping me awake for the past couple decades, and even longer, I guess."

"Nothing to be done, is that right?"

"Tried to get evidence not based on the confession. Came up with zilch. No one saw them together. Walker's never talked about what happened since. To anybody," Stephenson said.

They were both lost in thought for a while.

"You know, they went back a year or so ago to see if Walker's DNA showed up in the evidence they'd gathered from the crime scene. Lot of old cases been solved that way, as you know," Stephenson said. "Damned evidence was missing. Lost somehow. Never located. Complete dead end."

"How come no Miranda warning?" Thompson said, breaking a long pause. "That's the first thing they teach you during police training."

"Questioning was done by a new man. Just hired. Didn't tell his supervisor he was going to interview the accused. By the time they found out, it was too late. Walker kept his mouth shut when I tried to question him again. Read him the Miranda warning and he lawyered up."

"Who was the officer?" Thompson said. "Anybody I know?"

"Quit the force when the judge's decision came out. Guy lives in Billings, last time I heard. Security department at Walmart, Target, one of those."

The waitress showed up to pick up their plates, and refill their glasses.

When she was gone, Thompson was the first to speak.

"Here I've been worried about cases where it looks like the perps got what they had coming. What justice demanded."

"Yeah. And my problem is just the opposite. Case where the guilty party walked. Gets away scot free. Life's a bitch sometimes," Stephenson said. "Like my mother used to say, 'Life is fun, but rarely fair.'"

o0o

That afternoon Thompson couldn't get the Walker case out his head. A confessed murderer was carrying on like nothing happened. He had been in town for twelve years, and had never even heard about the murder of Pamela Whitedeer until now.

Ever since Stephenson had showed him the clippings about the Whitedeer case, and told him how Walker had gotten away with murder, the Montgomery case that had been keeping him awake had become a thing of the past.

CHAPTER 27

MONDAY AUGUST 31

He got up still thinking about the Walker case that had been bothering Ben Stephenson all these years. It seemed to him sometimes there is no justice. He remembered somebody said, "The law is an ass."

Could've been talking about the Walker case, he thought.

On the way to work he thought he'd come up with an idea. He called Stephenson just as soon as he was alone in his office.

"Ben, it's me, Bob," he said as soon as Stephenson picked up the phone and identified himself. Got an idea. Thought I'd run it by you."

"Sure, go ahead. I'm all ears."

"I'm going to make a photocopy of those newspaper items you showed me yesterday. About the Whitedeer murder. Plan to send it to Montoya out at the Boyd place. If he's the one behind those three matters we talked about, maybe he'll do something about Walker."

"You're not going to put a return address on the envelope are you?"

"I'm not that stupid. I'm not going to tell Montoya what to do. Just sending him some public information. Figure he was still in prison when the whole Walker thing came down."

It was quiet on the other end. Finally, Stephenson spoke up.

"You sure Montoya's the guy responsible for 'em all? Could've been Shay. For the last two, at least." He paused, before continuing. "Maybe they were working together."

As Thompson was considering this, Stephenson interrupted his reverie.

"Tell you what. You send your little message to Montoya. I'll send one just like it to Shay."

CHAPTER 28

THURSDAY SEPTEMBER 3

Irene was getting groceries out of her Ram truck when the rural letter carrier pulled up at the mail box at the end of the driveway. He beeped his horn in greeting and gave her a wave, then continued on his route.

When she had put everything in the kitchen away, Mully showed up from somewhere, and together they walked to the mail box, Mully trotting ahead, looking back from to time to see if Irene was keeping up.

"Going as fast as I can," she said. "What's the hurry, girl?"

Among the miscellaneous junk mail and bills were two other items. A letter addressed to Lleyellyn Shay and another to Manual Montoya. Neither had a return address, but they both had Miles City post marks.

o0o

Shay and Montoya entered the kitchen together.

Lleyellyn took a Mountain Dew from the fridge. Montoya asked Irene if she wanted anything, before he put some ice in a glass and poured an ice tea for himself.

"Not now," she said. "There's mail for you on the table. For both of you."

They both opened their envelopes and unfolded a single sheet of paper printed on both sides, and began reading.

"Lleyellyn checked the envelope to see if there was a return address on the back. Montoya did the same to his.

"Look at this," Lleyellyn said to Irene. "You ever hear of Terrence Walker. And Pamela Whitedeer, the girl he murdered?"

Montoya showed his letter to Lleyellyn.

"This the same thing you got?" he said.

Lleyellyn compared the two, and nodded.

They were copies of articles from the local paper. One headed *Murder Charges Dismissed*, and the other *A Killer's Confession*,

"Wonder who sent 'em."

"No way to tell. Sent from in town, though. Different type of envelopes. Different stamps. Beats me," Montoya said.

Irene had not answered Lleyellyn's question. She took Lleyellyn's copy of the articles about the Whitedeer murder and quickly read them through. There was a stricken look was on her face when she finally spoke.

"This all happened some thirty years or so ago," she said. "When you were way," she added, glancing at Montoya.

"I've been trying to put the incident behind me for years. And now this," she said, dabbing at her eyes with a tissue. "Pamela Whitedeer was one of my clients. Nice girl. Had to overcome a lot. Then that son of a bitch Walker killed her. He got away with it, too, as you can see from those," she said, pointing to the paper Lleyellyn was holding. Made a full confession, too."

No one said anything for a minute or two.

"A lot of people were affected by what happened," Irene said. "Pamela had no family, so there wasn't much said from her point of view. But Judge Peabody, poor man. Darn good judge. But, of course, people blamed him. Said he let a killer go free. He had no real choice. Cop screwed up. Peabody lost the next judicial election. Was so depressed, he killed himself. Let the car run in his garage until he was overcome with the fumes."

"Funny, I never heard about it at all," Montoya said. "Never heard of Walker. Or Whitedeer. The prosecutor and the public defender must have started after I was sent away. They aren't still around here, are they? Don't recognize their names."

"You were in Granite City at the time," Irene said. "The prosecutor and the public defender have both moved on. No choice after Walker was freed. They got blamed, too, like the judge. The cop that screwed up?" Just a kid then. Heard he was working loss prevention at ShopKo in Bozeman or somewhere."

After they had talked some more about what had happened, Lleyellyn asked a question.

"What about Walker himself, you know him?"

"Knew his father. His grandfather, too, come to think of it. Ran a real estate company in town. The dad still does. Mostly manage other people's land. Never heard a bad thing about them, until this," she said, holding up the paper Lleyellyn had received in the mail. "Really, Terry Walker has kept a low profile ever since. Know he still works at the family agency."

"Seems like a weird deal to me. Killer going free, and all."

"Tell me about it. I can tell you at the time, I was ready to gun down that Walker kid myself. Lots of other people felt the same way. And some of us still do, if you want to know the truth."

Lleyellyn looked at her, surprised that she still had such strong feelings about the case.

"There's a reason I didn't hunt him down," Irene said. "I knew I wouldn't get away with it. Everyone in town knew how I felt. Lot of people talked about evening the score. It wasn't just me. The investigator who tried to resurrect the charges promised me he would do everything to see he got what he deserved."

She was quiet for a minute or two, lost in thought.

"Investigator was Mr. Stephenson, a very nice man. Suppose he's long retired by now," she said. "People shun Walker. I know that. Doubt he has a friend in the world. Never married. Seen him in town a few times over the years. Always by himself, but," she added, "He's still walking around a free man. Guilty, but free."

CHAPTER 29

MONDAY OCTOBER 5

Back in high school Walker had gone pheasant hunting in South Dakota with a bunch of his friends. After his run in with the law it had gotten harder to get people to go with him. In the early days it had been an annual trip for six or seven of them every year.

He'd called around this year. His friends, the ones he used to consider friends at any rate, either didn't take his calls, or gave some lame excuse.

I was protected by my Constitutional rights, he thought. *Couldn't they see that?*

Friends or no friends, he made up his mind to go pheasant hunting. Good to get away. Get some fresh air. Maybe bring home a few birds.

o0o

The Big Sky wasn't a bad place to work. He had seen the Help Wanted sign in the window, applied, and was hired on the spot. It helped that the owner knew his uncle, Bob.

They had started him out washing dishes. Not too bad as long as he didn't fall too far behind.

When some guy tried to rape one of the waitresses, she put up a hell of a fight to escape. Cut up her feet getting away and had to take time off. LaDonna Mae was her name. He liked her. She shared tips better that some of the rest of the wait staff.

Two Shots Quick

When LaDonna Mae was away recovering from her injuries, he had started bussing dishes. He liked it better because he got to deal with customers sometimes, exchange b. s. with some of the people he knew, class mates and the like.

He'd been cleaning up a four top when he heard one of the customers talking about a pheasant hunting trip he was planning. He'd seen the guy around town once in a while, but didn't know his name.

The guy had asked several people to go with him. Said he could guarantee good hunting. Assured them they would limit out. Even offered to do the driving.

It sounded like a great trip, but everyone the guy talked to seemed to be busy and turned him down.

When the customer was alone, and he was setting out the cutlery on the table he had just wiped clean, he caught the customer's eye.

"Sounds like a great trip," he said. "Where 'bouts you going?"

"Hoping to get a couple guys to go with me back to South Dakota. Near a little town called Moreloft. Know it?"

"No, sir, I don't."

"There's miles and miles of abandoned rail road. Cuts right through primo crop land. Good cover along both sides. Had great luck there in the past. Not too many hunt it, especially after the opener," the customer said. "You hunt?"

"Used to, when my dad was still alive. Been trying to get my uncle to take me. He's usually busy on weekends."

The customer picked up his check and moved over by the cashier to pay his bill. When he was done, he walked back to where the busboy was busy working on another table, and caught his attention.

"Think you might want to go out to Moreloft with me? Opener's on a Saturday. That's October seventeenth. Plan to leave on Monday, two days later. Be back Wednesday evening. Probably late. Could be Thursday morning. Only expense you'll have is a motel room for one night and meals. I'll be driving out there any way."

"Be great," he said. "I'll have to check with my mom. And I'll have to make sure someone can cover my shifts here. Can I call you?"

"Let me know as soon as you can. Plan to leave that Monday morning at eight," the customer said. "That's my blue car out there, The Mustang. Here's my card. Try the house first."

He checked the business card. The customer's name was Terrence Walker of Walker Land Management.

"I'm Leonard Thompson," the bus boy said, extending his hand. "Friends call me LT."

"Nice to meet you, LT. You can call me Terry," he said, then added, "Hope you can go with. Look forward to hearing from you."

o0o

His mother was working in the kitchen when he got home. He set out the dishes as he told her about his day.

"Customer asked me to go pheasant hunting with him in a couple weeks. Going out to South Dakota. Plans to hunt a stretch of abandoned railroad. He's driving and paying for the gas. Be back late Wednesday night."

"Who's this customer?" his mother said. "Somebody you know?"

"Business man in town," Thompson said. "Gave me his business card."

His mother looked at the card her son handed him and read the name.

Her face turned pale. At first she didn't say a word.

Finally she asked him a question.

"You don't know who Terrence Walker is, do you?"

"Not really. Some land manager, I guess."

His mother looked like she was focused on putting the finishing touches on the evening's casserole, but he realized she was thinking about the hunting trip when she turned and looked at him.

"Call your Uncle Bob," she finally said. "The sheriff's department knows all about your Mr. Walker."

o0o

The receptionist at the sheriff's office told him she would contact his uncle and have him call back ASAP. The return call from deputy Bob Thompson came before they were ready to sit down for dinner.

After the usual greetings, his uncle got down to business.

"What's on your mind, LT?"

"Mom wanted me to call you. Guy's going to take me on a pheasant hunting trip to South Dakota. Said I should check with you first. Not sure exactly why."

"Who is this guy?" his uncle said. "Somebody I know?"

"Guy was eating at the Big Sky. Name's Terry Walker. Overheard him talking about the trip. Then he asked me. Nobody else could go," LT said. "Supposed to leave October nineteenth. Couple days after the opener. That's a Monday."

"Where exactly?"

"Motel parking lot across from the restaurant."

"No. I mean, where in South Dakota," his uncle said.

"Plans to hunt an old rail line near a place called Moreloft, I think he said. Said it's a great place. Good cover and stuff. Said after the opener it's never used if you get there early," LT said. "We'd stay at a motel in Moreloft. He's paying for the gas."

"What else did he say?"

"Said he's leaving that Monday morning at eight, whether I'm going or not," LT said. "You know I like pheasant hunting."

"I know you do son. Your dad and I did, too. This Walker guy, he know I'm your uncle?"

"I don't know. Didn't say anything."

His uncle remained silent for nearly a minute.

"If something sounds too good to be true, then it probably is. You've heard that before, I bet," Bob Thompson said. "Here's the problem with Terry Walker. He's a murderer. Killed a girl some twenty, maybe thirty, years ago. Confessed and everything. Case was dismissed on a technicality. People have been shunning him ever since. He'll never find anybody who knows his story to go with him. You shouldn't either. Make sense?"

"I guess so."

"You can see why your mother wouldn't want you to go, right?"

LT didn't reply.

His uncle said, "Tell you what. I've got a few days off next week. You and I can go hunting. Okay with you?"

"Great. Give me the dates. I'll clear it at work."

o0o

LT called the phone number on Walker's business card.

"Mr. Walker, this is LT. Just wanted to let you know I can't get off work to go hunting."

"Doesn't surprise me, kid," Walker said. "If you change your mind, I'll be across from the Big Sky ready to go at eight Monday morning. The nineteenth. On the dot."

o0o

Deputy Thompson called his nephew back about an hour later.

"One thing I'd like you to do for me. If you talk to Walker, see if he's still going on that trip even if you can't go."

LT told him he already had.

"Told him I wasn't able to go because of my work schedule. Walker said if I change my mind he's leaving from the Big Sky at eight in the morning on the day I said."

"OK. Good. I'll call you about our own little hunting trip. We can set a date."

CHAPTER 30

FRIDAY OCTOBER 9

The call from LT had gotten Bob Thompson thinking more and more about the Whitedeer murder case. Since he first heard about it, it had been on his mind every night and during quiet times when he was on routine patrol.

He thought Walker's trip to South Dakota was something he should share with Stephenson. When Stephenson picked up the phone, he told him what he had found out.

"Ben, just heard something interesting. Terry Walker's going pheasant hunting in a week or so. Supposedly by himself. Tried to recruit a few more to go along, but everybody begged off. Almost had my nephew going."

"Where's he going?" Stephenson said. "Any idea?"

"Out by Moreloft, South Dakota. Looked it up. It's in Clyde County. Northeast of Pierre. Maybe sixty miles or so, I think."

"When's he leaving?" Stephenson said.

"Supposed to take off from the Big Sky Café at eight Monday morning. That's the nineteenth. Coming back late Wednesday night. Told my nephew to be there at eight AM sharp if he changes his mind and wants to go along."

"Must be a six and a half to seven-hour drive to Moreloft," Stephenson said. "I've been out that way a couple times. He say exactly where he's hunting?"

"Abandoned rail road tracks near town. That's all I know."

"What are you thinking?"

"Well, if he's hunting alone, might be information we ought to share with our friends, don't you think?" Thompson said.

"If they do what we think they do, you could be right. Let me take care of it," Stephenson said. "Let me know if you hear anything else."

o0o

Stephenson called the Boyd Ranch from a pay phone at the Petrol truck stop. Didn't want his call traced if the shit hit the fan.

"Boyd Ranch," a woman said, answering the call.

"Manual Montoya there?"

"He's at the bunkhouse extension. Just a sec."

The line went dead for a few seconds, before an extension was picked up and someone said, "Montoya."

"Listen carefully," Stephenson said. He didn't identify himself. "Terry Walker's going pheasant hunting near Moreloft, South Dakota. Leaving from the Big Sky Café at eight in the morning Monday. October nineteen. Supposed to be making the trip all alone. Drives a blue Ford Mustang. Plans to hunt some abandoned rail road tracks near town. Figure he'll be in the field most of Tuesday afternoon. Thought you'd like to know."

"What the hell?" Montoya said. "Who is this?"

Stephenson paused before answering.

"You got the newspaper clippings about Walker in the mail recently. Right?" the caller said. "My gift to you."

He quietly hung up the phone. There was nothing else he could say. It was up to Montoya and his young friend now.

o0o

Montoya stood by the bunkhouse door watching Lleyellyn tossing a Frisbee for Mully to chase down and catch.

Teaching that dog new tricks, he thought. *Until the kid showed up, she'd never seen a Frisbee before in her life.*

Mully retrieved the Frisbee and brought it back to Lleyellyn. He saw Montoya out of the corner of his eye, and gave the Frisbee another toss, then turned to see what Montoya wanted.

"Dog never gets tired," Montoya said. "Can I talk to you for a sec? In my room."

Shay went inside, washed his hands, and went to Montoya's room at the end of the bunkhouse.

"Pull up a seat," Montoya said, from behind his desk.

Shay sat down and glanced around at the certificates on the wall. He was always amazed at the things Montoya had learned during his time in prison.

"Just got a call from the person who sent us those clippings about Walker. Male voice. Didn't recognize it," Montoya said. "Know what he said?"

Shay didn't reply, but shook his head as he stared at Montoya.

"Said Walker is leaving for a pheasant hunting trip Monday morning at eight sharp from the Big Sky. Driving to Moreloft, South Dakota. Hunting Tuesday along abandoned rail road tracks near town. Drives a Mustang, blue in color. Going alone."

"Why tell us? Think it's a setup of some kind?"

"I'm not sure exactly what it's all about," Montoya said. "He did send those clippings. Must think we had something to do with Montgomery's barefoot walk."

"Maybe he suspects me in Mal's death," Shay said. "Maybe both of us. And he must know what you did after Irene was raped."

Montoya didn't reply. He stood up from behind his desk and looked Lleyellyn squarely in the eye.

"I'm going to think about it for a while. You do the same. We'll talk about it again later."

Lleyellyn turned to leave. Montoya stopped him by touching him on the shoulder.

"One thing we know for sure. Walker is a murderer. So far he's gotten away scot free."

'Looks like somebody wants the score evened," Lleyellyn said.

CHAPTER 31

TUESDAY OCTOBER 13

It was Lleyellyn's turn to do the dishes. He was scrubbing baked on cheese from a casserole dish. Irene was in the other room talking on the phone. Montoya was still seated at the table nursing a cup of coffee.

"You been thinking about that hunting trip like I have?" Montoya said.

"I have," Lleyellyn said. "A lot."

"I think it's time Walker gets what's coming to him," Montoya said. "You can do what you want."

"Way I look at it, you helped me get justice for both my mom's murder and LaDonna Mae's attack. I agree Walker's gotten away with murder. There's no doubt about that."

"What are you saying?" Montoya said.

"I'm with you. You got a plan?"

"First thing, we go into town on the nineteenth. See if Walker actually shows up at eight and starts out."

"Follow him?"

"No need. We know where he's going. It's a six or seven-hour drive to Moreloft. We can leave later that day. South Dakota doesn't let you start shooting until noon. We'll locate his car near the railroad tracks. Go from there. Be back here Tuesday evening sometime. Maybe Wednesday morning. Easy."

"What'll we tell Irene? She'll wonder where we're going," Shay said.

"That's not a problem. She's going to an advocacy conference in Missoula. Leaves Friday. Be away several days. She's driving. Never mentioned it before. Saw it circled on her calendar. Just checked. Don't know when she put it on. Wasn't there the last time I looked."

CHAPTER 32

FRIDAY OCTOBER 16

Lleyellyn carried Irene's suitcase down the stairs from the second floor.

"Anything else to bring down?" he said.

"No that's fine. Can you put it in the back of my truck?"

He put Irene's suitcase in the bed of her blue Ram pickup and covered it with the tarp she had folded in the corner. When he was finished securing the tarp with bungee cords, Irene, Mully and Montoya came out of the house. Montoya was carrying a box containing bottles of water and snacks. Irene was carrying a garment bag and a jacket.

Montoya put the box he was carrying on the floor on the passenger side, and helped Irene hang the garment bag on a hook behind her seat. Irene folded her jacket, put it on the passenger seat, and turned to face them.

"I'm ready to go," she said. "Hope the movie crew's cleared out by the time I get back. And those damned porta potties. They're sure taking their good sweet time clearing them out."

"Livestock owner's just happy to let his herd eat up your grass. Don't know what's keeping Johnny on the Spot," Montoya said. "But don't you worry, we'll keep an eye on things. You have a safe trip. Enjoy the conference."

"Before I forget," Irene said, reaching behind the driver's seat and removing a gun case. "Better leave this here. Not sure if they'll appreciate guns on campus."

She handed the gun case to Montoya.

"I'll put it on the porch," he said. "Where's your twenty-two?"

"Put it behind the refrigerator yesterday. Forgot about the shotgun until now."

Irene climbed in and started the engine.

"Oh, and don't expect me back until a week from Sunday," she said. "They've got me down as a guest lecturer for a graduate seminar at the U."

She double checked, making sure her extra keys were in her purse.

"Then I'm going to spend a night with my aunt. Haven't seen her in ages," she said. "She's my aunt, but she's only six years older than I am."

"Have fun," Lleyellyn said.

Irene smiled at them and glanced at the dog.

"Mully! Keep an eye on things."

The dog wagged her tail and came over to the truck, put its front paws on the running board. Irene rubbed Mully's ears.

They waved back as Irene beeped the horn and moved forward. They watched her travel the length of the driveway and turn onto the paved roadway.

Montoya unzipped the gun case he had been handed.

"We can use this," he said. "Twelve gauge. Forgot she had one."

CHAPTER 33

MONDAY OCTOBER 19

They climbed into Lleyellyn's Ford Ranger at six fifteen Monday morning.

"If Walker is leaving the Big Sky at eight like the phone call said, we should have no trouble spotting him," Montoya said. "Want to make sure he takes off on his little hunting trip and he's alone."

Shay knew they weren't going to tail Walker to South Dakota when he left. Montoya had gone over the plan after Irene left for Missoula. Once they knew for certain Walker was on the way, they would get everything they needed to make the drive to Moreloft, locate Walker, and do what had to be done.

The Big Sky was busy with the breakfast crowd when they pulled into the parking lot at twenty minutes to eight.

A blue Ford Mustang GT was parked near the sidewalk in the motel parking lot across the street from the restaurant.

Lleyellyn headed for a table near a front window so they could keep an eye on the Mustang. Montoya and Shay had never seen Walker, but they had a general description of him, and they knew he drove a Mustang like the one parked out front.

One of the older waitresses Lleyellyn had seen before, came over to take their orders.

"Saw LaDonna Mae yesterday," she said by way of greeting. "Has the lunch shift today. Sure glad she's back. Brightens up the whole place."

"Know she's glad to be back. Been doing great," he said, giving her a smile. "Okay if we order now?"

"You bet," the waitress said. "You see the specials?"

"I'll have two eggs, bacon, hash browns and whole wheat toast," he said. "And a Mountain Dew."

Montoya ordered, and they both kept an eye on the blue car across the street, trying to figure out which customer was Walker. Several patrons fit his general description.

Their food arrived just as the wall clock showed eight. They looked around, waiting for Walker to make his move.

Two minutes later they saw someone leave the Men's room, stop at the cashier's counter, then go outside, cross the street, and stand next to the Mustang. They knew it was the man they were waiting for.

Walker looked back at the restaurant, lit a cigarette, climbed in, and drove off, heading for South Dakota, they knew.

"Okay, then," Montoya said. "It's on."

o0o

After they finished eating, Montoya directed him to a place north of the main business district. They pulled up in front of an old fashioned gas station. The gas pumps had been removed. Several older pick-ups were parked in the yard and a cab over tow-truck was parked near the front door. A rusted sign identified the place as *Gentry's Garage 24-Hour Towing*.

"Wait here," Montoya said. "Sal's bashful around people he doesn't know."

Montoya was gone for several minutes. Shay listened to the radio, scanning through the stations for something interesting. The weather report was just starting when Montoya came out carrying a tool box. He placed it in the trunk and went back inside. He was back a minute or two later carrying a gun case and several fishing rods. He placed them in the bed and got in.

"All set," he said. "Better get back to the ranch. Want the movie crew to be aware we're on the scene. Make sure they're getting ready to clear out for good."

Lleyellyn made a U-turn and they headed toward home.

"What's with the tool box and the fishing rods?" he said.

"Tackle box," Montoya said. "Anybody asks, we're going fishing," Montoya said. "Got us another shotgun, too. And some special ammo."

o0o

On the way to the ranch they overtook a semi with a trailer and a fork lift with the logo *Johnny on the Spot* neatly painted on the door of the cab. A van with a similar logo was following it.

"Looks like the portable toilet guys are right on schedule," Lleyellyn said.

"Hope they've started hauling out the livestock," Montoya said. "Nice to get them on their way before we take off after Walker."

He started slowing before he reached the ranch sign, *Boyd Ranch – Registered Herefords*, then made the right turn. They still had more than forty miles to go.

There was a cattle truck stopped at the stop sign, ready to head south with a load of longhorns. Another truck was following a few hundred yards down the road.

"Looks like they've started," Shay said. "How many head per truck you think?"

"Think they figure somewhere around thirty loads. Must be what?" Montoya said. "Probably less than twenty per. Those longhorns take up a heck of a lot more space than our usual Herefords do."

By the time they got to the ranch they'd seen fifteen or sixteen cattle trucks heading in the opposite direction.

They could see several cattle trucks in a line by the corral waiting to be loaded. They weren't wasting any time.

"I'm going over to the pens. Find out how close to being done they are," Montoya said. "You'd better wait around for *Johnny on the Spot*. Can't be too far back."

o0o

The wranglers finished with the cattle just after eleven. They took an early lunch in the mess tent, then began loading their horses and tack. Less than an hour later Montoya watched the last horse trailer disappear down the road.

When he started back to the house, Mully ran up to him and accompanied him the rest of the way. Shay was sitting on the porch polishing off a Mountain Dew.

"Porta potties will be loaded up and gone by three, three thirty, the guy said."

"What about the tents?" Montoya said.

"I called the tent guy little while ago. Promises to have his crew out here by ten tomorrow. Said they have to wait until the dew's gone. Told me they'd have their tents packed up and gone by mid-afternoon. Guaranteed. Need to set up them somewhere tomorrow. Didn't say where."

o0o

The semi loaded with portable toilets pulled up next to the house at a quarter to three. The driver got out of the cab, walked around the front of the truck and said, "Got done a little early. Crew's cleaning up a little spill. They'll be done in a few minutes."

As he turned to get back in the truck, the van with his helpers pulled in behind him. The truck driver motioned for them to get going and they did.

"Lleyellyn, think we'd better check things over. Take the Jeep. Check to make sure everything's gone from the cattle pens and parking lot. Check out the rest of the area. See what's left besides the tents and the remains of the spill the guy was talking about."

Lleyellyn stood up and started for the shed to get the Jeep, Mully at his side.

"I'll check the shot guns," Montoya said, as Shay started walking away.

.

oOo

"Only thing left are the two big tents and a dumpster full of trash. They rolled up the fencing they used for the cattle pen. It's gone," Lleyellyn said. "Whatever spill they had with the toilets was cleaned up pretty good. Saw a spot where they skimmed off and inch or two of dirt and spread some straw. Looked okay to me. Didn't see any of that blue stuff. Didn't smell any, either."

"Looks like we're good. Checked the guns. Cleaned them. Ready as we'll ever be. Anything you need to do?"

Lleyellyn shook his head no.

"What say we rest a little then head to town. Grab a bite to eat, then we can go hunting."

"How about Mully?"

"Dog's been left alone before. She'll be fine," Montoya said. "We won't be gone that long."

oOo

By the time they got to town it was after ten thirty.

Lleyellyn filled the tank at the Petro station, and then they drove down the frontage road to Pizza Hut for dinner. Luckily it was open to midnight. They were on the road east ten minutes before closing.

The headlight beams illuminated the highway ahead of them. Traffic was light. Lleyellyn set the cruise for seventy-nine.

He shot a sideways glance at Montoya, who seemed to be lost in thought. Shay couldn't get it out of his mind that they were on their way to shoot somebody. He wondered if Montoya had the same thoughts.

Finally Montoya broke the silence.

"You don't have to be involved in this, you know."

Lleyellyn wasn't sure just why Montoya was bringing this up now. It was all settled.

"You helped me track down Mal. And that asshole Montgomery. I'm in."

"There is a difference here. We went after Mal because he killed your mother. The cops weren't getting anywhere. Montgomery, same thing. Making him walk back was like what LaDonna Mae had to go through. Him getting trampled wasn't our doing. It just happened," Montoya said. "Pamela Whitedeer. We know Walker admitted killing her. But that was years ago. I didn't know her. You didn't either."

They were silent for a few minutes. Lleyellyn thought of saying something, but didn't. They were in this together. Just like before.

"What I know is that Whitedeer was one of Irene's first clients. She had no family. Walker admitted he killed her. Multiple stab wounds. One thing you can say, so far he's gotten away with murder because a cop screwed up. Just doesn't seem right, does it?"

Ross A. Phelps

"I can see that," Lleyellyn said. "And I agree." Then he paused, and added, "Who do you think sent us the newspaper clippings?"

"I've been thinking about that. Somebody who wants to see Walker gets what he deserves," Montoya said. "Somebody who must think we had something to do with Montgomery.

Maybe looked back in the records and found out what I did after Irene was attacked. Could even have a suspicion about that deal with your stepfather. Mal what's his name?"

"Like who?"

"Newspaper reporter, maybe. Maybe law enforcement."

Neither of them said a word for several miles.

"No matter who might suspect something, we have to make sure that we cover our tracks. Think we've done a good job of that so far," Montoya said. "Nothing ties us to nothing. Just have to make sure we keep it that way."

Two Shots Quick

CHAPTER 34

TUESDAY OCTOBER 20

As they approached Hammond, Montoya asked Lleyellyn if he'd like some relief.

"Only fair if I do some of the driving."

They changed places, then continued on, each lost in their own private thoughts.

Finally, Shay broke the silence.

"Montana have the death penalty?" he said.

"You wondering if Walker would have been executed if he'd been found guilty?" Montoya said. "He confessed to first degree murder. Then to burning her car to destroy evidence. He probably would have received the death penalty. Must've raped her. Death by lethal injection seems almost like a certainty in his case."

Lleyellyn seemed to mull this over.

"You are probably right," Lleyellyn said. "They ever give the death penalty to a white man killing an Indian?"

"Point taken," Montoya said. "Maybe, Maybe not."

"And I was thinking whether or not the death penalty might apply to us," Lleyellyn said. "You know. Worse case scenario."

"Just so you know, in case you're wondering, South Dakota has the death penalty, too," Montoya said. "From my time at Granite City I know it has been used only three times since the mid-seventies. Same method. Injection."

"Guess that means we'd better not get caught in South Dakota, right?"

Montoya glanced over at Shay.

"We won't, if we do it right."

o0o

I was just thinking," Lleyellyn said. "How'd you know hunting doesn't start 'til noon. Seems kinda late."

"Something else I learned during my time at Granite City. We used to print the hunting regulation booklets for the DNR," Montoya said. "We always thought the noon start was to let hunters recover from the hangovers they had from the night before."

o0o

They stopped to fill the tank at Sturgis, used the facilities, bought beef sticks and bottled water.

"Want to drive some more?" Montoya said.

Lleyellyn got behind the wheel. He followed Montoya's directions, taking SD 34 east until it joined US 14. It was nearing seven thirty when they pulled into Moreloft. Population 256 according to the sign. *The Pride of Clyde County. We do things right.*

They drove the main street and saw a sign that identified the Prairie Wind Motel.

"Bet this is the only motel, don't you think?" Shay said.

"Must be. Circle around the back. See if there's a Mustang GT around."

They spotted it in front of a room several doors down from the office.

"We've got plenty of time. Let's scout around, find the old rail line he's supposed to hunt," Montoya said.

They made the right guess, figuring the railroad had run east-west. The abandoned roadbed was a few minutes south of town.

They drove around the area and located side roads and places where the old rail line crossed other roadways in both directions. They guessed Walker would probably start hunting at the crossing nearest to town.

They drove back to Moreloft and checked the motel.

There was no Mustang, but Lleyellyn reversed direction, went down the main drag. He slowed at the intersection for a cross street, and saw cars parked diagonally along a stretch of sidewalk in front a café a half block to the west. He turned right and drove slowly past the Squeeze Inn. Parked near the entrance was a blue Mustang GT with Montana plates.

"You see that game warden's vehicle parked along there?" Lleyellyn said.

"I did. Not a problem. Must be grabbing a bite," Montoya said. "We could use some breakfast, but I think we should get the job done and get out of Dodge. Hate to have someone recognize us or your truck later."

Lleyellyn circled the block and parked a half dozen spaces beyond the Mustang.

"When he leaves, we'll see which way he goes. Nice to know exactly where he plans to start hunting," Montoya said. "It's still almost two hours before he can to start shooting."

o0o

They waited for Walker to finish eating his breakfast.

"Taking his damned time," Montoya said. "Doesn't seem to be in any hurry."

A few minutes later, someone came out of the café and got into the Mustang. They recognized Walker from the day before. The Mustang backed up, and headed down the street. They heard the rumble of the big V-8 as the car passed behind them. It was eleven sixteen.

It turned south onto the highway and then stopped to fill up at a Conoco station on the edge of town.

They circled the block and pulled over on a side street so they could see the Mustang at the gas pump. They watched as Walker left the gas station and continued south.

"I'll let him get a good lead," Lleyellyn said.

It was starting to get warmer. Shay waited until Walker was several blocks ahead. They could see the brake lights of the GT come on when it slowed at an intersection two or three hundred yards ahead.

The crossing for the abandoned railroad was seven miles south of town. When they bumped over the remnants of the tracks, they saw the GT on the side of the road. Walker was standing near the back of his car with the trunk open. He didn't look up as they passed.

"Go up here a little ways to the next road," Montoya said, pointing ahead. "We need to know what way he's going to go."

"Bet he'll start going west so he'll be going into the wind," Lleyellyn said.

Lleyellyn made a J-turn at a township road, and started back toward Moreloft. He slowed as they passed the Mustang, then crossed the tracks. The blaze orange of Walker's hunting jacket was a hundred yards off to the east.

"Fooled both of us," Montoya said. "Thought he'd go the other way."

"It's five after twelve," Lleyellyn said. "Must've started exactly at noon."

He continued driving north in the direction of Moreloft, then he took a right at the first cross road, one they had scouted earlier.

"We know there's a section line road a mile ahead," Montoya said.

Shay turned right at the section line road and proceeded south. They crossed the abandoned tracks and looked to the west to see if Walker was in sight. There was a tiny speck of orange in the far distance.

"Hasn't got very far," Montoya said. "But that's gotta be him. Coming this way."

"Can't park here," Lleyellyn said. "You see that old school building back there a ways?"

"Should work."

Shay turned around and drove back to where they had seen an old one room school building. The roof was sagging and the school yard was full of tall weeds.

"I'll park in back," he said.

He pulled around to the back of the building, trying to park out of sight, hidden from the road.

"They got out and put on camo colored jackets.

"We'll cut across that field," Montoya said, nodding to a corn field across the road. Can't be seen by no game warden. Could get stopped for no hunting license and no blaze orange. Anyone stop, just stay hidden in the corn until it's clear."

They each put a half dozen shot gun shells in their pockets, crossed the road carrying their cased shotguns, and stepped into the cover of the rows of corn which towered over their heads.

Following Montoya's instructions, they zipped open their gun cases and removed the shotguns.

"We'll leave the cases here," Montoya said. "We're directly opposite the school building, three rows in. Pick 'em up on the way back."

Montoya handed Lleyellyn the newer looking shotgun, a Winchester Model 1200, and kept the older one, a Model 12 Winchester, for himself.

Montoya showed Lleyellyn how to rack a shell in the chamber.

"Both these guns work alike," Montoya said. "Both very reliable. Keep the safety on 'til we get close," Montoya said. "Ready?"

Lleyellyn nodded. They moved off diagonally, stepping through the rows of corn at an angle heading toward the abandoned tracks.

o0o

Terry Walker sat in the Mustang with the windows down, trying to take advantage of the slight breeze in the bright midday sun.

In the far distance he heard the approaching distinctive cries of migrating Sandhill Cranes. Several large V-shaped flocks, high in the sky, barely visible in the bright blue background, were heading south, sounding for all the world like a grammar school yard full of screaming kids at recess.

He had seen only one vehicle pass by, a little red pick-up, which never slowed down. He was the only one there. He knew no one else would be hunting this stretch of the old rail line this afternoon. It was always first come, first serve.

He heard the faint wail of the noon time siren in Moreloft.

Satisfied that everything was ready, he locked the door, loaded his twelve gauge, and started off down the old railroad grade, now a long strip of prime hunting land.

Lush weeds had grown up along the abandoned right of way. On his left was a flat field of corn stubble. There was the remnant of a harvested soybean crop on the opposite side.

There has to be pheasants here, he thought. *There's no other place for them to hide.*

Almost immediately he saw two hens and a rooster dart across the old rail road bed eighty to a hundred yards ahead.

He moved at a slow steady pace, his Remington Wingmaster held at port arms, one finger on the safety. The wind was at his back.

As he got closer to where he had seen the birds cross, he moved slower, alert for movement.

Times like this, I could use a dog.

Suddenly the quiet was shattered by the racket made by a pheasant taking flight. He had his gun up, and the safety off, before he realized it was a hen. But then, seconds later, another bird arose making even more of an uproar. It gave the unmistakable call of a rooster. He pointed his gun at the bird, led it a few degrees, pulled the trigger, and watched as the bird's wings continued flapping several times, then stopped as the pheasant fell to the ground.

The rooster was laying a few feet to the side of the gravel rail bed in short grass. He retrieved it, shoved it into the game pouch in the back of his jacket, reloaded, and resumed his hunt.

Haven't lost the touch. I'll get my limit soon.

The road bed passed over a small stream, a mere trickle this time of year. A mallard flew up from the far bank, and winged off to the north. The stubble field ended at the waterway. There was a field of standing corn on the far side of the stream that hadn't been harvested. He could see the top half of a John Deere combine parked across the field near the road. Harvesting would be starting soon.

Whatever had been planted on the other side of the railroad bed had already been harvested, and the field plowed.

Ready for spring. Maybe winter wheat, he thought.

He flushed two more cocks that flew up and into the corn field. They were well out of range for a decent shot.

A good bird dog would really help here, he thought. *Maybe a Lab, or better yet, a German Shorthair.*

Two Shots Quick

He saw a cock pheasant stick its colorful head out from the weeds in front of him, then turn and move back into cover. He sped up, before veering off the roadbed, and began moving through thigh-high weeds. Suddenly the bird he was after burst into flight off to his left.

He turned, pointed and fired. A feather drifted to the ground, but the bird never wavered as it flew in a bee line over the corn field, gliding out of sight between rows of corn fifty yards away.

If they make it to the corn, they've made it.

He walked slowly, keeping alert, hoping he could flush a bird and get a decent shot at close range before it could get away to the safety of the standing corn.

Out of range ahead of him, another hen flew up and high tailed it to the safety of the cornfield.

Plenty of birds in here.

As he moved along, he could see he was approaching a swampy corner of the field. After that, it looked like more open ground. He knew he'd have better success along the railroad right of way when he got there. The only ground cover would be along the right of way of the old rail road bed itself.

There was a flash of movement off to his left. A rooster was flying from the side of the embankment toward the row of corn paralleling the rail line. Instinctively he fired, the bird dropped, obviously winged, and started running, disappearing between the rows.

"Shit!" he said in frustration. *I'll never find it. But I better look. Probably didn't get very far. Know I hit him.*

He zigged down the embankment and across the ditch that ran along side, then pushed aside some standing corn and stepped between the rows which towered several feet over his head. He could see nothing that looked like a dead pheasant between the first two rows. He moved to the next row, then the next. There it was, lying on its side thirty or forty feet to his left in the space between two rows of corn.

He retrieved the bird, put it in his game pouch with the one he had shot earlier, and started back through the rows the way he had come.

As he turned, he caught movement down between the rows. A man wearing camo was coming towards him, holding a shot gun. It was pointed at him.

"You Terry Walker?" the man said.

He didn't answer, not sure what was going on.

"Drop your gun!"

As the man moved a few steps closer, he saw another person step into the space between the rows behind the first man.

"I said, drop your gun!" the man said, jerking the barrel of his gun up an inch or two.

"What the fuck?" he said.

The two men were standing side by side, crowded between parallel rows of corn. Both had their guns trained on him.

"Drop it! Now!"

He did as he was told.

"Show us some identification," the first man said.

"Hey, I just followed a bird in here. I'm not hunting your land," Walker said. "Didn't mean to be trespassing, if that is what this is about. I've been hunting the tracks."

They didn't say anything, but the second man, much younger, held out his hand.

He removed his wallet, took out his hunting license and handed it to him.

"Terrence Spencer Walker. That's you, right?"

"Must be obvious. It's my name on the damned license."

"Driver's license," the younger man said, extending his left hand.

He fished the license out of his wallet, and handed it over. First the younger man, then the other one, looked at it.

"Nice picture," the younger man said, "What's your date of birth?"

"He told them his birthdate."

"It's him all right."

Nobody said anything for at least a minute. Finally he could stand it no longer.

"Now, what?" he said.

"You can go now. Enjoy your hunt," the older man said. "Better pick up your gun."

He wasn't sure if he was on the up and up, but took a step forward, picked up his shotgun by the barrel, then turned and slipped through the rows of corn that separated him from the old rail line, and started up the embankment.

Just before he reached the level roadbed, he heard one of them say, "One more thing."

He turned to see what they wanted.

Two shot gun blasts came at once. One hit him in the face, the other in the chest. He was dead before he fell to the ground.

His two assailants moved to him. The older one checked to make sure there was no pulse.

Without a word, they dragged the body to the side of the embankment and left it in the weeds.

o0o

They walked back through the corn field, and found the gun cases where they'd left them. Before stepping out of the corn field they made sure no vehicles were coming from either direction. They stowed the shot guns behind the seat and covered them with their jackets.

"Have to get rid of the shells," Montoya said. "We'll toss them in the weeds along the road."

Lleyellyn backed out from behind the old school building. He turned left when they reached the road.

"Plan to keep going south for a few miles, then I'll get back on the highway."

"Sounds good," Montoya said. "Keep her slow and steady. We're just a couple fishermen heading toward Lake Oahe."

Traffic all the way to Pierre was sparse. They didn't see a patrol car, a game warden, or anyone else that looked official.

"Think we should stop and eat or something?" Lleyellyn said.

"Better keep going. Some of those truck stops have video surveillance. Hate to have them find out we were here when they find the body," Montoya said. "Let's wait until we find a Mom and Pop place with no close circuit cameras."

Nearly four hours later at Belle Fourche they turned off the road and parked in a row of cars outside a place with a big sign on the roof. It said *EATS*, in gigantic red letters with the smaller words *Breakfast - Lunch - Dinner - All Day - Anytime* underneath.

Biscuits and Gravy was the special. They both ordered it. Montoya had coffee. Shay had his usual, Mountain Dew. They were back in the car in twenty minutes, this time with Montoya behind the wheel.

Lleyellyn was surprised how little the shooting was bothering him. He was thinking more about who had mailed the newspaper clippings.

"You still think it was some law man sent us those clippings?" he said.

"Seems kind of logical, doesn't it?"

Lleyellyn didn't respond at first. Something was bothering him. He wasn't quite able to put his finger on it. He thought about it for a while.

"You know, there's one person who knows more about what we've been doing than anyone else," he said. "Irene."

"What's your thinking?"

"First, she knows you're the one assaulted the guy who raped her," Lleyellyn said. "Second, she knows we both went to Minnesota and got back right after Mal was dead. Then, she knows we were upset about LaDonna Mae getting attacked. Knows we had plenty of opportunity to go after Montgomery. Probably figured out we found the proof."

Montoya looked at him and nodded in concurrence.

"She did say Pamela Whitedeer was one of her early clients. A favorite in fact. She felt real bad when her confessed killer went free," Montoya said. "Another thing, doesn't it seem funny Irene had to leave for that meeting in Missoula? She never said anything about it until two or three days ago. Never saw it on the calendar until then, either. Probably wanted to be gone so we would be free to do whatever."

Lleyellyn looked at Montoya, but didn't reply.

"She said she wanted to go after Walker herself, remember," Montoya said.

Lleyellyn nodded before speaking.

"Irene," he said. "She's something else, isn't she?"

"Sure is," Montoya said. "Found that out a long time ago. And she hired me when I got released from prison. Picked you up hitch hiking. Right? Offered you a job."

"Do we tell her what we know?"

"No, we do not," Montoya said. "That's like admitting murder. She'll find out Walker's dead soon enough. Won't anybody be able to prove we did it if we keep our lips sealed.

And remember, we say nothing. To Irene. Or anybody else. Ever."

He looked at Lleyellyn. His eyes intent.

"Agreed?"

"Agreed."

o0o

They drove several miles before either of them spoke.

"If you haven't already, be sure and get rid of those news clippings about Walker," Montoya said. "I tossed mine. Wouldn't want anybody to come across them and wonder why we were interested in a thirty-year-old murder."

o0o

He'd been up since six. Pheasant season was the busiest time of year in the game warden business, at least in South Dakota.

It had been a routine day. Hadn't found any hunters in the field before the noon start. Talked to ten or twelve hunting parties, checked licenses, examined guns and answered some questions. Issued one citation for inadequate blaze orange clothing. Guy was wearing full camo and a matching stocking cap with only a blaze orange top-knot.

He had lunch at the Squeeze Inn in Moreloft, then continued patrolling in the surrounding area.

He crossed the old railroad line on the State Highway, and saw a single car parked on the side of the road. He noted Montana plates. He could just make out an orange speck a half mile or so down the line.

Two Shots Quick

A single hunter, he thought. *Don't see a dog. Hunting pheasants the hard way.*

About three o'clock he had pulled up behind a slow moving pick-up with an elderly gent sitting in an easy chair in the back. He watched as the gentleman shot at several doves sitting on the telephone wires. He missed two or three times, but did manage to shatter a glass insulator on one of the poles.

He had pulled the truck over. An older woman was driving. Turned out to be the wife. The old codger explained that he just couldn't walk the corn fields any more. This was the only way he could get out hunting.

"Hey, they're a moving target," he explained. "But I have to admit, I'm the one doing the moving."

There was an array of options from a law enforcement point of view. Hunting from a motor vehicle. Uncased firearm in a motor vehicle. Criminal damage to property.

The hunter did have a valid hunting license. His age was eighty-five.

He let him go without a citation after telling them that what they were doing was illegal and could result in the loss not only of the firearm, but the truck as well. He hoped he wouldn't see them back dove hunting from the back of a pick-up any time soon.

Just before five he was patrolling the same stretch of State Highway again and approached the abandoned railroad right of way from the South. The same Montana vehicle was still parked where he had seen it before.

He pulled in behind the vehicle and looked inside. An empty canvas gun case was sitting on the passenger seat with a stainless steel Thermos next to it.

He called dispatch and found no wants for the car. Dispatch gave him the driver's name and said there had been no calls to 911 from or about Terrence Spencer Walker.

The car had been parked in one place for a lot more time than it would take to hunt the strip of abandoned railroad from this road to the next and back.

He got out of his SUV and scanned down the road bed with his binoculars. The roadway ran straight as an arrow. No one was in sight. He decided to investigate.

The warden drove onto the old rail bed past the *No Motorized Vehicles* sign and slowly moved east, visually scanning the embankments and ditches on both sides as he crept along.

He found Walker's body off to his left next to a field of corn that a combine hadn't gotten to.

His superficial examination of the body revealed two massive wounds. From past experience, he recognized shot gun damage to both the head and chest. Clearly there had been two shots. Either could have killed him.

He knew immediately Walker was dead without checking for a pulse. Insects were feeding on the exposed flesh.

He removed a billfold from a pocket near the chest wound. There were two pellets imbedded in the leather.

Looks like number twos, or maybe threes, he thought.

The driver's license verified the decedent's identity.

The dispatcher recognized his voice.

"Think I've found Walker. He's dead. Looks like two shot gun blasts."

"Hunting accident?" he was asked.

"Looks like two fatal shots," the warden said "Not too sure it was an accident."

He told dispatch where he was and waited a half hour for a sheriff's deputy to show up, and another twenty minutes for the coroner to arrive. An ambulance didn't get there to remove the body until a little before seven.

o0o

Two Shots Quick

They had been tossing the shot gun shells into the weeds along the way as they drove along.

"They were reloads," Montoya said. "Lead shot. Illegal on public land or for waterfowl. Don't know if you can buy new magnum shells with number two lead shot anywhere anymore. Shot we used was a mixture of two and threes. Most new ones all use steel bee bees. Doubt if they manufacture shells with different sized pellets."

They changed drivers one more time. While they were heading for Miles City, Montoya cleaned the barrels of both shotguns.

"Making sure there's no residue from the lead shot," he said. "Not going to say we used either gun. Returning them in same condition as we got 'em. Gentry won't ask any questions. Irene won't know we used her gun."

When they got to Gentry's, Lleyellyn stayed in the truck while Montoya made two trips returning the fishing gear and the shot gun.

"What say we stop at the Big Sky. Grab a bite," Montoya said.

Lleyellyn didn't reply, he just turned the truck around and headed to the restaurant.

"Anybody asks, we just came to town to pick up a few supplies," Montoya said.

o0o

The deputy sheriff's search of the crime scene turned up virtually nothing.

There were no empty shotgun shells nearby. He talked to several people who farmed in the area. No one had seen any vehicles in the area, except for Walker's. The game warden wasn't sure, but he didn't remember seeing anyone else in the vicinity during his patrols.

oOo

"Miles City Police department," the receptionist said. "We aim to serve."

"Can I speak to the duty officer," the caller said.

Someone picked up almost immediately.

"Sergeant Dipippo, Can I help you? I'm the duty officer."

"Evening sergeant, My name's Jack Bechtel. Chief deputy. Calling from Moreloft, South Dakota. Clyde County."

"Pheasant hunting's pretty good this year, I hear," Dipippo said.

"Yea. Well, one of your citizens was hunting here today and got himself killed. He was pheasant hunting. Took two shots. Died almost instantly. Name's Terrence Spencer Walker,"

Dipippo didn't reply immediately. When he finally spoke he said, "He's one of ours, alright. Suppose you want me to notify the next of kin, am I right?

"Yes sir, afraid so. I'll fax you the incident report."

"I'll go visit his parents soon as I receive it," Dipippo said. "You know the story on this Walker guy?"

"No criminal record, I know that from checking. That's about it."

"Quite a few years back he stabbed a woman to death. Burned her car. Confessed. Murder charges and everything else were dismissed on a technicality. Fact is, the rookie investigator took a full statement but forgot a Miranda warning," Dipippo said.

"That must be the case they talk about during our continuing education required training. Don't remember the perp's name, or where it happened. I'll be damned."

"This seem like a hunting accident to you?" Dipippo said.

"No comment. My boss'll be interested in knowing our vic was a confessed murderer," Bechtel said. "Not sure how we'll approach the investigation." After a pause, he continued with a question. "You're a pheasant hunter, you said. Ever hear of using a mixture of big pellets like twos and threes pheasant hunting?"

Dipippo didn't reply.

"I'll leave you with that thought," Bechtel said. "Putting our report in the fax machine right now."

o0o

Walker's parents took the news of their son's death stoically. Dipippo hated to be the bearer of bad news, but it was part of his job.

When he got back to the office he placed a call to the news editor at the Miles City Star.

"Thought you might be interested," he said to the editor without identifying himself, although he was pretty sure his voice was recognized. "Terry Walker was shot and killed while pheasant hunting this afternoon near Moreloft, South Dakota. Don't have many details. The Sheriff's Office out there in Clyde County is handling the investigation. You can check with them."

The news editor asked a couple of questions.

"Yes, I can confirm that the next of kin here in town have been notified," Dipippo said.

The man from the newspaper asked another question.

"Hell, I don't know what kind of name Moreloft is," Dipippo said. "Sounds like a perfect place to manufacture pitching wedges, though, don't you think?"

CHAPTER 35

WEDNESDAY OCTOBER 21

The next day the Capital Journal, the Pierre, S. D. newspaper, reported that a pheasant hunter had been shot and had died from his injuries near Moreloft. If anybody thought about it, they would have concluded the death was a hunting accident.

The coroner wrote 'death by shooting' on the death certificate, and then added in parentheses 'presumed hunting accident.'

There was an autopsy. The medical examiner confirmed the cause of death. His report noted that two different size shot were found in the massive wounds to the head and to the chest, both number two number size three shot. He concluded that either wound would have been fatal, and that the shells used in each instance were similar.

o0o

When the game warden read the autopsy report he asked himself, *Who the hell uses that size shot to hunt pheasants?"*

Two Shots Quick

CHAPTER 36

THURSDAY OCTOBER 22

The Moreloft Leader Tribune was a local weekly paper. The Thursday edition contained the following article, which appeared on page three under an article about the repainting of the town's seventy-six-year-old water tower.

PHEASANT HUNTER SHOT

By Cyndee Fosgrove, freelance reporter

(Moreloft) The body of Terrence Walker, a resident of Miles City, Montana, was found along the abandoned rail road tracks south of town between the State Highway and the Hutchins School Road.

This is the first hunting fatality this season.

The sheriff's office reminds all hunters to think SAFETY FIRST when hunting.

Hunting licenses are available at Reese's Feed and Hardware and the Co-op and Conoco gas stations.

Two Shots Quick

CHAPTER 37

FRIDAY OCTOBER 23

"Hear about Walker?" another deputy said when Thompson reported for work at the beginning of his sift.

Thompson gave the deputy a blank stare and shrugged.

"Bastard went and got himself shot. Hunting in SoDak. Hit twice. Killed instantly."

'There's a guy won't be missed," Thompson said.

"You can say that again. A copy of the faxed report from South Dakota is on the bulletin board."

Thompson read the report.

The report was short on details. So far the authorities weren't looking for any suspects. He thought that was a plus.

The office was empty. He made a copy of the report on the Xerox machine, then he called Benedict Stephenson.

Stephenson picked up the phone and identified himself.

"It's Bob," Thompson said. "Mind if I stop by? Got some information you might be interested in."

"I'll be here," Stephenson said. "You working your shift now?"

"Correct. It'll just take a minute."

o0o

Walker's obituary appeared on page four of the second section of the next day's Miles City Star.

Two Shots Quick

WALKER, Terrence S. ("Terry")

Terrence Walker, 53, a resident of Miles City, was killed in a hunting accident near Moreloft, South Dakota yesterday.

Walker, the son of Conrad and Harriet Walker, was preceded in death by an unnamed sister who died at eight days of age, and his grandparents.

A graduate of Miles City High School, Miles College, and a former student at the University of Montana, Walker was employed in the family land management business.

Funeral arrangements have not been announced and will be private.

o0o

On page one of the same issue of the Star was a short news article.

CONFESSED MURDERER SHOT TO DEATH

Moreloft, South Dakota (AP) Terrence Spencer Walker of Miles City was found shot to death while hunting in west central South Dakota yesterday, according to the Clyde County Sheriff's office in Moreloft. An investigation into the shooting continues.

Walker, 53, was the confessed murderer of Pamela Whitedeer. Charges were dismissed when it was discovered that the investigating officer failed to advise the confessed killer of his so-called Miranda rights.

CHAPTER 38

SUNDAY OCTOBER 25

Montoya had the grill fired up. They were expecting Irene back from the Missoula conference at any minute. She had called from a gas station in Forsyth.

Mully's ears perked up and her tail started wagging. Irene's blue Ram pickup made the turn into the drive way. She pulled up next to the house.

Mully put her front paws on her legs. Irene gave the dog's ears a good rub and walked over to Montoya.

"Trip's getting longer every year," she said. "Looks like I'm in time for dinner."

Montoya gave her a brief abrazo.

"Kid's inside making a salad," he said.

Lleyellyn came out the back door and hugged Irene.

"Seems like you've been gone a lot more than a week," he said. "How was the meeting?"

"It was a good one," Irene said. "Tell you more about it at dinner. Can you help me with my bag?"

He removed Irene's suitcase from the bed of the truck and followed her inside. He took it up stairs to her room and put it on her bed. He passed Irene on the way down the stairs.

"I'll just freshen up a little," she said. "See you gents on the front porch. Get some drinks. I'll be down in a jiff."

Lleyellyn poured iced teas for Irene and Montoya and grabbed a Mountain Dew for himself. He put them on the rail of the porch and told Montoya Irene was coming down to join them.

When they were all together, Irene was the first to speak.

"I can see the portable toilets are gone," she said. "How about those tents?"

"Crew's coming tomorrow," Montoya said. "Delayed because of the shower we had. Guess they didn't need 'em anywhere else. Should be gone by three or so, they said."

Irene took a sip of her beverage.

"Moved the cattle out Sunday. Last load left about four," Montoya said. "Lleyellyn, how many truck loads we figure?"

"Lots. Lost count. Know they can only carry fifty thousand pounds per trailer. Twenty-five tons. Can't be more than twenty head per load, we're guessing. Max. Mr. Montoya said longhorns take up more space. So there's that. Must've been twenty, twenty-five loads, if you can believe that."

Irene smiled at them.

"Looks like everything's under control. You must have been busy keeping an eye on things."

Mully went from person to person begging for a treat. Finally Lleyellyn went inside and returned with the dog's chew toy. It seemed to occupy the dog while they continued their conversation.

"Tell us about your meeting," Montoya said.

"You know, I've been going to these meetings, they call them institutes, for twenty-three years. Almost didn't go this time. Decided at the last minute. But you know what, think I enjoyed this one more than most of the others."

They waited for her to tell them why.

"They had me give a presentation at the banquet Tuesday evening. Seemed to be pretty well received. Most of it was shown on Missoula public TV the next day," Irene said.

She took a sip of iced tea and smiled at them.

"There's a printed program talks about it. I'll put it in the kitchen," she said. "Then they gave me an award. Program tells about that, too."

"Can't you tell us more now?" Lleyellyn said.

"Hey, I'm starving," she said. "You gonna put the meat on the grill or what," she added standing up and giving Montoya another smile.

oOo

Irene said it was the best meal she'd had since she left. Rather than talk about herself, she turned the conversation to other topics.

"Hon, how's LaDonna Mae coming along?" she said, directing her question at Lleyellyn.

"Much better. She's back at work. Full time, too," Lleyellyn said. "And guess what, she's thinking of enrolling at Miles College in the spring."

"Good for her," she said, before turning to her foreman.

"Mr. Montoya, when they get those tents out of here tomorrow, what's left on your agenda?"

"Plan to double check everything. See if the movie company left anything behind or did something we don't know about. Better have Lleyellyn check the fences again. Want to grease the windmill and the pump. Routine stuff, really," Montoya said. "Anything you have in mind?"

"Not really. Lleyellyn can ride fence, he's done it before. Then maybe you can show him what has to be done to maintain the windmill."

"Good idea. Weather man says sunny and clear," Montoya said. "Okay with you?" he added, looking at Shay.

"Remember what LaDonna Mae said at the picnic? There was a longhorn steer wandering around by the windmill," Lleyellyn said. "Big son of a gun. Wonder if it's still loose."

"Their foreman told me every head was accounted for. Only one missing is the one had to be put down. Critter you saw out there must've rejoined the herd," Montoya said. "We won't have to go looking for it."

Irene waited to see if Montoya had more to add. When he didn't, she said, "Why don't you go into town, hon. See LaDonna Mae. Take her to a show or something. You can use a break. I'm sure she'll be happy to see you."

o0o

Lleyellyn called LaDonna Mae and talked to her brother.

"She's not here," Jimmy said. "Went into town. Going to a baby shower for one of the waitresses at the Big Sky. Don't expect her back until after ten."

CHAPTER 39

MONDAY OCTOBER 26

Chief Deputy Jack Bechtel had completed filling the gas tank in his unmarked squad car and was returning to his office when he spotted the game warden's tan SUV parked diagonally in front of the Squeeze Inn. He swung a U and parked next to the game warden's car.

The warden was in a booth reading a newspaper. He sat down across from him.

"Morning," he said. "Mind if I join you for a minute?"

The game warden folded his paper and smiled at Bechtel.

"Be my guest. Just finished breakfast. I can use a refill on the coffee. Want some?"

The waitress brought a clean cup and filled both their mugs.

"Just following up on our little shooting accident," Bechtel said.

The game warden took a sip of coffee, and watched the officer over the rim of his cup.

"Medical examiner says our shooting victim was hit twice. Found both number two and number three shot in both wounds. Either blast could have caused immediate death," Bechtel said. "Use of those size pellets make sense to you if you're after pheasants?"

"No doubt reloads. Probably work pretty well for your high flying geese. Some of the Sandhill Crane hunters use threes. Maybe twos sometimes. Be hell on pheasants, though. At normal range they'd tear the bird to shreds."

"That's what I was thinking," Bechtel said. "Makes a hunting accident seem unlikely, don't you think?"

"That's your department, I guess. Got any suspects?"

"No. I don't," Bechtel said, "But I'll tell you something interesting. Walker was a confessed murderer. Happened some twenty, maybe even thirty, years ago. All charges were dismissed. Confession was obtained without a Miranda warning. Only evidence they had was his statement."

The warden mulled this over, realizing there may have been a reason Walker was shot.

"The woman he killed had no family. I talked to the chief investigator in Miles City. He couldn't think of any suspects. Said most people have pretty much forgotten about the case."

They turned their attention to the coffee mugs.

"You discovered the body because it seemed strange to you that his vehicle had been parked there so long, right?" Bechtel said.

"Yes. Knew it wouldn't take more than a couple hours to hunt that stretch of the old track."

"Did you see any other hunters or vehicles around there during your patrol that day?" Bechtel said.

"There were no cars or anything parked near Walker's pickup both times I drove by there that day. I'm sure of that. I crossed over the old tracks at the next crossing to the east at least once that day. Think that's Hutchins School Road. Don't remember seeing any one parked there either. Would have been a good place for a poster if someone was hunting along the road bed coming his way."

The warden paused as the waitress refilled their cups.

"You know, I think I might've seen a vehicle parked near the old school. One road east of where I found Walker. Like I said, Hutchins School Road. Can't remember if I saw it the first time I drove by there, or later. If I did go by there twice, that is," the warden said. "I think I must have. Wouldn't bet on it, either way."

"How far is the school building from the old rail line?"

"I'm thinking a half mile maybe. Seems to be on the corner of the quarter section line," the warden said. "Like a lot of those old one room schools used to be,"

"Remember anything about the vehicle?" Bechtel said.

"It was parked mostly behind the school house near the privy. Just got a glimpse. Didn't pay much attention to it really. Seems to me it was a smaller truck. Maybe a Chevy S-10. Ford Ranger. Something like that," the warden said. "Red. I'm pretty sure. Red. Maybe maroon. Hell, could've been orange."

"See a plate? Was it local?"

"Never noticed. Didn't mean anything at the time."

"Anybody in the area?"

"Must've been. But I didn't see 'em."

o0o

Chief Deputy Bechtel located the Hutchins School on the Clyde County map in the hallway outside his office.

He drove out to the site and looked around the perimeter of the abandoned one room school building.

There were numerous tire tracks on three sides of the building, but they were indistinct in the flattened weeds where vehicles had knocked them down.

School kids have been using the place for parties, he thought.

He got out and looked around hoping to find spent shot gun shells or other clues. He came up empty handed.

o0o

Two Shots Quick

Bechtel didn't think the reference to a red, orange, or maroon Chevrolet S-10 or Ford Ranger was much of a lead. He supposed it was a possibility that whoever was driving such a truck was the shooter, but he didn't have much to go on.

Moreloft had a population of less than three hundred. He knew everybody in town. There was only one truck that fit the general description.

He placed a call to the owner of a red Chevy S-10.

"Blake, this is Jack at the sheriff's office, how you doing?"

"Not bad. Doc says I should get the cast off next week. Start rehabbing my leg about then."

"Bet you miss getting after those roosters, huh?" the deputy said.

"You betcha. Can't wait 'til next year," Blake said. "What can I do you outta?"

"You still got that little Chevy pick-up?"

"Technically. Wally at the garage says it's not worth fixing. Insurance company says it's totaled."

"That's what I thought," Bechtel said. "Trying to locate a smaller reddish pick-up. Wanted to make sure it wasn't yours."

"Far as I know, not another one like it in town. Only pick-ups I know color of mine are full sized rigs. And those at the co-op. As I'm sure you know, all their vehicles are painted red," Blake said.

o0o

Back at the sheriff's office, Bechtel thought he'd better follow-up on the pick-up a little more. He found the number of the Miles City Police department in the file and placed a call. The same receptionist he had talked to before answered the phone.

"Miles City Police Department," she said. "We aim to serve."

"Can I talk to Sergeant Dipippo?"

She put him through.

"This is Jack Bechtel again. Clyde County sheriff's department in Moreloft, South Dakota."

"Sure. I remember. We talked earlier. How can I help?" Dipippo said.

"We're not sure if your man Walker was killed in a hunting accident or shot on purpose. Murdered," Bechtel said. "I'm trying to follow up."

"Go ahead. What do you need?"

"First. You got anybody with a grudge against Walker. Somebody you'd expect would want to see him dead?"

There was a long pause before Dipippo relied.

"Walker killed that girl some twenty-five years or so ago. Even more, I guess. I've been in town almost fifteen years. Never heard of the murder until maybe a year or so ago when I was talking to an old retired member of the force. No one talks about it around town. Girl had no family. Her parents were never located. No next of kin for her. Can't think of a soul."

Bechtel considered what Dipippo told him.

"How about this? You know anybody driving a small size reddish pickup that could have been out here and did the shooting?" Bechtel said.

"That's all you got?" Dipippo said. "No plate number. Make? Model?"

"I don't have shit, if you want to know the truth. Just checking to see if anything comes to mind. Not even sure of the color. Maroon. Red. Orange. In there somewhere," Bechtel said. "Seems to me, if he was shot on purpose, the shooter is probably from your area. No one out here knew him."

"Makes sense, but I don't know if I can tell you more. You might want to talk to the sheriff's office, they cover a lot more area on their rounds than we do."

"Got a name for me?" Bechtel said. "Someone who won't think I'm half bonkers for asking?"

"Can't guarantee what he'll think, but Bob Thompson's been around for quite a while and patrols most of the county. Nice guy, too. Deputy sheriff," Dipippo said, then gave Bechtel deputy Thompson's phone number.

o0o

Lleyellyn was finishing up with the supper dishes, when Montoya came in and sat at the table. He had the program from the Institute Irene had attended in his hand.

"She received an award," he said. "Look at this."

Lleyellyn dried his hands and sat down to read the page Montoya had been marking with his index finger.

PERSON OF THE YEAR *** IRENE BOYD

Irene Boyd of Custer County (Miles City) is a graduate of Miles City High School and the University of Montana. She has been a counselor and social worker in that county since graduation, specializing in counseling and assisting women who have been physically and sexually abused.

Currently she is a part time sex abuse counselor who is always "on call" when needed.

Irene has a special empathy for her clients helped no doubt by her openness concerning her personal story. She was raped as a high school student. She maintains that her most rewarding duties are helping her clients and assisting law enforcement in bringing their abusers to justice.

In addition to her profession as a social worker of high acclaim, Irene is the proprietor of The Boyd Ranch, a more than 20,000-acre cattle ranch where she has specialized in the production and development of registered Hereford cattle.

The Boyd Ranch is the scene for a soon to be released motion picture produced by one of her college class mates, Will DeLong, the Golden Globe award winning director.

Irene is tonight's keynote speaker. Her topic will concern one of her first clients, Pamela Whitedeer, and her untimely tragic death. A client whose sad story has been an inspiration for Irene Boyd ever since.

o0o

In the back of the booklet Montoya saw a folded sheet of paper with the handwritten words, *My Address,* written across the top. He opened the paper and two news clippings fell to the table. They both recognized them at once. They were copies of the same two articles about Terry Walker they had received in the mail.

The outline was bare boned.

Growing up (ranch life)
High School (& being sexually assaulted)
Missoula (University of Montana)
Professional Career (social work)

Pamela Whitedeer
> Her story
> Her assault
> Her murder
> Her killer (Terrence Spencer Walker etc.)

The Boyd Ranch
My motto: "We do what we can. We can't fix everything, but we can try."

"Pretty succinct," Montoya said.

"She ever tell you about Whitedeer and Walker?" Lleyellyn said.

"Never," Montoya said. "Must have stayed with her all these years, though. You're probably right. Maybe Irene's the one sent us those clippings."

"Should we say anything about Walker?"

"No. Wouldn't want to make her an accessory to murder, would we?"

Lleyellyn just looked at Montoya and gave a slight nod of agreement.

Montoya folded up Irene's outline and put it and the clippings back in the booklet, then put it on the counter.

"She'll read about his shooting when she goes through the papers we saved for her," Montoya said. "Play it cool. We know nothing about Walker being killed. Our lips are sealed. Comprende?"

"You bet. I do."

o0o

Irene spent the day housecleaning and doing the laundry.

She retired early. She hadn't got around to the stack of accumulated mail and newspapers waiting for her.

CHAPTER 40

TUESDAY OCTOBER 27

Irene stayed in bed a little longer than usual. Montoya had fixed a baked egg dish and had it ready when she came downstairs. Other than compliments for the meal, no one had anything much to say while they ate.

When they finished breakfast, they sat around the table making small talk. Lleyellyn and Montoya were waiting for Irene to say something about Walker.

"Mail man brought a lot of stuff," Lleyellyn said. "There's a package for you. Left it on the clothes dryer."

"Put the newspapers out there, too," Montoya said. "Knew you'd want to catch up on the local news."

"Read anything of interest?" Irene said.

"Never even looked. There're still in the wrappers," he said.

They watched Irene leave the room to get the newspapers and the mail. She came back carrying a green package and a stack of mail in both hands, and with several orange vinyl newspaper bags under her right arm.

"Post man's been busy," she said before sitting down at the table.

She sorted through the mail, stacking the bills in one pile, letters, junk mail, and magazines in others.

"Mail builds up doesn't it?" she said. "Here's something for each of you," she added, handing a postal card to Montoya and sliding another one across the table to Shay without glancing at the pictures on the face of either one.

Two Shots Quick

She took the newspapers out of their bags and stacked them in chronological order. The Saturday October 17 issue was on top.

Irene had handed Lleyellyn a full color postcard with the image of a Ringneck Pheasant flying. There was a corn field in the background. He turned it over. It was addressed to him in block letters. The brief message said *Your efforts are much appreciated*. There was no signature.

He looked at Irene. She was absorbed in the Miles City Star, scanning the Saturday paper quickly, before moving on to the bloated Sunday paper.

When he glanced toward Montoya he saw him holding up another postcard, this one with the front divided into several sections showing deer, ducks, pheasants and so forth and the words *South Dakota – Hunter's Paradise*.

They exchanged post cards. The message on the back of the one addressed to Montoya was exactly the same as the one he had received.

Irene was still engrossed in the papers.

Montoya put his card in his shirt pocket. Lleyellyn folded his in half and handed it to Montoya.

"I've got the dishes again today, right?" he said.

He stood up, then started clearing the table and putting the dishes in the sink.

Montoya picked up the papers Irene had finished scanning, pretending to read, but keeping an eye on her, waiting for her reaction to the big story in the Friday edition, the one about Walker's shooting.

As Lleyellyn finished drying the last of the breakfast dishes, Irene held up the front page of the Friday newspaper for them to see.

"Did you see this!" she said. "Terry Walker's dead. Why didn't you tell me?"

They both looked at her, feigning surprise.

"Went and got himself shot! Hunting."

"Wasn't there anything in the paper in Missoula?" Montoya said.

"Not as far as I know. And I never watched the news either. You know how those hotels are," Irene said. "Only thing I saw at the Radisson was the USA Today they leave at your door every morning. The only Montana news I saw was about some darned elk got into a post office somewhere near the park. Knocked over a bank of mail boxes."

"Walker's the guy murdered that client of yours, right?" Lleyellyn said. 'The one you mentioned in your talk."

Irene nodded.

"Doesn't really say how it happened," she said. "Paper doesn't say accident. Hope it wasn't. Someone finally evened the score, I bet. Should've been done years ago."

Irene stood up and poured another cup of coffee for herself.

"You know, I think I'll sleep good again tonight," she said. "Who says there's nothing good to read in the paper?"

o0o

Lleyellyn and Montoya headed toward the bunkhouse.

"I'll deep six these postcards," Montoya said. "Same reason we dumped those old news articles about Walker."

"Walker?" Lleyellyn said. "Who's he? Never heard of him."

o0o

As soon as Montoya and Lleyellyn had gone outside, Irene picked up the phone.

"Is Benedict Stephenson there?" she said to the woman who answered.

She recognized his voice when he said hello.

"Mr. Stephenson, this is Irene Boyd. I just heard about Walker's death."

Stephenson didn't respond at first. She heard him breathing, the muffled sound of music from the radio in the background.

Finally he said, "That was something wasn't it?"

"Who shot him?"

"Can't help you there," he said. "Cops at the café were talking about it. Said he took two blasts from a shotgun. Died instantly. Authorities out there have no suspects."

"Accident?" Irene said.

"They don't think so," the retired investigator said, then after a pause continued. "When they learned Walker was a confessed murderer, they decided not to expend too much time and money on their investigation."

There was a long pause. They were both lost in thought.

"You know, I always wanted him to get what he had coming," Irene said.

"You weren't the only one."

"I remember you told me you'd never give up trying to bring him to justice," Irene said.

"Well, I never closed my case file, if that's what you mean," Stephenson said. "After I retired there wasn't much I could do except think about it."

"Just so you know, I appreciate everything you've done," Irene said. "If you had any part in this final outcome, I thank you."

Irene thought Stephenson might say something, but after a few seconds he quietly hung up the phone.

o0o

Benedict Stephenson was sitting in his car in the Sheriff's Office parking lot behind the courthouse when Deputy Bob Thompson skipped down the stairs and headed toward his department SUV.

"Ben! What are you doing here?"

"Just checking to make sure there's no loose ends."

"Meaning?" Thompson said.

Stephenson glanced around to make sure no one was nearby.

"You've closed your file on that Montgomery stampede thing, right?"

"I have."

"Remember that list of things that were bothering you. Those coincidences with Montoya and that kid at the Boyd place, and so forth?"

Thompson responded with a nearly imperceptible nod.

"Just want to make sure your list has been shredded. And those old news articles about the Walker case, too. Don't want anyone to come across them in the file sometime in the future and start digging around. Stir something up," Stephenson said. "Make sense to you?"

They looked at each other for a moment, then shook hands to signal their mutual understanding.

o0o

Bob Thompson saw the law enforcement table at the Big Sky was vacant. The usual contingent of local cops, sheriff's deputies, and state patrolmen were gone, leaving a table of dirty dishes behind.

He sat down just as his nephew came out of a swinging door from the kitchen to clear the table and wipe it down.

"Unk," Leonard Thompson said, "What's up?"

"Stopped in to grab a bite," he said. "Looks like I missed everybody. Want to talk to you for a bit."

LT sat down across from his uncle, placing the tray of dirty dishes on the table next to them.

"I've got three days off starting Sunday," Bob Thompson said. "Think you can get off Sunday to go after some pheasants?"

"No problem. I'm off anyway. Where we going?" LT said. "Not Moreloft I hope."

"No. No. Not there," he said. "I know a guy with a half section of CRP land next to some corn acreage they just finished up combining. Birds pretty concentrated in there. He's had it posted so he and his family plus a few friends can hunt it. We're invited."

"If it sounds too good to be true …" Lt said, before his uncle cut him off.

"This is true, believe me. Guy's got two good dogs, too."

LT stood up to finish wiping down the table as LaDonna Mae, the waitress, came up to take the deputy's order.

"Miss Ritchie," he said. "Sure glad to see you back. Doing okay?"

"Feel great. Glad to be back on my feet and back here," she said, holding her order pad at her side. "There is something I'd like to ask you."

Bob Thompson looked up at her and waited, sure she was going to ask about her missing belongings, and when she would be getting them back. But what she said caught him by surprise.

"Do you know if Mr. Walker was murdered?" she said. "Or was it a hunting accident?"

He looked down at the table, then met her eyes.

"Did you know him?"

"Well, he was a regular customer. Always nice to me. Tipped well," she said with a smile. "Left me a twenty-dollar tip on the day before Christmas last year. Nobody else ever did that."

"Well, all I know is he was killed while hunting in South Dakota somewhere," he said. "I've heard the authorities back there have closed their file. Consider it an accidental shooting, I guess."

LaDonna Mae shifted her weight from one foot to the other before speaking.

"I saw that stuff in the papers about him, but he seemed awful nice and polite around me," she said. "He was a good customer. I miss him."

He looked at her for a moment. She spoke up before he could think of an appropriate reply.

"Can I take your order," she said. "The pork tenderloin sandwich is the luncheon special. Comes with fries and coleslaw. You can substitute cottage cheese, if you want."

A WORD OF THANKS

I had proof-reading help and editorial suggestions from my wife Barbara, my daughter Lara, and Wick, an author colleague. Many thanks to you all.

My father-in-law, Daniel K. Stern, published a book about Savage automatic pistols. It was called *Ten Shots Quick*. You can guess where the idea for the title of this book came from.

Cover drawing by the author.

No animals were harmed in the making of this book.

Ross A. Phelps and his wife, Barbara, divide their time between the bluffs overlooking the Mississippi River in southeast Minnesota and the lee of the Santa Catalina Mountains in the *Old Pueblo*, Tucson, Arizona.

This book was printed in Tucson, Arizona
by AlphaGraphics Commercial Printing Services
www.tucsoncps.com